# Heidi's Faith

RUGGED CROSS RANCH
BOOK FOUR

JILL DEWHURST

JILL
DEWHURST
FAITH FILLED FICTION

Copyright © 2024 by Jill Dewhurst. All rights reserved.

Book cover design by Greg Hewitt and Briana Spence (Spence Studios, Inc.)

Cover portrait by Amy Fondriest.

Barn photograph by Jill Dewhurst.

Author portrait by Robert Dewhurst.

This is a work of fiction. Names, characters, events, cultural traditions, and incidents are products of the author's imagination. Any resemblance to actual persons, living or dead, or actual events is purely coincidental.

Scripture quotations are from The ESV* Bible (The Holy Bible, English Standard Version*), copyright 2001 by Crossway, a publishing ministry of Good News Publishers. Used by permission. All rights reserved.

No portion of this book may be reproduced in any form without written permission from the publisher or author, except as permitted by U.S. copyright law.

ISBN 978-0-9995228-2-0 Paperback

ISBN 978-0-9995228-7-5 eBook

# Dedication

*In Memory of my Mom, Jeanne Tison, whose much-read collection of novels inspired my love of reading—and writing*

Fear not, for I am with you; be not dismayed, for I am your God; I will strengthen you, I will help you, I will uphold you with my righteous right hand.
   ~ Isaiah 41:10 ~

## Contents

| | | |
|---|---|---|
| | Prologue | 1 |
| 1. | Shattered Peace | 11 |
| 2. | Covert Move | 15 |
| 3. | Jacob's Birthday | 29 |
| 4. | Home | 37 |
| 5. | Cheesemaking | 47 |
| 6. | Harvest | 57 |
| 7. | Christmas | 65 |
| 8. | Quarantine | 71 |
| 9. | The Milking Help | 81 |
| 10. | Frederick's New Brother | 89 |
| 11. | Sketches | 103 |
| 12. | The Meeting | 107 |
| 13. | The Painting Speaks | 117 |
| 14. | The Promise | 131 |
| 15. | Johann's Approval | 143 |
| 16. | A Budding Friendship | 151 |
| 17. | Calligraphy Lessons | 163 |
| 18. | God's Heritage | 175 |
| 19. | Courting | 181 |
| 20. | The Picnic | 195 |
| 21. | Back to Church | 207 |
| 22. | The Empty Cradle | 217 |
| 23. | Kathryn O'Brien | 227 |
| 24. | Nathan's Reaper | 233 |
| 25. | Jacob | 237 |
| 26. | Fighting Self-Pity | 251 |
| 27. | Recovery | 263 |
| 28. | Anger | 269 |
| 29. | Selfless Love | 275 |
| 30. | The Protector | 283 |

31. Traditions 293
32. The Waltz 303

*Acknowledgments* 313
*About the Author* 315
*Also by Jill Dewhurst* 317
*Rugged Cross Ranch* 319

# What Readers are Saying

What an amazing storyline! I can't wait to read the sequel! Bravo to Mrs. Dewhurst on developing these unique characters and painting such vivid descriptions along the way.
~ Deven, Amazon Review

I couldn't put it down! Can't wait for the next book to find out how the saga continues! Love the twists and turns life throws at Julie as her destiny unfolds in love and tragedy.
~ ND, Amazon Review

I have been an avid reader for many years and read many authors. This book has been exceptionally well-written with a solid, Godly perspective. I am very eagerly awaiting Jill's next book! It is a joy to see her gifts and talents so beautifully expressed as she writes from her heart.
~ Beverly, Amazon Review

I fell in love with Julie's Joy, but I have to say Emily's Hope was a perfect continuance of this special family. The author has a way of pulling you in and allowing you to feel the joy and heartache of each character. Highly recommend!
~ Vickie, Amazon Review

Jill does a great job weaving a portrait of Christ into the storyline.
~ Cindy, Amazon Review

# Families ~ Rugged Cross Ranch

*Daniel* and Emma Taylor, owners of the Rugged Cross Ranch
    James McAllister, married to Emily (Kendrick) McAllister
    *Buck Matthews*
    Tim O'Brien, married to Laura (Kendrick) O'Brien
    Luke Hamilton, married to Julie (Peterson) Hamilton,
    Matthew
    Jacob Collins
    Josiah Collins

Johann and Ingrid Müller
    Heidi, Frederick

David and *Eloise* Kendrick, Pastor and his wife
    Emily (wife of James McAllister), Laura (wife of Tim O'Brien), Robert, Susan, Sarah, Beth

Seth and *Susanna* Carter, blacksmith and his wife
    Louisa, Jonathan, Anna

Nathan and Molly Lange
    Thad, Amy

Jeremy and Martha McClintock, owners of Rafter C Ranch
    Clara

(Deceased characters are *italicized*.)

# Prologue

## KANSAS TERRITORY, ELEVEN YEARS EARLIER

The creak of the kitchen door signaled the entrance of ten-year-old Jacob Collins. Both hands were wrapped around the handle of a pail full of milk, and his face was scrunched in concentration as he tried not to spill a single drop. Behind him, the door snapped shut as he hefted the pail onto the counter.

Jacob's mom folded her dish towel and stepped toward him. She reached out to ruffle his hair and bent down to kiss his forehead. "Thank you, Jacob. You're a good helper."

Jacob's eyes glinted in appreciation of the compliment.

A rush of stamping feet sounded just before his younger brother Josiah ran into the kitchen. "Now that you're finished with the milking, wanna play catch with me?"

Jacob looked to his mom, who was tucking a large basket of laundry against her hip. "Is there anything else you need me to do? Do you want me to carry that basket down to the creek for you?"

A sweet smile formed. "No, Jacob. You have done a man's

work today. Now it's time to play. Enjoy your childhood. Your dad is chopping wood by the barn, and I'll be washing clothes. Keep an eye on Josiah and stay close to the house."

"Yes, Mom."

Josiah grabbed his hand and pulled, unsuccessful in his attempt to move his brother with physical force. His enthusiasm bubbled over with every word. "Come on. Play catch with me."

"All right, I'm coming." Jacob opened the kitchen door, and Josiah scooted outside. He continued to stand there and hold it for his mom to slip through with her burden.

"Thank you, handsome, for being such a gentleman."

Jacob's heart swelled. "You're welcome."

"Jacob! Hurry up!"

His mom's soft laughter surrounded him like a warm blanket. "I think the last two days of heavy rain have given Josiah cabin fever. Go, enjoy the sunshine with your brother."

Jacob watched as his mom waved a greeting to his dad before starting down the path to the creekside.

"Jacob!"

"Patience, Josiah. I'm coming!" He trotted over to the side yard to where Josiah was waiting.

---

Miriam Collins worked her way carefully down the steep descent to the creek and placed the basket on a flat boulder near the water. Closing her eyes, she lifted her face to the warmth of the sun and breathed deeply of the fresh air. "Thank you, Father, for the sunshine." She understood Josiah's need to be outdoors, for he was like her in many ways—generally quiet, thoughtful, creative. Jacob was more like his father—hardworking, strong, dependable, outgoing. The brothers complemented one another, just like her and Jed.

Miriam and Jedediah Collins had met when he came to work on her family's farm. His dedication and hard work had earned her father's approval. His charm and his enduring faith in God had won her heart. Of course, his handsome face and honed muscles didn't hurt either.

Both of their boys resembled their father, with their dark brown unruly hair, their freckles sprinkled across their noses and cheeks, and their adorable dimples when they smiled. Jed's dimples could still make her heart melt.

Enough reminiscing. There was work to do. Miriam reached for the first garment and the bar of lye soap and began scrubbing while she hummed.

Half an hour later, she stood, placed her fists in her lower back, and stretched backward. The birds were twittering, and the water flowing by gurgled around the larger rocks in the creek bed. While she was listening, a low rumble added to the sounds of nature. "Is that thunder?" She studied the sky, but not even a wispy cloud dotted the azure expanse above her. The rumble gained volume.

Her attention darted upstream. A wall of water was coming toward her like a locomotive, and for a few precious seconds she froze in panic. The torrential rains had sparked a flash flood! She blinked, and the instinct of survival turned her toward the sharp ascent. She began to climb.

Her feet kept slipping in her haste, her shoes kept getting tangled in her long skirt, and the water kept coming like a quickly rising tide. "Jed!" Her scream tore from her, but the growing volume of the flood and the walls of the creekside muffled the sound.

Jed swung his axe and split the wood in a single stroke. In the seconds of silence that followed, he heard it—the roar of water. A flash flood! And Miriam had gone to the creek! His heart pounded in his chest as he abandoned the axe still embedded in the stump and ran. "Miriam!"

The volume of the rushing water increased with every footfall. As he neared where the ground gave way to its steep descent, he heard his name. His wife's terror was etched in the single syllable. "Jed!"

"Miriam! I'm coming!" He climbed halfway down and extended his arm. "Grab my wrist!" She stretched and wrapped her hand around his arm just as the water reached her hem and pulled her feet from beneath her.

The force of the water was so strong he had to lean backward with all his weight to find enough leverage to keep them from getting swept away.

Jacob appeared at the crest of the creekside. "Dad!"

Jed secured Miriam's arm with his other hand and looked up into the terror-stricken face of his eldest son. "Jacob! Do not come down! Go! Get Josiah to higher ground!"

Another wave of water hit, and Jed lost his footing. He released one arm and lunged for the massive branch that extended over the creek. Miriam screamed, but Jed hooked his arm around the branch while maintaining his vise grip on his wife's arm.

"Dad!"

Jed saw yet another swell of water storming toward them and knew the outcome. Without fear, he yelled up to his boy. "Jacob! I love you! Take care of Josiah. He is your responsibility now! Get to higher ground! Run!"

"Miriam! Take a deep breath!" The destructive force of the water snapped the sturdy branch as if it were a mere twig. The surge yanked them both under and swirled them swiftly downstream.

"Dad!" Jacob's chest tightened as he searched the raging river for any signs of his parents. They were gone! Gone! The water level was still increasing fast. His dad's words resounded in his mind: "Get Josiah to higher ground!"

Jacob turned toward the house and ran, his footsteps heavy

as if they were cast in dried mud. He grabbed Josiah's hand, "We need to go to Flanders' Hill."

Josiah's face scrunched in confusion. Chaos had erupted all around him, and his mind clung to the last command he had been given. "But Mom said to stay near the house."

"Dad said to run. Come on!"

Other families had gathered with Jacob and Josiah on Flanders' Hill. From that vantage point was a clear view of the rising flood. In silence, everyone watched in horror as the power of the water pushed through the countryside. Josiah searched the faces around them in desperation before he lifted his hazel eyes to Jacob and whispered, "Are Mom and Dad coming?"

Tears streamed down Jacob's face. The raging river held his eyes captive, making him unable to meet Josiah's gaze. "No, Josiah. The river took them." Their pastor was standing just behind Jacob and overheard him. He rested his hand on Jacob's shoulder, the gesture trying to convey wordless comfort.

The next few days passed in a daze. When the floodwaters began to subside, the destruction was made evident. Several low-lying homes had been lost, along with quite a number of livestock, and crops near the creek had been washed away. All of the members of the community, other than Miriam and Jed Collins, had been accounted for with only minor injuries.

Pastor Henry had invited the boys into his home until they could safely inspect their family's homestead. When the time came, he offered, "Why don't we drive the wagon to your home, and you can collect some of your things?"

When they approached the house, it appeared untouched. The effect was oddly eerie, knowing everything had irreparably changed. The flood had crested a few feet below their front door, but the shredded ground leading downhill echoed Jacob's shredded heart.

The brothers entered their home, found a carpetbag, and

filled it with their clothes and the coins from the extra cookie jar. Josiah grabbed his baseball, and Jacob's eyes landed on his dad's Bible, its cover worn from use. Jacob reverently stroked his hand across the engraved title and lifted his dad's most cherished possession from the nightstand. From his mom's desk, Jacob gathered both his and his mom's calligraphy pen cases and with them collected all the memories of her teaching him her special script.

Pastor Henry peeked into the carpetbag. "Don't you have more clothes than this?"

Slowly shaking his head, Jacob answered, "The rest of our clothes were in the laundry basket by the creek."

Pastor's chin dipped in understanding as the meaning of those words settled on his mind.

The search parties reported to the pastor and sheriff every evening, but there had been no sign of either Miriam or Jed. Each day, the fragile thread of hope that they had survived came nearer to breaking. On the fifth day, the lead searcher asked Pastor Henry to step outside, but Jacob slipped outside with him. The man began to protest his presence, but Jacob argued with a passion that belied his youth, "If you have found something, I deserve to know."

The searcher paused, then nodded his assent. "Miriam's and Jed's bodies were found seven miles downstream. They were still holding on to one another, even in death. They are being transported back for burial." And with that, the tenuous thread of hope snapped.

That evening, the sheriff and the banker came to visit the pastor, and they conversed as if Jacob were not visibly sitting within earshot. The banker began. "The house is structurally sound, and the barn and animals are in good condition. Selling the homestead and the livestock should cover the balance of the bank loan."

"At least the boys won't have debt hanging over them. Where will they live?" the sheriff continued.

Pastor Henry joined in. "The boys have no other family. If we split them up, we might be able to find homes for them."

"Josiah stays with me." All eyes turned to Jacob.

"Son, no one will be able to afford to take both of you. Every family in the valley has been affected by the flood. Your only other option would be the orphanage."

"Then we'll go to the orphanage," Jacob responded without hesitation. "Dad told me to take care of my brother and made Josiah my responsibility. I'm not going to let him down."

"Your responsibility? You're what? Twelve?" scoffed the banker.

Jacob chose not to correct his age. "My age doesn't matter. I'm the man of the house now, and I will protect my brother."

Compassion glistened in the pastor's eyes. "Very well. I'll send a telegram to the orphanage in the morning."

For the next three years, the Collins brothers found food and shelter at the mission orphanage in southern Kansas Territory. The other children there all bore their grief differently, but the embittered ones found an easy bully's target in quiet Josiah. Jacob took Josiah's protection seriously, and delivered many a black eye as a message to leave his brother alone.

Occasionally, food had to be rationed, but Jacob always shared his portion with Josiah. He would rather endure hunger pangs himself than listen to Josiah's stomach growl in empty protest all night long. Josiah was content to live in Jacob's shadow, and Jacob wore the mantle of his responsibility with a formidable determination.

When more children arrived at the orphanage, there simply wasn't enough room for everyone. Jacob overheard the minister speaking to his wife. "I don't want to turn the little ones away, but we're bursting at the seams at it is. I don't know what to do."

Jacob entered the kitchen. "Let the younger ones stay. Josiah and I will leave to make room."

The chair scraped against the wood floor as the minister turned to face him. "I appreciate your generous spirit, son, but you are only thirteen, certainly not old enough to provide for you and your brother."

Jacob lifted an eyebrow in challenge. "Don't you always say that God will provide?"

"Yes, so I do," the minister conceded. "Let me send out a couple of telegrams before we make any final decisions, shall we?"

A few days later, a telegram was delivered, and the minister called Jacob and Josiah into the kitchen. "A pastor friend of mine from Prairie Hills in Oklahoma Territory has found a family who has invited you to live with them."

"Both of us?" The glint of steel in Jacob's eyes communicated that he would accept nothing less.

Admiration for this young man swelled in the minister's heart. "Yes, both of you. Daniel and Emma Taylor will be arriving tomorrow to meet you."

"What do you think, Jacob?" Josiah asked.

"If they are willing to keep us together, I think we should hear them out. Staying together is the only acceptable option."

Late the following afternoon, Jacob stationed himself on the front porch and leaned his shoulder against the support beam. His relaxed stance belied the tension building in his gut. When the distant puff of dust on the road appeared on the horizon, Jacob's eyes fixed upon it. The growing rumble of the wagon joined the enlarging dust cloud until the conveyance's destination was certain. Soon the driver pulled into the yard and set the brake. Jacob took a deep breath and stuffed his hands into his pockets, unsure how their lives might change in the next few hours.

The minister walked past him to meet the wagon and shook hands with the man driving. The petite woman beside him had her kind eyes locked on Jacob. Her penetrating gaze began to untwist the knots in his gut. The connection was broken momentarily when the man helped her down, but she walked straight toward him, a basket in hand.

"Are you one of the brothers thinking about coming to live with us?"

"Yes, ma'am." He extended his hand as Josiah came through the front door. "I'm Jacob Collins, and this is my brother Josiah."

Emma Taylor ignored his outstretched hand and pulled him in for a hug. The sweet floral scent of her hair transported him back three years to the embrace of his mother. When she pulled back, his eyes held a sheen of moisture that he quickly blinked away. She released him and immediately reached for Josiah.

Over dinner and a slice of Emma's homemade apple pie, Daniel introduced himself and his wife and described their home, the Rugged Cross Ranch, and the four older brothers already waiting for them. Jacob glanced at Josiah and lifted his eyebrow in a silent question, and his younger brother nodded. "We'd be grateful to come and live with you."

The four of them left just before dawn the following morning. After a long day of traveling, they arrived at the Rugged Cross Ranch as sunset filled the sky. When their new brothers filed out of the bunkhouse, Jacob stiffened. If he had to defend Josiah against these guys, he'd have his hands full.

His hesitation was short-lived, for James, Buck, Luke, and Tim helped them get settled and eagerly adopted them into their family. For the first time in three years, Jacob felt himself begin to relax.

He and Josiah had found a new home—and better yet—a family.

# CHAPTER 1
## Shattered Peace

*God's creation sings on days like this.* The sun shone on Heidi Müller's straw-colored hair as she paused on the porch of the general store and tugged her shawl a bit tighter around her shoulders. One hand rested on the stair railing while the other clutched the edges of her shawl. An empty basket recently overflowing with fresh cheese bundles hung loosely from her elbow. Tipping her face toward the warmth of the sun, she breathed deeply and exhaled a happy sigh.

The autumn day was crisp, but beautiful, with the sunshine glinting off the yellow birch leaves like gold. As she strolled along Main Street on her journey home, she studied those leaves, immersing herself in the sound of the rustling breeze and the crunch of fallen leaves under her shoes. Even the fragrance of fall was unique to this season.

*How did one describe the scent of fall?* She smiled at her musings. *Leave those details to the writers and philosophers.* Capturing the scene on canvas or sketch paper was all about the visual details—colors, textures, shading, movement. If those elements were perfect, the other senses would follow.

Wishing she had her sketchbook with her, Heidi slowed her pace to memorize the details of the nearest birch tree with its thin dark lines and dramatic knots against the stark white bark. The contrast would be a lovely subject for a black and white pencil drawing. Her eyes skimmed over to the lowest branch of the maple tree across the street—the tree she would climb if she were not required to be a lady. Boys had more fun.

When she passed by the milliner shop, a hand reached out, grabbed her upper arm, and yanked her forcefully into the shadowed alley between the buildings. She had been startled so thoroughly her scream was held captive inside her. Lifting her panic-stricken eyes, she discovered her attacker. *Peter?*

The young man pinned her against the wall and growled menacingly, "You refused me. Your father refused me. You just don't understand that I don't take 'no' for an answer. I always get what I want."

Peter's sinister sneer turned his normally handsome face into something dark and evil. Heidi tried to pull her arm away, but his grip only tightened. Her heart rate soared as she realized her perilous situation. Without premeditation, she threw the power of her weight behind her sharply lifted knee, striking him with all the force she could muster and leaving him incapacitated enough to release her arm. As soon as she was free, she raised the hem of her skirt and ran, her shawl lifting from her shoulders and fluttering to the ground in her wake.

Home was two miles away. Perhaps she should go to the sheriff. No, he would be on Peter's side. Not even the preacher could be trusted to protect her. Her only hope was to reach her papa. She didn't know how long Peter would be doubled over, but he was surely a faster runner than she was. If he could get to his horse, she had no chance at all. *Lord, give me the endurance to make it home before Peter catches me!* She ran with the intensity of prey being chased by a wolf. The analogy was not far from the truth.

Heidi's lungs were burning. Even her heaving breaths could not grasp enough air. Never had two miles felt so far. Just when the boundary of her farm came into view, the distant thundering of hooves began to grow louder. Wide-eyed, she looked behind her and caught a glimpse of Peter's horse.

The stitch in her side had escalated to stabbing pain, and her feet were blistered in the shoes not designed for running. Her energy was fading. Though her lungs were desperate for a respite long enough to catch her breath, she pushed herself forward. *Lord, give me strength. Give my feet wings.* Keep going. One step at a time.

---

Johann Müller wiped his shirtsleeve across his sweaty brow, an empty water bucket dangling from his other hand. The horses' water trough was full. A frantic movement in his peripheral vision caught his attention, and he focused on the distant fence line. *Heidi!* Why was she running and continuing to look back over her shoulder?

The water bucket was dropped and forgotten as he sprinted toward his daughter. When he reached her, Heidi's eyes were wide with terror. She ran at him and flung her arms around him. Between heaving breaths, she managed a strangled, "Protect me, Papa!" Her relief at reaching him melted into weakness, and her legs began to buckle. Then her entire body began to tremble violently. Without a word, Johann scooped Heidi up in his arms and hurried to the house.

## CHAPTER 2
## Covert Move

That scoundrel would never touch his daughter again! Protective anger surged through Johann as he gently cradled his daughter's bruised arm in his hands. *How did Peter Montgomery think he could grab Heidi and not suffer the consequences?* As soon as the thought formed in his mind, Johann knew the answer: Peter was the mayor's son, and the mayor's family owned most of the town and coerced the other citizens into doing whatever the mayor wanted. Well, they were not going to coerce him.

In this moment, everything in him wanted to hurt Peter for what he had done. In one violent act, he had ripped away Heidi's sense of safety and security. Heidi wore the imprint of his fingers on her arm, and she would not soon erase the imprint of this nightmare from her memory. If she had not reacted as she did, Peter would have harmed her irreparably. Johann closed his eyes and clenched his teeth as the familiar words whispered to his soul: *"Beloved, never avenge yourselves, but leave it to the wrath of God, for it is written, 'Vengeance is mine, I will repay, says the Lord.'" Lord, give me the self-control to obey.*

Sitting at the kitchen table next to him, Johann's seventeen-year-old daughter misread the twitch in her father's jaw. Her voice was barely above a whisper. "I'm sorry, Papa. I should have taken Frederick with me to deliver the cheese."

"No!" The word exited more bark-like than Johann intended, and he repeated in a gentler tone, "No, Heidi, you did nothing wrong. There is no reason you should not have been perfectly safe walking to the store alone in broad daylight." He glanced at his eight-year-old son also sitting at the table. "Your brother is a courageous lad, but he would have been no match for Peter." He huffed loudly, trying to dispel the tension in his chest. "I am proud that you remembered what I taught you and were able to get away from Peter, but I fear this will incite his anger and make him even more determined and desperate to get his way."

His wife Ingrid draped a thick quilt around Heidi's shoulders and gently urged her to sip on the hot tea. She must recognize that Heidi was in shock from the trauma even though the outcome could have been so much worse.

That Heidi had been subjected to the attack at all left Johann with a twisted gut. He had traveled to America with his family to find freedom and opportunity, not to trade one form of tyranny for another. From their home region along the border of Holland and Germany, the Müllers had tried to live quiet lives, but the heavy taxation, political unrest, and religious oppression were an increasingly intolerable burden that finally became too great to bear.

The Müllers had sailed across the Atlantic Ocean to America, the land of promise, and settled in a beautiful region of southern Pennsylvania nestled between the bustling metropolis of Philadelphia and the quiet Amish communities. The rolling hills of lush grassland were perfect for his cows to produce rich milk for their family's cheese-making business.

Though their nearby town provided many conveniences, it also introduced new challenges. To secure the bank loan for their land required the approval of the mayor. To sell their cheese at the general store required approval of the mayor. Everything seemed to require the approval of the mayor, and he enthusiastically reminded everyone he conversed with that he was ultimately in charge of everything in *his* town. The Müllers had endured the mayor's high-handed influence, that is, until today.

When Peter Montgomery had declared to Heidi that he was going to court her, she had refused on the spot with a kind firmness only she had the skill to convey. When the mayor came to their home a week ago to "suggest" that Johann allow Peter to pay suit to Heidi, Johann immediately rejected the demand. His reply was blunt and undoubtably not diplomatic enough, for the mayor's smug smile had transformed into a sneer. The threat that followed was unexpected; though, considering it now, Johann should not have been surprised. "If you refuse to allow Peter to be Heidi's suitor, you will regret it."

"My answer will not waver. Peter will not now or ever receive my permission to court my daughter."

"We shall see."

Now Peter seemed to be taking matters into his own hands. No doubt his father would be close behind.

That evening, Mayor Montgomery rapped on the Müllers' wooden door during dinner. When Johann answered the door, filling the frame with his height and breadth, the mayor's face somehow managed a condescending sneer while looking up at a man a head taller. "Your daughter humiliated my son in pubic today. What does she have to say for herself?" The mayor tried to peek around Johann, but he remained firmly planted in the doorway.

"Your son forcefully grabbed my daughter."

"And you believe the words of a girl?"

"My daughter has proven herself to be honest, and she bears the bruises as evidence."

The mayor lifted his chin and sniffed as if a few bruises were of no consequence. "Peter is willing to overlook her arrogance and desires to court her anyway." The words were spoken as if Heidi were the one at fault, and she should be grateful Peter was still interested.

Johann responded with the exterior appearance of calm though his voice held the strength of iron, "No man who lays a hand on my daughter will ever receive my blessing."

"I see. If I rescind the permit for you to sell your cheese in the general store, you will go bankrupt. If you go bankrupt, the bank will foreclose your loan, and you will lose your home and property."

"Your son needs to stay away from my daughter." Though Johann understood Reginald Montgomery was plotting to undermine his ability to provide for his family, he refused to acquiesce to the mayor's demand. Johann knew he was answerable only to God, and God had promised to provide when he could not. Johann chose to trust Him.

The mayor's expression hardened into a scowl. "Out of consideration for our future family ties I will give you one more week to recant your decision. If you refuse, you will be sorry!"

Not wanting to spout something he would regret, Johann stood silently until Ingrid gently nudged him over a bit. She addressed the mayor as if he were any other company arriving at their home. "We are having dinner. Would you like to join us?"

If the situation were not so tense, Ingrid might have laughed at the expressions of utter shock on the face of the mayor and her dear husband.

The mayor sputtered, "No, thank you. I am needed at home." He turned abruptly and walked away.

When he had departed, Johann closed the door, still speechless, and gently lifted his wife's chin so she would meet his gaze. His furrowed brow communicated his confusion.

Ingrid answered the question in his gaze, "Kindness is the antidote for meanness."

"You, my wife, are stronger and wiser than I, though even your abundant kindness may not be enough to soften his hardened heart."

---

Though Heidi was physically and emotionally exhausted, she lay in bed unable to sleep, her thoughts in a jumble, landing only on impressions, feelings, and flashbacks from today's horrific event. Subconsciously certain she would have nightmares if she succumbed to slumber, she stared at the sliver of moon visible through the upper windowpane. She prayed quietly, "Lord, I do not want to be controlled by fear. Teach me to trust You more." Verses from her youth floated into her thoughts. *"Do not fear, for I am with you; be not dismayed, for I am your God; I will strengthen you, I will help you; I will uphold you with my righteous right hand. I will never leave you or forsake you. God is my fortress; in Him I will trust."* Heidi sank further into her pillow. "Thank you, Father."

The soft click of a door told Heidi that her parents were retiring for the night. The murmur of their indistinct conversation on the other side of the wall soothed her nerves and lulled her to sleep.

---

"Is Heidi going to be all right?" Johann lowered himself onto the corner of the bed while his wife sat in front of the mirror and unbraided her long hair.

"Yes, in time, Heidi will once again find her confidence and her contagious joy. Those qualities were shattered today, but God will glue them back together into a masterpiece even more beautiful than before." She picked up her brush and turned in her chair to face her husband. "You were exactly what Heidi needed—a guardian, an empathetic listener, a defender. You have always been able to connect with her in ways that even I cannot. Keep fulfilling those roles in her life and give her time." Ingrid commenced the smooth brushing motion. "She will heal, but the mental wounds will flare up at unexpected times, especially at first. Sudden sounds or movements may spook her. We'll keep her close and be there when she needs us."

Johann reached over and rested his hand on Ingrid's shoulder. "God has blessed her with a mama who has walked in similar shoes and understands the burden she carries."

After becoming lost in thought for a few moments, Johann leaned forward and rested his forearms on his knees. "Ingrid, we need to be prepared. I fully expect Reginald to follow through on his threat. If I know him, this threat will not be his last. First, let's devise a solution to our dairy farm's profit should our market in the general store be denied. Then we should initiate plans to move."

The hand holding the hairbrush stopped mid-stroke. "Move? Move where?"

Shrugging his shoulders, Johann replied, "Further west? I have heard of successful dairy farms in Minnesota and Wisconsin, but the Montgomerys would look there first. Maybe more southwest toward Kansas or Oklahoma. There is plenty of open land, and our business would have opportunity to grow without as much competition."

"Do you really think the Montgomery family would be able to reach us in Wisconsin?"

"They are determined to get their way. To the mayor, this is another power struggle he cannot lose. I wouldn't put it past them to have connections throughout the Midwest. There are rumors of a connection to the Mafia in New York, though I do not know how credible those rumors are. If a move becomes necessary, we must do everything we can to ensure it is our final move. We will need to pack secretly, travel light, and leave under cover of darkness. They will not get my girl."

Ingrid absorbed the idea and nodded. "We will plan for the move and pray it will become unnecessary. For the immediate need, how do we save our farm?"

Johann kissed his wife's forehead. Only she could be this strong in the midst of potential upheaval. "Our cheeses are our livelihood. If we are forbidden to sell them to the general store, how else could we distribute cheese to our current patrons and reach new customers?" Johann and Ingrid spent a couple of hours fielding ideas of alternative ways to sell their cheeses.

Just as Johann reached to turn off the wick of the oil lamp on the bedside table, Heidi's scream ripped through the silence. He bolted to her room. His daughter was sitting upright, drenched in sweat. Her wide eyes and staccato breathing tore at his heart. Sitting on the edge of her bed, Johann gathered her in his arms and soothed her. "Shh. You are safe. I am here to protect you. Peter will not hurt you."

Heidi's terror turned to sobs. The more she tried to stop shaking, the harder she shook. Her father never let go. His strong arms enveloped her like a fortress with impenetrable walls. Many minutes later, the effects of the nightmare waned. She breathed into his shirt, "Thank you, Papa." Only then did he release his hold on her.

"Lie down again, Heidi. I will not leave you." She looked as if she would protest, but he gently urged her, "Rest. I will protect you." Heidi lay back down, and the weight of her eyelids pulled them closed. Johann glanced over to the doorframe and found his wife wrapped in a shawl, leaning against it. Ingrid gave him a small smile and nodded in silent approval.

Throughout the night, Heidi awoke three other times, but each time she found her father still sitting there, his head bowed in prayer, a stalwart guard facing her invisible enemy. Restful sleep finally claimed her for the last few hours of the night.

---

The next morning, before the time to make cheese with her mother, Heidi placed a blank canvas on her easel. She desperately needed to release her emotions, yet she could do nothing but stare at the blank white of the stretched fabric. The sunlight streaming through the window seemed to taunt her with its cheerfulness. A gray, stormy day would have suited her churning thoughts more aptly.

Heidi felt her mother's hand on her shoulder. "I don't know what to paint, Mama. My thoughts are so jumbled—full of hurt and frustration and fear—mostly fear. How do I find my way back to joy?"

"You are not alone, my dear. Many who have come before you have experienced those exact emotions. Even King David, in the forty-second Psalm, spoke to his soul: 'Why are you cast down, O my soul, and why are you in turmoil within me? Hope in God; for I shall again praise Him, my Salvation and my God.' Your grief is real, but in God there is hope and praise." She considered her daughter for a moment, then asked, "What was the last beautiful scene you studied before Peter grabbed you?"

Heidi had to consciously force herself to remember the sketch she had planned to draw. "The birch trees along Main Street. The gilded leaves would translate well to a painting."

"Immerse yourself in that image. When you find the sunshine in your portrait, you will find it again in your soul. Pray as you paint. God knows your path to joy. Allow Him to lead you there."

When her mother left, Heidi donned her bespeckled apron and opened her Bible to Psalm 42 to read David's words again. Committing the fifth verse to memory, she recited it as a prayer to God while she mixed the paint on her palette. When the blue matched the azure of the sky, she brushed the first bit of color onto the canvas.

Day after day, God worked in her heart while her brush worked on the unbleached cloth. Her mother had been right, for the scene before her seemed to infuse color into her bleak and stormy soul—a cathartic healing deep within. Focusing on the beauty of God's creation enabled her to catch a glimpse of His glory. Healing had begun.

Heidi finished adding the golden highlights to the first cluster of leaves and sat back, absorbing the truth that had been revealed to her heart. The source of the sunshine was evident, but she could merely see the results of that sunshine as it reflected off the leaves. Even when God seemed far away, the reflection His presence could still be seen around her and in her.

---

The following Saturday, Ingrid received a blunt refusal when she delivered cheese to the general store. If the clerk had expected a spirited argument, he was sorely disappointed, for Ingrid simply nodded, lifted her basket of wrapped cheeses, and quietly departed.

Fortunately, the Müllers knew their most faithful customers, and they visited each one throughout the following week and arranged home delivery for their wares. Unfortunately, when

Mayor Montgomery discovered what he considered to be their deception, he was furious.

The owner of the apothecary had made an appointment to discuss the expansion of his business and had brought a gift basket to put the mayor in an accepting mood. The basket, however, had the opposite of the intended effect, for lying on top was a large wedge of Müller cheese.

Mayor Montgomery pointed accusingly to the forbidden cheese and demanded, "Where did you get this?"

The small balding man before him paled and sputtered, "The Müllers have been making home deliveries to their customers."

The mayor gestured angrily toward the office door. "Out!" The confused apothecary owner all but ran from the room. Reginald pounded his fist upon his desk with such force the neatly stacked papers jumped and scattered. Seething with rage, he spoke to the two men standing in his office. "They will not get away with this treachery. Visit every farm that bought their cheese and threaten them with higher taxes if they ever purchase even so little as a wedge from the Müllers again!"

When news of Mayor Montgomery's response reached Johann, he began to put together the final pieces of their clandestine move.

Reginald Montgomery pounded on the Müllers' door. Ingrid quickly scanned the room to ensure the packing crates were not in view and nodded to her husband. Johann took a deep breath to diffuse his anger and opened the door to their adversary, whose face reddened with the intensity of his wrath.

"Your petty side business has been destroyed. Will you consent to allow Peter to court Heidi now?"

Johann responded without hesitation, "No, I will not."

"Barn fires happen more often than you would think."

The mayor's scathing undertones were not lost on Johann,

who stared back and clenched his jaw. "Fires set intentionally are against the law."

The rage was pouring from the mayor so profusely he began spitting as he punctuated each word. "You have forgotten that I own the law in this town!"

"Be that as it may, I will not change my mind."

"Fool!" the mayor screamed before he stomped off.

---

Johann kept a keen eye on the mayor's back until he was out of sight. When he had closed the front door, he turned and locked his gaze with Ingrid's. She understood his unspoken question and nodded. He decided to postpone the evening milking for a few minutes and call the family meeting immediately.

Once Heidi and Frederick had joined them, Johann spoke with quiet intensity. "Mayor Montgomery is planning to torch our barn. The time has come. After milking, we will turn the cows out to pasture and latch the barn door to keep them out. Once darkness has come, I will bring the wagon around to the back door. Finish your packing now and be ready to help me load. The cloak of night will hide our departure."

"What will happen to our cows?" Frederick asked, clearly concerned about the animals so important to their family.

"Gordon Reeves has already agreed to purchase our home with the barn and cows, and he has promised to keep the transaction a secret until we are gone. Mr. Reeves conducts no business in town, so the mayor should have no reason to retaliate against him as long as our mortgage loan is paid in full."

Frederick nodded. He liked Mr. Reeves and trusted him to care for "his" cows.

"Our wagon will certainly not hold all of our belongings, and we must be careful to pack light for the horses' sake. Bring only what is absolutely necessary."

Heidi stared at the wall holding several of her favorite paintings, each landscape infused with a little piece of her, knowing that they fell into the category of unnecessary. Her gaze lingered on her most recent work, and she tucked the promise in the painting deep in her heart. A quiet tear trickled down her cheek. Johann wrapped her hand in his own. "I am so sorry, Heidi."

"As am I." Heidi brushed the tear away and sat a bit straighter. All of her family were making sacrifices for her safety. They were uprooting their lives for her. Her oil paintings could be recreated; her family could not.

Everyone rose to perform their assigned tasks. Heidi packed only her most serviceable dresses and stockings, one bar of her rose-scented soap, a nightdress, and her Bible. She slowly fingered the art supplies on the desk next to the easel her papa had built for her. After closing her eyes for a moment to regain her composure, she reached for her sketchbook and pencils. There was just enough room on the top of her trunk, and they did not weigh much. To Heidi, having the ability to express herself on paper or canvas was as necessary as breathing. Papa would understand.

Loading the wagon happened in a flurry of activity. Heidi and her mother settled on the front seat while Papa made one final walk through the house. He must have found something they had missed, for Heidi heard him opening and securing one of the crates in the wagon bed before he climbed up beside her. With a command to Frederick to stay seated in the back, they embarked on their journey.

Heidi's eyes burned with the tears threatening to fall. Her words were a little above a whisper. "I wish Peter had never noticed me. All of this is my fault."

Johann reassured her with impassioned resolve. "None of this is your fault. Though you have never done anything to encourage his affections, Peter would have to be blind not to notice you. You are beautiful because God has made you beautiful. You are a priceless treasure—one meant to be cherished and protected. Peter has no idea how to either cherish or protect. He only knows how to steal and destroy." Johann waited until she lifted her eyes to him. "There is a young man specially chosen by God for you, and He will bring him to you. Until then, you must trust me to protect you."

## CHAPTER 3
### Jacob's Birthday

Jacob strolled from the barn to the kitchen door, his fingers wrapped around the handle of the milk pail. From his first day here at the ranch, he begged for milking to be one of his assigned chores. Somehow, the familiar chore connected him with the memory of his parents. Those memories were tickling his thoughts more than usual today. After setting the pail carefully on the kitchen counter, he scrubbed his hands and pulled out the chair next to his brother by birth.

Jacob's heart was full—mostly. The table in the ranch house was buzzing with conversation and laughter. Emma enjoyed having her family together for Sunday dinner, and Jacob felt blessed to be considered a part of this family.

Resting a hand on Jacob's shoulder, Emma stretched around him to place another bowl of mashed potatoes on the table.

Jacob lifted his face toward her profile. "Thank you."

"You're welcome, son."

*Son.* Arriving here at thirteen, he had thought himself too grown up to need another mother. After all, life had forced him to leave his boyhood behind and accept the responsibilities of a man at age ten. Emma had proven him wrong with her care and compassion, her hugs, and especially her prayers as she implored the God of Heaven on his behalf with the ardency only possible of a mother for her son.

Despite the role she filled in his life with such grace, Jacob had never been able to call her "Mama." Motherly titles belonged to the memories of the woman he had lost in the flood so many years ago. Emma understood. In fact, only James, his oldest brother here on the ranch, consistently referred to her as "Mama." The rest of them usually called her by her given name.

Jacob's eyes roamed over those present and landed on the empty chair at the head of the table—Daniel's chair—and thanked God again for the fatherly influence Daniel had been in his life. Now he and their brother Buck were buried on the Hill, the rise behind the house where Daniel had taught them to get alone with God. Tim was absent, too, having moved away.

Those remaining still filled his heart with belonging—Josiah, Luke with his wife Julie and their son Matthew, and James with his wife Emily. A knock sounded, and Emma called, "Perfect timing. Come on in and have a seat." Seth Carter, the widowed blacksmith and former rancher, had joined them with his three kids. Jonathan grabbed the chair next to Josiah, and Louisa and Anna sat between Emily and Emma. Seth unknowingly pulled out Daniel's chair and sat at the head of the table. Jacob waited for Emma to protest. When she didn't, he raised an eyebrow at Luke, who nodded that he had noticed, too. Interesting. Seth might not technically be family, but he had stepped into the hole left when Daniel died and had mentored him and his brothers through some rough times.

When Emma was seated, Seth prayed, "Dear Father in Heaven, thank you for Your unconditional love. Give us eyes to see Your many blessings, even when our hearts still hurt with sorrow. You promise that your mercies are new every single morning, and for that we are truly grateful. Thank You for this food and for those who worked to prepare it. As we celebrate Jacob's birthday, we thank You for the blessing he is in our lives and pray that You will bring Your blessings into his life in the coming year. In our Savior's name, Amen."

Seth's petition to God regarding Jacob both encouraged and humbled him. When Jacob kept his head bowed to absorb the words of his prayer, Josiah nudged him with his elbow. "Are you okay?"

Lifting his head, Jacob answered, "Yes, I'm fine."

"Good. Pass the potatoes." Jacob dropped a heavy dollop onto his own plate before handing Josiah the bowl.

After dinner, Emma brought out two apple pies. When everyone's eyes turned toward her, she responded with a mischievous grin. "These aren't just any apple pies. These were made by special request from Tim for Jacob's birthday."

Jacob laughed, his dimples on full display. The rest of the family understood the significance, but Seth raised a quizzical brow. When Jacob caught his breath, he explained to the Carters. "Tim absolutely loves Emma's apple pies. He would always get one on his birthday in August. By my birthday in October, he could only guarantee another apple pie if he convinced me to ask for one. So I did, every year, just for him."

His smile dimmed. "I miss him."

Emma walked over and placed a wrapped gift in front of him. "From Tim."

Jacob tore off the paper and opened the box to reveal a toy sheriff's badge. Lifting it from the tissue paper, he rubbed his thumb across the front. Lost in thought for a moment, Jacob then cleared his throat. "When James married, Tim bought this badge and teased Josiah and me that he was the sheriff of the bunkhouse, and we were his deputies. 'Only a real man can be sheriff,' he would say."

Josiah pointed to a slip of paper still in the box. "What does that say?"

Unfolding the paper, Jacob crooked his mouth and read aloud, "The time has come to pass this badge to you. You've earned it. Only a real man can be sheriff. I'm so proud to call you my brother. Happy 21$^{st}$ Birthday. Tim"

Josiah reached over for the badge and pinned it on Jacob's shirt. Thumping him on the back, Josiah declared, "The badge looks good on you."

His family presented thoughtful gifts, including a painted handprint from his nephew. His final gift was a narrow hinged wooden box with his initials surrounded by scrollwork carved on the lid. Inside was a new whittling knife. Examining it closely, Jacob found the tiny initials SC engraved on the Damascus steel blade honed to a sharp edge. Seth was gifted at forging blades. The wooden handle had been stained and polished to a flawless sheen, obviously Josiah's handiwork. Wrapping his fingers around the evenly-spaced grooves in the smooth handle, Jacob found the knife to be well-balanced and designed to fit in his hand as if it had been molded there. Jacob shifted his gaze from Josiah to Seth and back. "Thank you to both of you. It's beautiful."

When the dishes were washed and the family dispersed, Jacob wandered over to the pasture fence. He propped his boot on the bottom rail and leaned his forearms on the upper rail. A moment later, Seth appeared beside him, mirroring his stance. Comfortable silence passed between them. When Jacob acknowledged him with a nod, Seth sensed his invitation. "Other than missing Tim today, is there anything else on your mind?"

"I'm not sure. Maybe." Jacob expelled a mirthless laugh. "I've been rather introspective today."

"Did your musings reveal any insights?"

"Not really. What I know is that my relationship with the Lord continues to grow, and I love my family here. I just feel as if there is a puzzle piece missing from my life, and I'm not sure what it is."

Seth had the uncanny ability to peer straight into his inmost thoughts. Oddly, the inspection never felt intrusive, just thorough, and his conclusions were seldom wrong. As Seth studied him, Jacob was curious what he would find. Heaven knew he was at a loss.

Seth evaluated him for a moment before the edge of his mouth quirked upward. "I've got a pretty good guess." He rested a fatherly hand on Jacob's shoulder. "God is faithful. He will answer your heart in His timing. I'll be praying, too. In the meantime, focus on becoming the man God wants you to be, and God will bring the right young lady into your path."

A brow arched upward in surprise. *A girl. Huh. Interesting. Could he be right? Maybe.* Jacob turned his thoughtful gaze back toward the cows grazing in the pasture and considered the wise advice in Seth's words. "Be the right one, and I'll find the right one."

Dropping his voice to a whisper, Seth added with a glint in his eyes, "The right one is worth the wait." He clapped his hand on Jacob's shoulder and left him in the privacy of his thoughts.

With Seth's conversation playing in his mind, Jacob meandered into the barn and saddled Shadow for a ride. The blue roan horse's dark gray coloring and black mane and tail had earned him his moniker. Though Jacob had no specific destination in mind, he found himself approaching his favorite quiet spot. He dismounted and wrapped Shadow's reins around a low-hanging branch.

This place could always soothe his jumbled thoughts. Jacob rested his back against a tree near the river's edge and closed his eyes to absorb the sound of the cascading water as it tumbled over a three-foot waterfall into the pool below. He and his brothers here at the Rugged Cross Ranch had chosen this place as their swimming hole and had spent many hours here cooling off and horsing around after a hard day's work.

Jacob was the fifth of the six orphaned brothers who had been given a loving home here. All of them except Josiah, his younger brother by birth, had come from different families. Their differing backgrounds had not deterred them from forging a strong bond as brothers. Now they had grown into young men, and the oldest four had married. Now only he and Josiah still lived in the bunkhouse. He was thankful for Josiah, but if he were completely honest, he had felt a bit lost since Tim married Laura and moved to Kansas to become a pastor of a growing community in Kansas while working as the foreman of the Rafter C Ranch.

Of all his brothers, Tim understood him best and had been instrumental in leading Jacob to a personal relationship with Jesus Christ. God had strategically ordained Tim to be his older brother: Jacob was convinced of that truth. He had been honored when the brother he most admired asked him to be his best man. His mind returned to Tim's wedding day.

---

Jacob stood at the front of the church to Tim's left. Though Jacob was a couple of inches shy of six feet tall, he never felt out of place next to Tim's six-and-a-half-foot frame. A quick upward glance showed that Tim's mischievous grin had been replaced by a genuine smile, a smile that grew the instant the back doors opened to reveal his bride.

When Jacob turned his gaze to Laura as she walked down the aisle, something inside him shifted. The way her eyes glistened with love and adoration for her groom alone uncovered a hole in his heart he had not known existed. Would he ever have a woman walk an aisle toward him?

---

His thoughts had been tucked away so they would not detract from Tim's special day. Now he untucked them to examine them more closely. He was too pragmatic to be a romantic, although he would have said the same of Tim before Laura claimed his heart. Yet he could not deny the tug to imagine his life with a lovely woman on his arm—a lady to love and protect and share the rest of his days.

A sigh erupted unbidden from deep within. Who was he kidding? Their town of Prairie Hills was a small community, and none of the few eligible young ladies were near enough to his age, though age wouldn't necessarily be a limiting factor if one were "the one." Thinking through the unattached ladies in their church brought the same conclusion he came to every year during the time of the annual church social and the reason he had been attending alone for the last several years.

Jacob loved the ranch—his work and his family—and he had no desire to leave it. Unless God Himself brought a woman to Prairie Hills to be his wife, he should get used to the idea of staying an eternal bachelor. Truly, he was mostly content. He had been blessed when Emma and Daniel added him and Josiah to their family. He just needed to turn "mostly content" into "completely content."

"Lord, I don't know why my desire for a wife has been pressed upon my mind, but I cannot deny it, for you know my thoughts. The verse from Proverbs that says 'He who finds a wife finds a good thing and obtains favor from the Lord' keeps playing in my mind. If your plan for me is to remain unmarried, please remove this desire from my heart."

A verse from the Gospel of Luke invaded Jacob's thoughts

as if it had been spoken aloud. *"With God, nothing is impossible."* He opened his eyes and watched the frolicking water spill from above and splash into the quiet pool below while he ruminated on those words like a cow chewed her cud. He had seen God do the impossible in his life before. God had kept him and Josiah together and had provided them a family here at the ranch. Besides, many times in Scripture, God performed the impossible. Surely God was able to bring the right woman into his life if He chose to do so. Until then, he would follow Seth's advice and strive to be the man God wanted him to be.

## CHAPTER 4
## *Home*

Peter Montgomery and two of his father's "personal escorts" rode to the Müllers' farm under cloak of nightfall with only the moonlight to illuminate their villainous mission. The "personal escorts" could not even be accurately labeled "bodyguards," for they were "henchmen" in every sense of the word. For this reason, they were exactly who Peter needed this night.

Approaching the farm, Peter noted that every window in the house was dark. The edges of his mouth lifted in a sneer, and his heart rate rose in answer to the adrenaline rush of anticipation. Leading his entourage around to the rear of the barn, Peter began to sense that something felt amiss. Before he ignited his torch, he paused to listen and realized the soft lowing of the cattle came from around him rather than inside the barn.

Peter dismounted and flung open the latch of the barn's back door with such force that it nearly ripped from its hinges. The barn was empty. *Empty!* He stormed through the barn and did not slow his steps as he barged through the front door and across the clearing to the house. His anger rose to full fury. Not pausing to knock, he rammed the door open with his shoulder and searched each room one-by-one. *Empty!*

A growl emanated from deep within, and his jaw was clenched as tight as a vise clamp. *They were trying to escape. No matter.* His seething anger wrapped its noose around his heart. *He would catch them, and when he did, he would make them pay. Heidi would be his, and her moron of a father would be stopped, one way or another.*

Peter stomped back to his horse and remounted. Addressing the other two men, he fumed, "The entire family is gone, and their wagon is missing. They cannot be too far ahead of us. The question is: where would they go?"

One man barely kept himself from rolling his eyes at the ignorance of this man-child. "Logically, they will be heading for a train depot."

"Obviously, but which one? They have no family on this side of the ocean or acquaintances beyond the borders of our town."

The second man piped up, "If they want to stay in the cheese business, they will probably head toward Wisconsin."

"There are three train stations within a few hours' ride." Peter thrust his finger at the first man. "You, head south toward Maryland." Turning to the second man, he commanded, "You, head east toward Philadelphia. They may go that direction first to throw us off. I'll head west toward the spur that heads into Pittsburgh. If you find the Müllers and bring them back, I'll make it worth your while. Go!"

---

Knowing that winter was not far off, Johann was thankful for modern modes of transportation that would speed their twelve-hundred-mile journey and planned accordingly. The morning following their hasty departure, they arrived in a small town just across the Maryland border. To offset travel expenses, Johann sold the wagon and team to an elated livery owner. The family boarded a train heading west, choosing to stay in the freight car with their belongings to decrease the threat of anyone spotting them and reporting back to Reginald Montgomery. For an added measure of protection, Johann decided to purchase only one leg of the journey at a time, hoping their broken trail would be harder to follow.

As Johann helped Ingrid into the freight car, the hair on the back of his neck bristled. He glanced over his shoulder and spotted one of Mayor Montgomery's men standing on the platform searching the throng of travelers for them. Before the pursuer's gaze swept down the line past the passenger cars, Johann hopped aboard and shut the boxcar door. His breathing quickened, and he prayed he hadn't been seen. Johann's grip remained on the door handle while he schooled his features, for he did not want to alarm the rest of his family.

His chosen route was south to Baltimore, then west through Cumberland, Cincinnati, and St. Louis before their final train stop on the border of Kansas. Johann scrutinized everyone at each station along the way, but he never again recognized anyone familiar. With each leg of the journey, his tension abated a bit more.

Once the train pulled into the station in Kansas City, Johann still needed a final destination. *Lord, guide me. Where do you want us to go from here?* When he eyed the loading dock, he spotted a flyer tacked to the bulletin board. Closer inspection revealed an invitation to attend the community church. The corner of Johann's mouth lifted, *Yes, Lord, church is a great place to find answers.*

Realizing it was Sunday morning, he took his family to the church near the teacher's college for the morning service. Pastor Witherspoon had a welcoming demeanor and introduced the Müllers to his father, the former pastor, who invited them for dinner after church. In him, Johann found a man of wisdom, and he was in need of advice.

Following the meal, Johann confided in the elder Mr. Witherspoon and asked for recommendations. "Actually, I do have a good recommendation for you. The town of Prairie Hills lies in northwestern Oklahoma Territory. I mentored the pastor of the church there when he was in training. David Kendrick is a godly man. The town is relatively small, yet it contains all the necessities including a newly established school. Available farmland stretches in all directions. You could maintain anonymity in the short-term, but Prairie Hills would be a beautiful place to call home. Allow me to write to David and inquire about any farms for sale. He is a man to be trusted and would prove to be a good ally."

Johann pondered Mr. Witherspoon's request and agreed to the letter.

The elder pastor smiled his approval. "Until you receive a reply, you are welcome to stay in our home."

"Oh, we wouldn't want to impose."

"Nonsense. This house can be too quiet. A bit of company is just what we need."

A week later, a letter arrived from David Kendrick. Mr. Witherspoon settled in his favorite chair and donned his half-rimmed spectacles before he opened the envelope and unfolded the papers within. Johann was eager for news, and the elder man's methodical movements tempted him to be as impatient as his children on St. Nicholas' Day. He studied the man reading and witnessed the edges of his eyes crinkle when he smiled and lifted his gaze to Johann. "Who says the Lord doesn't answer prayer? David has an older couple in his church who want to sell their dairy farm and move East to live near their children and grandchildren before winter hits, but they haven't been able to find a buyer. The sale of the farm would include twenty milk cows with a barn large enough to hold twenty more. Would two hundred acres be enough pastureland for forty cows?"

"Yes," Johann answered simply, concealing the excitement building within him. "Does David mention the farm's price?"

The retired preacher skimmed the letter again. "Here it is in the post script." He handed the letter to Johann. "Is that a fair price?"

Ingrid had come to stand behind her husband. He wordlessly held the letter so she could see the printed figure. Her response was to lay her hand on his shoulder and squeeze lightly. "God has indeed answered prayer. Few times in my life has God's direction been so clear." He turned and captured his wife's hand in his own. "Our family is moving to Prairie Hills."

---

The nefarious trio united again with Reginald Montgomery in the mayor's office. Peter spread a rudimentary railroad map on the worktable and followed his route with his finger. "I followed the route through Pittsburgh and Chicago to where the line ends in La Cross, Wisconsin. No sign of them along the way."

The mayor glared at the next man, who added, "I covered points east to Philadelphia and north to New York."

"I thought I had a lead on them at the spur depot to Baltimore. A man had just sold a wagon and team to the livery."

"Was it the Müllers'?" demanded Peter.

"No way to tell. Every wagon looks the same, and the horses had no identifying brand. The livery owner thought the seller might have been tall, but he had purchased three wagons that day and couldn't remember for sure. Either way, I searched the passenger cars but didn't find any of them."

Mayor Montgomery slammed his fist against his desk, the poor wooden surface taking a beating from its owner's lack of self-control. "We must find them! When word of their deceit gets out, more citizens will be emboldened to rebel."

---

Heidi was weary of travel. Frederick's grouchy attitude told her he was, too. Her papa stoically kept the wagon moving toward Prairie Hills. That was the name of the town, right? Her mama was tired, but she just hummed and made the best of it. *Lord, help me to be more like my mama.*

---

They arrived on the outskirts of Prairie Hills just before dusk and set up camp one last time. The following morning, Johann rode into town toward the steepled church. When he did not find the pastor there, he tried the home adjacent to the church building, hoping it was the parsonage. When a young man answered the door, he asked, "Is this the home of Pastor Kendrick?"

Robert Kendrick, the pastor's son, answered, "Yes, it is. Come on in." Turning his head, he called, "Dad, someone is here to see you."

A middle-aged man with greying at his temples emerged from a side room to greet the stranger. Johann extended his hand. "David Kendrick?"

Pastor Kendrick returned the handshake. "Yes, and you are?"

"Johann Müller."

Instant recognition crinkled David's eyes as he smiled. "Ah, yes. Welcome to Prairie Hills." He gestured toward the room he had just exited. "Join me in my study, and I'll show you the map of the area and the location of the Coopers' farm."

David picked up a rolled parchment from his credenza,

smoothed it out on his desk, and pointed to the building marked with a cross on the map. "Here is our church." He glanced up at Johann. "Your family has an open invitation to worship with us." His expression sobered as he continued, "Though I understand the safety concerns you expressed in your letter, I just want you to know you are welcome."

"Not right now, but perhaps soon. We do desire a church family, and the Lord knows I could use a friend to confide in. Allow me to get a feel for the town and put down some roots first."

David nodded in understanding. "Of course." Returning his focus to the map, he circled the cluster of buildings near the church with his finger. "This is the town of Prairie Hills, and two miles to the northwest is the Coopers' homestead. The farmhouse sits here with the pastureland beyond."

Johann studied the drawing and noticed a large parcel of land due west of town that abutted the Coopers' farm. He indicated the spot and asked, "Are the folks here good neighbors?"

David smiled. "That is the Rugged Cross Ranch. They raise some of the best beef cattle in Oklahoma Territory, and yes, they will be excellent neighbors. My oldest daughter Emily is married to James, the oldest brother and foreman on the ranch." David tapped the map where the land parcels joined. "There is a thick stand of fir trees just on their side of the boundary line, so you'll have a good visual of where the dairy farmland ends and theirs begins."

As an excellent judge of character, Johann needed only this brief exchange before he readily agreed with Mr. Witherspoon's assessment that David Kendrick was a man to be trusted. After showing him the lay of the land on the map, David procured his horse from the livery and escorted Johann to the Coopers' dairy farm for a tour. The buildings needed some minor maintenance, but nothing that needed urgent attention before winter.

Johann took the most time with the cows. Charles Cooper was white-haired and slightly bent with a face lined with the wisdom of long life. He led Johann from one stall to the next, giving an introduction and a brief summary of each animal, including age, temperament, feeding habits, and milk production. Mr. Cooper's care for his herd rivaled his own.

Conversely, Johann sensed that Charles was equally impressed with Johann's knowledge of dairy cows and was relieved to be selling them to someone who would continue to care for them.

After Mrs. Cooper insisted on feeding them all a hearty lunch, Charles joined them for a meeting at the land office in town to complete the real estate transaction. When the last document had been signed, Charles shook Johann's hand. "Thank you, son, for being an answer to prayer. Sissy and I will pack up the last of the kitchen supplies when I get home so your family can move in."

"Then I'll plan to start the milking tonight," Johann offered.

Johann returned to his family's camp with a smile that radiated his enthusiasm. "Let's pack up. We're moving into our new home tonight."

---

Frederick cheered, and Heidi had to rely on her ladylike composure to keep herself from cheering with him. Her papa had just used the most wonderful word—home.

The wagon's rumbling wheels skirted the town, but Heidi observed the buildings from a distance and was filled with both excitement and fear. Panic stole her breath like an ambushing thief, and all color drained from her face. Ingrid wrapped her arm around Heidi's shoulders and pulled her close as the tremors began. Just when she was feeling as if this fear were finally waning in intensity, the unbidden attack of panic would seize her. She clutched her stomach to still her nerves and filled her thoughts with the familiar verses—God's message to her—that He would never leave her.

The fierce grip of panic began to release one finger at a time as they took the road heading west and veered right at the fork until they reached the farm. Beyond a generous front yard lay a two-story farmhouse with a welcoming porch that wrapped around the front and side. The barn stood to the right, facing the house, and the fence line stretched far into the distance. The pastoral sight was both peaceful and healing. When Johann pulled the horses to a stop close to the front door, Heidi felt herself begin to relax for the first time in weeks. She was home.

Feeling as if she could empathize with the roaming gypsies of Europe, Heidi's soul ached to have her life firmly planted in one place again. Would this town be like the last? She shivered as the icy fingers of fear wound around her pounding heart. The memory of those awful moments with Peter continued to haunt her. Closing her eyes and focusing on her breathing helped to dispel the feeling, but they never seemed to quell it completely.

Desperate to find a distraction, Heidi turned her attention to helping her family unload their crates of belongings from the wagon. Papa used a crowbar to unfasten the lids of each crate before he took Frederick to the barn to start evening milking. Finding the crate marked "kitchen," she busied herself unpacking each item and helping her mama clean and fill the cupboards.

When that crate was empty, Heidi lifted the loosened lid from the next one. A rectangle-shaped parcel wrapped in canvas lay on top. The instant she picked it up, she knew. The beveled edges discernible through the covering were a familiar friend. Reverently, she opened the protective sheathing.

Behind her, the door hinges squeaked and heavy footsteps entered. Heidi looked up at her papa as tears filled her eyes. She gingerly laid her birch tree painting back on the crate and ran to her Papa, flinging her arms around him. "Thank you, Papa! Thank you."

The warmth of his strong arm curved around her, and his lips pressed against her hair. "You are welcome, my sweet girl. You need this place to feel like home, and that painting is my favorite."

Deep within, Heidi understood her papa had chosen the one tangible thing to continue her healing—not the painting itself, not really, but the promises of God's presence the scene represented.

"Underneath your painting, you will find your paints and brushes. I will order more blank canvases tomorrow when I head to town for supplies." He released his daughter. "Now, for the pertinent question: Where would you like me to hang your birch trees? I was thinking the space over the mantel might be nice."

Glancing over at the stone that surrounded the hearth and extended to the ceiling, she envisioned the landscape centered above the rough-hewn wooden mantle. "Yes, Papa, that would be the perfect spot."

The corner of his mouth lifted. He reached for the toolbox in one hand and the framed scene with the other. A few minutes later, he stepped back next to Heidi. "What do you think?"

"It's perfect. Now it feels like home."

## CHAPTER 5
## *Cheesemaking*

Before the first fingers of dawn had pushed back the blanket of night, Heidi stretched and opened her eyes. The immediate tight cinching of her chest and the knots in her stomach ratcheted her heart rate, propelling her upright in bed. A glance around her brought understanding. She was in her new bedroom. Safe. A hand lifted to her chest as she willed her heart to cease its pounding, and she focused on her breathing—in through her nose and out her mouth—just as her mama had taught her.

Peter's continued hold on her needed to be broken. She refused to remain a victim even when her trauma became a fodder for her fears and nightmares. The Lord was her Shepherd, her Rock, her Fortress, her Protector, and He had given her a tangible representation of those qualities in her papa. "Lord, thank you for my papa. Please continue to work in my heart as I grow from fear to peace and joy."

The final breakfast platter was laid on the rough-hewn table as Johann and Frederick returned from morning milking. Sliced challah bread, still warm from the oven, fresh-churned butter, strawberry jam, fried eggs, sliced ham, and their own homemade cheese waited at the center of the table, and tall glasses of milk stood like pale sentries beside each plate.

When the men had shrugged off their jackets and washed their hands, they joined Ingrid and Heidi at the table. Johann held out open hands. Once the ladies had grasped one of his and one of Frederick's, Johann prayed, "Almighty God, our hearts praise You for our new home and this bountiful feast. Please protect our family and give us wisdom as we establish our business in this community. We will give You all the glory. In Jesus' name, Amen."

"Since our cheese is a family business, your mama and I would like your opinion on a new brand name."

"Why can't we still call it Müller cheese?" Frederick inquired.

"We are hoping to eventually expand our distribution to the region and beyond, and we do not want a name that would be easily tracked back to us."

Understanding clicked, and Frederick continued, "Because Mayor Montgomery and Peter may be looking for Müller cheese to find Heidi."

"Yes," confirmed Johann. "Now for a new name. What do you think about Segen Farm cheese?"

"The German word for *blessing*—I like it," Heidi responded.

Frederick's brow furrowed slightly. "Ja, I like it, too, but wouldn't a German word be a clue as well?"

Johann considered his son's comment. "To anyone who is not German, Segen sounds like a Scandinavian surname, and there are many cheesemakers from that region. I think the name would protect us from suspicion." He glanced around the table. "We are Americans now. Let's practice democracy and vote. Who approves of changing our business to Segen Farm cheese?" Every hand raised. The vote was unanimous.

"After breakfast, Frederick and I will begin a thorough inventory of tools, hay, and feed while both of you are making cheese. This afternoon, your mama and I will drive into town and request a meeting with the owner of the general store."

Addressing Heidi, he continued, "For now, I want you and Frederick to stay on the homestead. Though highly unlikely, if anyone comes while we are away, stay hidden. For your protection, we want to keep your existence a secret until we know whom to trust. Your seclusion will be temporary, but I believe it to be necessary for a short time."

"Yes, Papa. I understand."

---

By the time Heidi finished clearing the table and washing the breakfast dishes, Ingrid had warmed the milk. Heidi carefully removed the sealed jar of Gouda culture from the packing straw and measured a precise amount into the first pot.

Not unlike the starter for sourdough bread, their cheese cultures had originated in Germany and Holland and had been carefully grown and bloomed through the years. The cultures had become a family legacy, handed down from mother to daughter for several generations.

Ingrid observed the clock and jotted down the time on a nearby piece of paper. "Thirty minutes of ripening will finish at 9:07."

Since the citric acid, crystallized from lemon juice, had already been added to the second pot, Heidi added the rennet, an enzyme procured from the fourth stomach lining of a calf, stirred it gently, and pulled it off the cookstove and covered it.

She also glanced at the clock. "Time to cut the mozzarella will be 8:50."

When the time came, Heidi cut the mozzarella into a grid pattern and lifted the pot back onto the cookstove. As she stirred for a few more minutes, the curds began to separate from the whey. Using a slotted wooden spoon, she scooped the curds into a cheesecloth bag and tied the bag to a frame, allowing the excess whey to drip into a bowl beneath it.

Five minutes later, she dumped the curds back into the pot of heated whey and warmed them until they became the right consistency. Removing the curds a final time, Heidi added a liberal sprinkling of salt and began to stretch the mozzarella like taffy seven times before she formed the cheese into a ball and laid it in a bowl to cool.

Heidi finished the mozzarella while her mama was adding the rennet to the Gouda. Ingrid again consulted the clock. "Forty minutes to develop the curd."

Cheesemaking was much like baking bread. Each working step was important, but the periods of waiting were just as important. Aged cheese like Gouda and cheddar needed time to develop in the same way as yeast bread needed time to rise.

The mother-daughter pair often prepared cheddar along with the other two cheeses, but Ingrid had wanted a double batch of Gouda today to begin the aging process and build their future inventory.

"Heidi, since cutting and stirring this curd doesn't require two of us, why don't you get some fresh air? Maybe take your sketchpad?"

Heidi hugged her. "Thank you, Mama."

After procuring her paper and pencils from her bedroom chest, Heidi wandered around the homestead, never straying far from the buildings. The open barn door beckoned her, the door itself telling a story. It was strong and sturdy, but the exterior showed definite signs of weathering, and the sunlight was striking it at just the right angle to emphasize the battered texture.

Resting on a stump probably used for woodcutting, Heidi turned to a blank page in her sketchbook and lined her pencils in order from softest to hardest graphite. Choosing a medium hardness pencil, she began outlining the door with its crossbuck pattern, the surrounding wall of the barn, and the cluster of flowers still defying the onset of autumn.

Alternating the softer and harder graphite, the darker and lighter details came to life on the page. The rough texture of the door juxtaposed with the smooth petals of the flowers. The dark opening to the barn's interior seemed curiously welcoming. Heidi breathed deeply of the cool autumn air. *Yes, welcoming like a new beginning.*

Lost in her drawing, Heidi forgot the time until her mama poked her head out of the front door. "Are you ready to help me press the Gouda?"

"Coming, Mama."

Working together in companionable silence, they divided the curds evenly into four cheese molds lined with cheesecloth, fitted the top part of the mold, and tightened the cheese press just enough to squeeze the whey from the curds. In prescribed intervals, they flipped the cheese and repeated the process with twice as much pressure. The Gouda would stay under pressure for twelve hours. Then the round of cheese would sit in a brine overnight and lay out to dry for two or three days before it would be dipped in wax and aged for six weeks.

The Coopers had left furniture and several items for their use, including a broom Heidi found in the pantry closet. Making herself useful, she swept the front porch, musing on the idea that life was a lot like cheesemaking. Periods of heat and pressure with intervals of rest and the right amount of aging yielded a delicious result. Her struggle with fear definitely felt like heat and pressure, but trials were a necessary part of life along with intervals of quiet rest. God's greatest blessings, though, often required patience, waiting for His timing with a happy heart.

---

Later that afternoon, Ingrid packed one round each of Gouda and aged cheddar from the crate they had brought with them from Pennsylvania and included Heidi's fresh mozzarella from that morning.

"Are you ready to go, Meine Liebe?" Johann asked his wife.

"Ja," Ingrid answered as Johann took the basket from her hand. "Let us hope the store owner likes cheese."

"How can he not when you made it?"

Ingrid blushed under his praise. With another reminder for Heidi and Frederick to stay out of sight of any strangers, Johann commanded the team into motion toward town.

Johann might look imposing with his height and broad, well-muscled shoulders, but Ingrid was the mastermind when it came to business negotiations. Once they were introduced to Levi Hensley, the store owner, Johann handed Ingrid the basket and excused himself, allowing her the freedom to promote their cheese.

Ingrid followed the portly man with a friendly countenance behind a curtain-covered doorway into a back room used primarily for storage. In one corner was a small desk with a flurry of scattered papers on its surface, proclaiming the room's secondary purpose as an office. Mr. Hensley gestured to a chair, and Ingrid lowered herself and pulled the basket onto her lap.

"Our family has made cheese for generations. We specialize in three cheeses: Gouda, aged cheddar, and mozzarella. The cheeses use milk that comes from Jersey cows that have been fed grass fortified with additional nutrients from alfalfa and clover."

"We have recently moved from Pennsylvania, where our cheeses were popular and sold quite well, bringing the shopkeeper there a tidy profit."

"If your business was doing well, why did you move?"

An astute question, if their move had been motivated by business. However, to say their move was not motivated by business would not be entirely honest, for the mayor had crippled their ability to reach their customers. That explanation would only breed more questions. Ingrid replied, "God directed our move here, and we are eager to meet a need for artesian cheese in your community."

Reaching into her basket, she withdrew her cheese knife and sliced a sample of each cheese. "Try these and see what you think."

Mr. Hensley took the time to savor each one. "Mmm. These are really good. My only hesitation is that several of our townsfolk make homemade cheeses, not this delicious, mind you, but I'm not sure if there would be much of a demand for your cheese in our store."

"Take the rest of these cheeses, free of charge, and offer them for sale in your store by the slice or by weight. There is no financial risk to you, for anything you make from these will be entirely profit. When your customers ask for more, we will gladly bring you additional inventory. Here is our price list." Ingrid pulled a neatly penned paper from her basket and added it to the top of his disheveled pile.

He perused the prices and nodded. "These prices are reasonable with potential for a nice profit margin for the store. Let's see how these sell, and we'll go from there."

"Thank you for your time." For the first time in the conversation, Ingrid smiled. She knew her cheeses could practically sell themselves. With a profit incentive from the free samples, the owner was sure to promote them well. Knowing her ongoing pricing, he could set the price competitively from the beginning, ensuring himself a continued profit when he was paying for the inventory.

"I'll stop by in a few days in case you need more cheese."

"Excellent. See you then."

---

When Heidi's parents pulled away toward town, she gathered her sketch paper and pencils and began wandering, staying close to the house, of course. Her eyes scanned for just the right subject for her next drawing. She would have to continue this morning's sketch on the morrow, for the sun and shadows needed to be the same.

The breeze lifted the wisps of hair around her face and tickled her cheek. She absently raised her hand and tucked the wayward strands behind her ear. *There.* Around the corner of the barn stood an aged rain barrel, the light enhancing its weathered surface. The stark shadow on the barn wall would create depth in the sketch. Heidi returned to the front of the barn and entered, giving herself a moment for her eyes to adjust from the bright sunlight outside. She found a short wooden box. "This will work nicely." Heidi carried the box and chose just the right position from which to draw. Then smoothing her skirt, she lowered herself onto the makeshift chair.

The corners of Heidi's eyes narrowed in concentration while her focus bounced back and forth between the scene before her and the faint outline growing on the paper. With her tongue held captive between her teeth, the barrel began to take shape. When the shading revealed the wood's rough texture, her pencil paused mid-stroke. Her brow furrowed as she shifted to anchor her elbow on her knee and rest her chin in her hand.

*Why am I drawn to weathered surfaces today? First the barn door, now the barrel.* She pondered her choice of subjects. *This whole incident with Peter certainly has my soul feeling battered and rough. Perhaps that's why I'm inspired by these things. What lesson can I learn?* Her thoughts scrambled for an answer. *Though the barn door and barrel have endured harsh conditions, they are still strong and useful. Lord, give me strength to overcome my fears and use me for Your glory.*

After an hour or so had passed, the stiffness in Heidi's back forced her to stand and take a break to stretch. When she set her drawing on the wooden box, Frederick called to her from inside the barn. "Heidi! Come see this."

The barn door released a rusty squeak as Heidi entered. Her eyes were veiled again with the change in ambient light, and she couldn't see her brother. "Frederick, where are you?"

"Up here in the loft. There is a window about halfway back. Whoever heard of a window in a loft? Come on up."

After another minute, Heidi's eyes had adjusted enough to visualize the barn's interior. She lifted her hem to secure her foot on the bottom rung of the ladder and began to climb. The loft was tall enough to stand with several inches to spare. Surveying the beams overhead, she asked, "Do you think Papa could stand straight without hitting his head?"

"Probably." Frederick's dismissive answer proved her question was unimportant to him at the moment. Heidi was obviously not moving quickly enough to soothe his impatience, for Frederick approached her and grabbed her hand. "This way."

About halfway back, a stripe of light shone between two stacks of hay. Sure enough, a transom window approximately five feet in length was fitted below the eve. Frederick beamed up at her and announced with enthusiasm, "This could be your secret studio!" He had repositioned the bales of hay to create a chair with a table beside it near the window and cleared the space across to the edge by the railing overlooking the barn floor below. He had even adjusted a hay bale at a slant to give her a back rest if she chose to sketch from this vantage point. "Your very own private space. What do you think?"

Heidi's lips tipped upward in a smile, and she turned slowly in a circle to survey Frederick's handiwork. Her mind was already envisioning her studio. "It's wonderful. You are so thoughtful! Thank you." She grabbed her brother in a quick hug, glad that he still allowed them from time to time. Soon, he would be too big for such displays of affection.

When the siblings heard the rumble of a wagon, tightness instantly gripped Heidi's chest and her fist pressed against her sternum. They peeked from the loft window and saw their parents approaching, and the tightness began to unwind. Frederick studied his sister and his concerned face brightened with a sudden idea. "This could be a great hiding place for you, too. You could see anyone coming toward the house, but they would never see you."

"Hopefully, I will not need to stay hidden for much longer. Staying sequestered for too long will give my fear the ability to change my place of safety into a prison that I am too afraid to leave."

"You are too strong to let that happen."

Heidi released a sigh. "I fear the change has already begun."

## CHAPTER 6
### *Harvest*

The time of harvest was near at hand. Farmers throughout the community of Prairie Hills had a short window of time to reap and store their crops. Since work on the ranch was not as busy this time of year, the brothers volunteered their time to be a blessing to the farmers around them.

While James was meeting with three of the farmers in their congregation after church to plan which days he and his brothers should help at each farm, Emily stood in the shadows observing the young mothers with their children, some cradling infants, some with toddlers clinging to their mothers' skirts, and some busy trying to keep the older ones out of mischief. The ache in her heart for a child of her own intensified to an almost palpable pain. Emily closed her eyes and focused on the distant indistinguishable hum of her husband's voice.

The words of Mrs. Margret Lange penetrated her thoughts. Mrs. Lange was refined but endowed with enough padding for a grandmotherly effect, that is, until one glimpsed her perpetual scowl. Rather than speaking kindhearted words, she tended to wield her tongue like a saber, cutting others down to cause her short stature to appear taller.

Standing with her back to Emily, Mrs. Lange was speaking to one of her many confidants in a loud whisper, a sound that pretended to be confidential but in reality beckoned all within earshot to listen. "By the time I had been married three months, I was already in the family way. Emily has made no such announcement yet, and she has been married for two years. Motherhood should be a higher priority than teaching."

Mrs. Lange's friend replied, "I read in my women's magazine that some women are choosing careers over motherhood these days. I'm just surprised Emily is one of them. She was so good with her siblings after her mother passed."

"Maybe they put a bad taste in her mouth," Mrs. Lange commented with a mirthless laugh and a dramatically sad shake of her head. She and her friend meandered toward the church doors, leaving a wounded young woman in their wake.

A few minutes later, James approached and noticed his wife fighting back tears. His brow furrowed. "What's wrong?"

Resting her hand on James' arm, Emily answered, "Nothing I wish to discuss here."

James lifted her hand, tucking it into his elbow and covering it with his own. "Let's go home, then, so I can listen without interruptions."

On the way home, Emily shared her heart. "I know Mrs. Lange wasn't meaning to attack me personally, but her barbs hurt just the same."

James' ire ignited. "That woman's gossip causes nothing but pain and destruction. I'd like to give her a piece of my mind." Emily laid a quieting hand on his forearm, and the fire in his eyes dimmed slightly. "I'm sorry I was not with you in that moment to defend you. Anyone who knows you at all knows your heart for children, both in the classroom and in our home."

Emily rested her head against his shoulder. "I love you, James."

"I love you more." James pressed a kiss into her hair.

---

While Sunday dinner was underway with the entire family around Emma's table in the farmhouse, James turned the conversation to harvest. "Tom Wilson's fields are ready to begin harvest tomorrow. Nathan Lange's and Walter Moore's crops are nearly ready, maybe as early as midweek. Luke, will you be available to help?"

"Yes, Doc is giving me the next two weeks off for harvest, though I'm still on call to assist in any emergency surgeries."

"All right. Why don't you cover barn chores tomorrow? Jacob, Josiah, and I will head over to Tom's in the morning. We'll rotate barn chores each day and split up when the other fields are ready."

Luke nodded. "Sounds good."

"Did you hear Nathan discussing Cyrus McCormick's mechanical reaper?" Josiah inquired. "Now that the design includes a self-raking feature, more farmers are investing in the contraption. He's seriously considering the purchase of one before next harvest, saying he can double his crop and still reduce harvest labor."

"That's interesting," Jacob commented. "With the farms ready for harvest at different times, I wonder if a coalition of local farmers would want to contribute toward the purchase and share the machine."

"Not a bad thought. Although if two crops ripened simultaneously, the need for the reaper might cause contention," Luke reasoned.

"I suppose they could decide the terms of use ahead of time to avoid conflict," James offered.

"If Nathan is considering a harvester, he might want to consider Hiram Moore's combine. In addition to reaping, it will thresh and winnow the wheat." All eyes turned to Emily in surprise. "Of course, it wouldn't be effective with corn or hay. McCormick's reaper might be more versatile if the machine is to be shared."

Josiah asked what most were thinking. "How do you know all this?"

"When you teach students in a farming community, including instruction about the latest agricultural inventions is an important part of their learning."

Josiah chuckled. "Of course, it is."

Next to Emily, James wrapped his hand around his coffee cup and glanced down at his wife with unmasked admiration. When Emily turned her face toward him, he winked.

After lunch, Jacob strolled up to the Hill and sat on the bench beneath outstretched branches. He rested his forearms on his knees and loosely clasped his hands. For a few moments, he sat in silence, unsure how to pray. Focusing on his hands gave his heart inspiration. "Lord, my soul feels as if it's wandering aimlessly. I need purpose. Give me the opportunity to use these hands You've given me to be a blessing to others above and beyond just helping with harvest. Help me to be alert to the needs of those around me. Use me for Your glory. I want to become the man You desire me to be."

---

After chores the following morning, James crossed behind his doctor brother to hang the pitchfork on the wall. "Luke, may I see you for a minute?" When Luke joined him in the foreman's office, James closed the door behind them and rounded his desk to sit in his chair. Luke sat in the chair on the other side of the desk and leaned back, extending his legs in front of him, expecting a run-down of his delegated tasks for the day.

"Luke?" James began, uncharacteristically lost for words.

Luke noticed the change and shifted to sit forward. "What is it, James?"

James splayed his fingers and ran his hand through his thick dark brown hair. "May I ask you a medical question?"

"Of course." Concern crinkled Luke's brow. He waited while James continued to collect his thoughts.

"Emily and I dream of having a houseful of children." Luke nodded but kept silent. "We've been married for two years, and . . ." James released a stream of air through pursed lips. "Well, is there a way to know if something is wrong, and if so, is there a way to fix it?"

Luke rested his elbows on his knees and hung his head. "Unfortunately, no. Maybe one day enough research will be done to know what to test for and how to treat infertility. Until then, all we can do is pray and wait."

When Luke raised his eyes to James, James saw pain there beyond the expected compassion for James and Emily's hurt. Suddenly he realized, "You said 'we,' but you and Julie have Matthew."

Luke slowly nodded, "Yes, and I know you will understand when I say I am proud to claim Matthew as my son, and I could not love him more, but he is not from me. Julie and I have been married longer than you and Emily, but she and I haven't been able to have children. Julie conceived twice during the year she was married to Buck, so whatever 'problem' there is must be with me. The burden of responsibility is a heavy weight."

James whispered, "I had no idea."

"Julie and I are beyond thankful for Matthew, and we don't take him for granted, but our hearts' desire is to have another baby . . . or two or three."

James relaxed a bit knowing Luke truly understood.

Luke hastened to add, "I know what you and Emily are going through is even tougher in many ways because your arms are still empty. Julie and I have been praying that God will answer both of our families' requests, and we will continue praying. I wish I had more medical hope to give you, but our God creates life, and we must be patient."

"Waiting is hard," James replied.

"Yes. Yes, it is." Luke bowed his head and began to entreat their Father in Heaven. "Father, we are hurting. Our hearts are aching to hold your gift of little life. In Your Word, you proclaim that children are a treasure, a heritage from You. Please bless our families with babies and help us to be patient while we wait for your timing. In Jesus name, Amen." Luke lifted his gaze to his brother in time to see James swiftly swipe away a tear from his cheek.

"Thank you, Luke."

---

When Josiah finished saddling his horse, he called over to Jacob, "Does James want us to head over to the Wilsons' farm now or wait for him?"

"I'm not sure, but I'll ask." Jacob approached the office door, but before his knuckles rapped on the wooden surface, Luke's voice wafted to him. Not wanting to interrupt, he paused to listen and closed his eyes when Luke began to pray. Inwardly, he added, "Lord, I did not know my brothers were hurting so deeply. I have no idea how to help or encourage them, but I will pray with them that You will bless their families with children."

The sound of Luke's boots thumping the floor was Jacob's cue to knock. When Luke opened the door, Jacob peered around him to address James. "I saddled Trigger for you. Are you riding over with us?"

"Yes, I'll be right out."

Jacob grabbed Luke's arm as he passed through the doorway and lowered his voice. "I did not intend to overhear your prayer, but I will be praying for both of you, too."

Luke's gaze softened. "Thank you. That means a lot."

---

The next few weeks flew by in a flurry of activity. Despite a couple of days with clouds that threatened a storm, the rain held off until after the last field was harvested. A good harvest was a boon to the entire community, not just the farmers themselves.

The annual church social was a celebration of the end of harvest. Just as he had the last few years, Jacob attended alone and entertained Matthew so Luke and Julie could dance together. This year, however, something within him ached as he watched the myriad of couples dancing. Even Josiah, though he had not invited a young lady to attend with him, asked several of the younger girls for just one dance before dancing with Emma for the rest of his time on the dance floor. Josiah had heard the rumors that several of the young ladies were sweet on him, and he desired to show kindness and impartiality without encouraging their affections.

About halfway through the event, Matthew pointed to the dance floor. "Uncle Jacob, why do they dance?"

"It's fun, and if you're dancing with someone you love, it's even better. Watch your mom and dad smile at each other. They love each other a lot."

"Do you not know how?"

"To dance? Sure, I know how. I'd just rather be here with you."

"You should dance, too."

"I should, huh?"

When Josiah and Emma took a break for punch, they sat next to Jacob and Matthew. "Emma, after you catch your breath, would you dance with me?"

"You know how?" Emma teased.

Jacob rolled his eyes toward the ceiling. "Matthew is skeptical, too. I guess I need to show you both that I haven't forgotten my amazing dancing skills." One side of his mouth lifted in a mischievous smile as he waggled his brows.

Emma laughed. "Oh, dear." She turned to Matthew and whispered, "Wish me luck." Matthew giggled.

Looking over Emma's head to his brother, Jacob tilted his head toward Matthew. "Don't let him talk you into more ice cream. He's already had two scoops."

"Two scoops?" Josiah exclaimed in mock surprise.

With that, Jacob stood and offered his hand to Emma. Once they were moving in rhythm to the next song, Emma commented, "You are as good of a dancer as Josiah. Why don't you ask any of the young ladies to dance with you?"

"For me, dancing with non-family should be reserved for—well—someone special, and God hasn't brought my 'someone special' yet."

Emma nodded in understanding. "When God does bring her into your life, she will have won the affections of a wonderful young man."

His smile crooked. "Thank you, Emma. Though you are my mama, and you might just be biased."

"Not a bit, Jacob. Not a bit."

## CHAPTER 7
### Christmas

Soon Luke was back to work in the clinic, and Jacob was petitioning God for another way to help his neighbors now that harvest was complete. Humble prayers for occasions to serve others mirrored God's heart. Those are requests He loves to answer.

After a conversation with Pastor Kendrick asking him to keep his ears open for opportunities to serve, several families around town asked him to help with random jobs, most related to winterizing homes and storing feed and firewood for the colder months. The odd jobs kept him busy throughout the Thanksgiving and Christmas seasons, and being a blessing to others eased the outcry of his heart to a subtle hum. He was doing what God had asked of him, and he would strive to be content as he waited for God's timing in his life.

The Sunday before Christmas, Jacob sat in the church pew next to Josiah immersed in the carols being sung around him. He loved Christmas. Jesus was born as a baby to experience humanity firsthand with all of its joys, sorrows, and growing pains. There was nothing we would ever face that Jesus wouldn't personally understand. Then He gave His perfect life on the cross to pay the penalty for our sin, thereby making us justified—legally righteous—in the Father's eyes. With His resurrection three days later, He claimed victory over spiritual death forever. What a promise to those who choose Him!

Pastor Kendrick's Christmas sermon focused on the wise men who visited Jesus when he was a year or two old. "We know from studying Old Testament prophecy that God's sovereign plan for Jesus' birth was revealed as early as the fall of Adam and Eve in the Garden of Eden. That prophecy, however, was given primarily to the Jewish people, beginning with the covenant to Abraham."

"The wise men were from Persia, about nine hundred miles from Bethlehem. How did they know to look for a star? The answer? Daniel. His influence four hundred years earlier lasted for generations. The Persians were astronomers who studied the stars, and the wise men remembered Daniel's prophecy and looked for the sign in the heavens that signaled the time had come for the prophecy to be fulfilled. That star would have been created in Genesis 1, but the light from that star shone over Bethlehem at just the right moment in history. God's timing was perfect."

"Many nativity stories include the wise men in Bethlehem just after Jesus' birth, but the word *child* in Matthew 2:11 means just that: *child* not *baby*. Our other clue is that after Herod asked these men when the star appeared, he ordered the murder of every male child two years old and under, not just the infants. Besides, from the time the star appeared the evening of Jesus' birth, the wise men had to travel a great distance with their treasures before they arrived in Jesus' home to worship Him."

"How can this story encourage us in our walk with God today? Consider these three things. First, just as Daniel left a spiritual legacy, your testimony should cause others to desire to glorify God. He knew from personal experience that God's sovereign hand will take life's hardships and use them for His perfect plan. Daniel was removed from his family as a teenage boy and brought to Babylon, the cultural capital of the world at that time."

"Through Daniel's faithfulness to God, his presence there influenced three reigning monarchs in ways Daniel would have never dreamed. Nor could he have known his legacy would result in three significant gifts for the Messiah he worshipped. God has a perfect plan for your life, too. He has not forgotten you or the hardships and sorrows you may be facing. Trust Him."

"Second, the wise men were wealthy men who left the comforts of home for a long, arduous journey. What comforts are you willing to sacrifice to worship Him? They brought treasures, a portion of their riches, for the newborn King. They brought their best—gold, frankincense, and myrrh—gold for Jesus' status as King, frankincense for worship as God, and myrrh for his burial as our Messiah. What can we give him? Our hearts, our worship, our gratitude. Psalm 86:12 says, 'I give thanks to you, O Lord my God, with my whole heart, and I will glorify your name forever.'"

"Finally, how do we know the way to God? In His Word— Just the way the wise men knew from Daniel's prophecy to look for a sign. God promises in Jeremiah 29:13, 'You will seek me and find me, when you seek me with all your heart.' Wise men still seek Him and find Him and worship Him."

Jacob soaked in Pastor's message, marveling anew that the Christmas story could still challenge his life today. *Lord, take my whole heart. Teach me to faithfully seek and worship You. Help me to fulfill the purpose You have planned for me.*

Across the aisle and one row up, James and Emily prayed similar silent prayers for trusting God's timing in their lives. *Lord, You know the overwhelming desire of my heart for a baby,* Emily prayed, *but help my trust in You to overshadow my impatience, for Your will is more important than my sorrow.*

On Christmas morning, James found Jacob in the barn. "After chores, would you ride over to the Johnson's ranch with me in the buggy? I may need your help with Emily's gift."

"Sure." Jacob's curiosity was piqued.

A short while later, the brothers arrived at the Johnsons' barn. The rancher had heard their arrival and met them with a fluffy ball of gray and white fur. James paid him and shook the man's hand in gratitude.

Jacob's grin could not be any bigger. "A puppy?" James handed the wriggling body to Jacob who hugged him close during the ride home. The puppy responded by licking Jacob's nose. "Oh, he's too cute! Emily is going to love him."

"Yeah, I hope so. He's a blue merle border collie, so he'll be a help on the ranch, too."

"You know Emily's going to spoil this little guy, right?"

James' eyes softened, and he smiled. "Yeah, I know."

---

The highlight of Christmas was Emily's gift. When the other gifts had been given, James leaned over and whispered into Emily's ear, "I'll be right back." He disappeared to the barn and reentered the house with an armful of fluff. The instant the furry face with the brown eyes and the little pink panting tongue lifted from the protected space against James' chest, Emily's hands flew to her face in surprise. Her sheer delight overflowed in happy tears streaming down her face as she stood to meet her husband and stroke the warm fur.

"May I hold him?"

"Of course. He's yours. Merry Christmas."

Emily reached for the puppy and snuggled him against her.

He wiggled, trying to catch her salty tears with his tongue on her cheek. "Thank you, James. He's an adorable little guy."

Her pure joy melted James' heart. He had missed this side of his lovely wife. "What are you going to name him?"

Emily studied the pup. None of the other family suggested any names, silently concurring that this auspicious task belonged solely to her. Emily's thoughtful expression suddenly gave way to a broad smile. "How about Asher? The name is Hebrew for *blessed*, and his gray fur is the color of ashes. What do you think?"

"It's just right." James reached over to scratch the puppy's head. "Asher, you have yourself a new family." Emily rolled up on her tiptoes and kissed her husband on the cheek.

Jacob chuckled, "I think you found Emily the perfect gift."

James smirked at Jacob. Then he smiled at Emily and whispered something in her ear that made his wife blush.

Watching James and Emily's interaction made Jacob's heart twinge, but he stuffed the feeling away. Someday God would bring his special someone. Seth's words rang in his memory: *The right one is worth the wait.*

## CHAPTER 8
## *Quarantine*

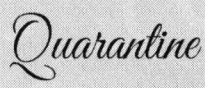

Ingrid's mind was whirling with plans to fill the new cheese orders from Mr. Hensley at the general store. Her thoughts were so distracted she almost forgot to plate the dinner rolls before the men returned from evening milking.

When Johann and Frederick came through the door and joined Ingrid and Heidi at the table, their movements were slow enough to earn Ingrid's notice as out of the ordinary. Then she noticed that both of their faces were flushed. After Johann's simple prayer, Frederick stared at his empty plate before asking, "Mama, may I go to bed?"

Reaching a motherly hand to his forehead and finding it hot, the corners of Ingrid's mouth tightened with concern. "Of course. I'll check on you in a little bit." As his steps faded down the hallway, she laid a hand on her husband's face. "You're feverish, too."

"Ja." Johann always became a man of few words when he wasn't feeling well, though Ingrid could count on one hand the times he had been sick since they married.

"Do you need to retire early, too?"

"Ja." Her husband rose and plodded toward their bedroom.

Ingrid turned her attention to Heidi. "Do you feel all right?"

"Yes. I don't feel ill at all."

"Good. Let's try to keep it that way. Stay out of their rooms tonight. I've already been exposed to your Papa, so I'll check on them overnight."

"Yes, Mama."

The next morning, father and son trudged to the barn for morning milking, but Frederick returned half an hour later and went straight to bed. When Ingrid checked on him, she noticed that a red, blotchy rash had developed over his face and behind his ears.

By the time Johann finished, his pinched brows, deep frown, and achingly slow footsteps proclaimed his utter exhaustion. When he entered the bedroom where Ingrid was folding clothes, she spied the same rash beginning on his face. "I should go for the doctor."

"No, Ingrid. Not unless absolutely necessary." What Ingrid heard was an opening for medical treatment if she deemed it "necessary."

Ingrid and Heidi scrubbed their hands and forearms mercilessly before making their morning batch of cheese. By lunchtime, Johann's and Frederick's rashes had traveled down their chests and were creeping around to their backs. Both were still running fevers and acting lethargic enough to ignite alarm within Ingrid's chest.

Ingrid made her choice. They needed to be examined by a doctor. Johann would probably not approve, but she was concerned with the rapid progression of their illness. As she rolled down her sleeves and buttoned the cuffs, she addressed her daughter. "Heidi, I'm going to town for the doctor. Stay in your loft studio until I come and get you. Your papa will be displeased enough that I am purposefully bringing a stranger to the farm, but he will be comforted knowing you are hidden."

"What if they need something while you're gone?"

"I just refilled their water pitchers and refreshed their cooling cloths. They should be fine until I return. Go, and stay out of sight."

"I'll collect my Bible and go to my studio now."

"Thank you for understanding."

While Ingrid traveled toward town, the weight of her choice felt heavy, and she prayed she had made the right decision. "Dear Lord, heal my husband and my son and protect my daughter from further harm."

---

In the clinic, Luke was taking inventory of the medicines in the glass cabinet when an unfamiliar woman entered. Her face wore a blend of wariness and determination, yet she stayed firmly planted near the door, her hesitation forcing her to keep a means of escape close at hand.

He turned and queried, "How may I help you?"

"I was hoping to speak to the doctor."

Noting her German accent and crisp English, Luke stepped forward with a friendly expression, "I'm Dr. Hamilton, but folks around here usually call me Dr. Luke. His brow furrowed slightly. "Are you ill?"

The woman took a moment before answering, as if she were assessing his capabilities. She must have found him acceptable, for she answered, "I'm Ingrid Müller. No, I'm not ill, but my husband and son are."

"Describe their symptoms for me."

The tension in Ingrid's stance abated. "They have both been running a fever with chills since yesterday afternoon. This morning after chores, they both developed a red rash that feels like sandpaper on their skin. It began on their faces and has now spread to their chests and backs."

"Have you noticed anything unusual with their tongues or the skin in the crease of their underarms?"

"No, but I didn't check there specifically." She hesitated. "Nothing ever slows Johann down, but this morning, he could barely make it to the barn to milk the cows. I fear something is seriously wrong. Would you be willing to make a house call?"

Luke reached for his bag and gestured to the door. "Of course." Before he exited, he flipped the sign to "Will be back soon."

Approaching Dakota, Luke hung his medical bag on the saddle horn and mounted in one smooth movement. Addressing Ingrid as she climbed aboard her buggy, he said, "You lead, and I'll follow."

As they traveled the road out of town toward the ranch, Luke had to reign in Dakota when he repeatedly tried to quicken his gait. Luke bent forward and rubbed Dakota's neck. "We're not going home yet, buddy." Dakota shook his head in disappointment, and the jangling of his bridle caused a chuckle to bubble in Luke's chest.

Glancing at the third side road they passed, Luke raised an eyebrow in curiosity. Only a mile from the turnoff to the Rugged Cross Ranch, Ingrid turned her buggy into the Coopers' lane. "Huh, I guess these are our new neighbors." Dakota was reluctant to turn yet, but a nudge from Luke's heels provided the motivation he needed.

The farm looked relatively unchanged from his prior visit to the Coopers a few months before. Luke tethered Dakota to the hitching post and followed Mrs. Müller to the front porch. She rested her hand on the door latch and turned slightly to face him. "I'm not sure how Johann will react to my bringing a stranger onto our land. He is protective for good reason, but I cannot explain why. Please forgive him if he gives you a gruff welcome."

The corner of Luke's mouth lifted. "Men are usually gruff patients anyway. I'll be forgiving. I promise."

"Very well. Right this way." Ingrid led him through the house and opened a bedroom door. "Johann, I brought the doctor."

The voice from the bed was deep and rough, like a growl, "You shouldn't have brought him here."

"Hush now. I've never seen you so sick. Of course he needed to come."

Ingrid opened the door wide enough for Luke to pass by. The bedroom lamp was dim, but the light was enough for Luke to see the massive form of the man in the bed. Luke guessed him to be nearly as tall as Tim's six-and-a-half feet and twice as broad. "Mr. Müller, I presume?"

Johann nodded, but eyed Luke skeptically. "You look too young to be a doctor."

One side of Luke's mouth crooked upward. "I'm Dr. Luke Hamilton. Though I am the younger of the two physicians in Prairie Hills, I have been a doctor for several years. Your wife is concerned about your illness, and her description has garnered my concern as well. Allow me to complete a physical assessment and determine what has you feeling so poorly."

At Johann's grunt of assent, Luke set his bag on a nearby chair and pulled out the thermometer, shaking down the mercury with sharp snapping motions of his wrist. "Put this underneath your tongue while I examine your rash. I'm going to brighten the lamp to better visualize your skin, so feel free to close your eyes if the light bothers them."

Ingrid stood at the foot of the bed with her arms crossed over her chest while Luke performed his thorough examination. When Luke pulled out the thermometer to check the mercury level, Johann turned his head and expelled a bark-like cough. Luke nodded, as if that cough was the final symptom to solidify his diagnosis.

"My greatest concern when your wife mentioned your rash was the possibility of scarlet fever, a disease that leaves lifelong ill effects and is often fatal." Ingrid drew in a sharp intake of breath. "Fortunately, your tongue is not swollen or lumpy, and the skin under your arms and in the bend of your elbows is not scarlet red. The barking cough and your sensitivity to light in addition to your generalized rash confirms that you have the measles. I'm going to guess your son is suffering from the same disease. I will assess him next."

"Though there is not a cure for measles, I do have some medicines that can alleviate some of the symptoms. Measles is highly contagious. For that reason, you should stay quarantined in your bedroom until your rash is gone." Luke glanced at Ingrid. "Even though you have already been exposed to your husband and son, please avoid additional contact unless absolutely necessary."

Johann growled again, "How long will that be?"

"Seven to fourteen days. Adults tend to keep their rash longer than kids, so plan on the fourteen days."

"Impossible. My cows need to be milked twice a day." He moved to get up then fell back on his pillow with a groan. Luke could see the frustration written on Johann's features, the hallmark of a strong man zapped of strength. Thankfully, Luke knew how to attend to more than just physical ailments.

"Were they all milked this morning?"

"Yes."

"You stay in bed. I'll send my brother to do your milking until your quarantine is over."

"No, not another stranger on our farm."

Ignoring her husband's protest, Ingrid entered the conversation. "Is your brother a good man?"

"Jacob? Yes, he's a hard worker who loves the Lord and

serves others. He could be a huge help if you allow him to come."

"No, we must stay hidden for a while longer." Johann's position was unchanging, but his vehemence was waning.

Luke drew his brows together and tried to ascertain the situation. "I do not understand the reason for your seclusion, but I do respect your privacy. My family at the Rugged Cross Ranch are your nearest neighbors. Since I will check on you each day on my way home, no one needs to know I have been here. Jacob is a man of his word and is worthy of your trust. You need him."

Johann capitulated, too tired to argue anymore. "All right. Let him come."

---

Luke performed a physical assessment on Frederick and confirmed that he, too, was suffering from measles.

Despite his illness, Frederick's thirst for non-familial conversation fueled his interest in Dr. Luke. His simple questions came in a steady stream. "Are you really a doctor?"

"I am."

"Where do you live?"

"With my family on the Rugged Cross Ranch. We are your nearest neighbors."

"How big is your family?"

"I have five brothers, though only three still live on the ranch."

Frederick noticed the ring on Luke's hand. "Are you married?"

"Yes, my wife's name is Julie, and we have a little boy named Matthew."

"That's nice."

The burst of energy had been drained. "I've always wanted brothers, but all I have—"

"Are parents that love you very much," Ingrid interrupted and finished for him. "Rest now, and give the doctor some peace."

Luke patted the boys knee through the blanket and gave him a subtle wink. He recognized Frederick's inquiries for what they were—the offer of a friendship of sorts. "I'll be by again tomorrow afternoon, Frederick. If you think of any more questions between now and then, feel free to ask."

Turning to Ingrid, he added, "They are both going to have a miserable week, I'm afraid, but they are stable. The medicines I left will combat the fever and help their immune systems fight their illness more effectively. If anything changes and you need me overnight, our ranch is the next turnoff about a mile up the road."

"I wouldn't want to disturb you or your family."

"Nonsense. Caring for physical needs is what God has called me to do. My family understands that emergencies often happen at inopportune times and is supportive of my need to be available at all hours."

"Thank you, Dr. Hamilton."

"My pleasure. I'll send Jacob for evening milking. What time should I tell him to be here?"

"Johann usually begins at 5 pm."

"Shall I have him come a few minutes early for any instructions?"

Ingrid nodded, but concern creased her brow. "I won't be able to pay him until our next batch of cheese sells."

A chuckle from Luke startled her. "Not to worry. Jacob wouldn't let you pay him anyway. He enjoys being a blessing."

A fire of determination lit in her eyes. "Of course, I will pay him."

Luke's eyebrow lifted, and he grinned. "Good luck with that."

## CHAPTER 9
## The Milking Help

Jacob and Josiah were riding fence in the north pasture when they spotted Luke turning onto ranch land and met him halfway. Jacob piped up, "You're home early. Is everything okay?"

"Yep. I'm just stopping by briefly before heading back into town." Dakota's ears pricked in displeasure as if he had understood Luke's words. Luke casually crossed his wrists on the saddle horn and explained, "The family that moved into the Coopers' place is also running a dairy farm. In fact, I have a sneaking suspicion that they may make the new cheese Emma has been buying in town. The husband and son have come down with the measles, and I've put them under quarantine for the next week or two. They need someone to milk their cows morning and evening."

"For two weeks, huh?" Jacob turned his attention to Josiah and raised an expectant eyebrow.

Josiah swallowed hard. "Um. Well, I guess I could—"

The brotherly hand to the back of Josiah's shoulder stopped him mid-sentence. Jacob laughed. "I'm just teasing,

Josiah. I'd be happy to help." After all, milking had always been his primary chore.

Luke's smile broadened into a mischievous grin. "Good, because I already volunteered you. Ingrid Müller is expecting you a bit before five o'clock."

"What? Hey, that's not funny!" Jacob's laughter died in an expression of mock indignation.

Now it was Josiah's turn to laugh.

The expression on Luke's face sobered. "One more thing. The Müllers are private people and quite wary of strangers. Johann was upset that his wife had brought me onto their farm at all. They do need you, but I had to convince them you were trustworthy before they would even allow you to come."

"Do you suspect criminal activity?" Jacob's brow crinkled in concern.

"No, nothing like that, but they are definitely hiding something, and it's more than just the family cheese recipe. Their eight-year-old son Frederick nearly spilled the beans, I think, but his mother cut him off. Whatever they're protecting, I did promise them my discretion, and I'll ask you to do the same. Just stay alert."

"Sure. You've always had a gift for reading people, so I trust you, but I'll be careful anyway."

Luke turned a reluctant Dakota around with a wave and "Thanks, Jacob." He pointed to his brother. "Before five o'clock. Don't forget." With that, he rode back toward town.

When Jacob lifted his shirt to his nose, the smell contorted his face and made him cough. "Whew, that's bad." He turned back to Josiah. "Would you be able to finish checking the last section of fence so I could clean up a bit? There's only one chance to make a first impression. I don't want this new family to think some vagrant is prowling around their barn."

"Sure, go ahead. I'll finish up."

At precisely 4:45 pm, Jacob dismounted Shadow in front of the Müllers' barn. It looked the same as it had a few months back, and he nearly expected the elderly Mrs. Cooper to appear with a tray of freshly baked cookies. "For milking stamina," she would say. But this wasn't the Coopers' farm anymore. He patted Shadow's neck and glanced around, unsure whether he should knock on the front door of the house and introduce himself or reorient himself to the barn and start milking.

---

Alerted by the sound of hooves outside, Ingrid approached the front window and nudged the corner of the curtain aside. A young man dismounted from a beautiful gray horse and tethered him in front of the barn. Ingrid observed him for just a moment as he rubbed his horse's neck and spoke to him in warm tones. He seemed capable enough, and he was recommended highly by the doctor. She took a deep breath and blew it out to steady her thoughts.

With a sudden realization, her hand flew to her forehead. *Oh, no! Heidi!* She had forgotten to call her daughter after the doctor left the farm. *Heidi is still in the barn!* Ingrid squeezed her eyes shut. *Please stay hidden in the loft, sweet girl.*

The man looked around as if trying to decide whether to go to the house or the barn. When he chose the latter, Ingrid slipped from the house and approached him cautiously. "You must be the doctor's brother."

"Yes, I'm Jacob. Luke sent me over to help with the milking until your husband is back on his feet again." The woman's posture was straighter than a two-by-four, and her smile was strained. In fact, everything about her radiated tension. Jacob sensed it and desired to set her at ease. "I've been in charge of milking the cows since I was five, and I've filled in here before from time to time when Charles Cooper was ailing. I promise I'll do a good job." He felt as if he were under scrutiny, but he found himself biting back a smile. *"I don't think I've ever had to work this hard to convince someone to let me help them."*

Despite Ingrid's concern over Heidi's presence in the barn, Jacob's sincerity and his eagerness to do the work began to allay her misgivings. "Right this way." Ingrid led him into the barn.

---

From Heidi's vantage point near the window in her new studio, she had witnessed the young doctor come and go. Twice she had nearly climbed down from the loft, but her mama's clear command to wait until she called her kept her there. With two books, her Bible, and her sketching supplies, Heidi had everything she needed to pass the time.

An hour later, another rider approached the homestead. From a distance, his dark hair and build with broad shoulders reminded her of—*it couldn't be*—Peter? Her breathing and heart rate escalated to a feverish pace. She clutched her chest as the panic erupted there. *How could he have found me here?* Her mind screamed, *Hide!* but her body stayed frozen in terror.

When the rider drew near enough for her to see him more clearly, she released a humorless laugh, the only audible indication of her relief. Whoever he was, he wasn't Peter. Heidi leaned back against the bale of hay and closed her eyes to catch her breath.

Though Heidi could not understand the words, she could hear the voices of her mama and this stranger in conversation. Her mama sounded reserved, but not unwelcoming. There was no imminent threat. *Lord, please take this fear away. You promise in Hebrews 4:16 that I can come confidently before Your throne and "find grace to help in time of need." Please increase my faith in your promise to be with me.*

The creak of the rusty hinges and the shaft of afternoon light preceded the increased volume of her mama's and the stranger's voices and heralded their entrance. Despite her trembling, Heidi determined to face her fear, at least in some approximation. Using the scuffling of their entry to cover her movements, she crept across to the angled hay Frederick had arranged for her comfort and settled herself next to the railing. Closing her eyes, she berated herself. *This is ridiculous. Calm down! This man is not Peter.*

When Heidi gathered her courage to peer over the railing, the sight of the young man crippled her resolve to be brave. *Focus on the camber of his voice.* It was smooth and warm like melted chocolate, friendly but not falsely so, confident but not condescending. The combination soothed her frayed nerves.

As if the cows knew how to read a clock, they all meandered in from the pasture and found their respective places for milking. Jacob turned toward the first cow, allowing Heidi to see his face for the first time. His growing smile showed off a dimple. Her breath caught for another reason. Heaven and earth, he was handsome! He strode over and scratched the cow between her ears while she nuzzled his chest with her nose like a horse. "Bessie, I'm glad to see you, too. Are you still the matriarch of this bunch?" His attention shifted back to her mama. "Did you keep all of the Coopers' cows?"

"Yes, we purchased them with the farm."

"These ladies are as gentle as they come. Bessie and I have been friends for years. Haven't we, girl?" Bessie looked at him expectantly with her large brown eyes. Jacob reached into his pocket and pulled out half a carrot. Leaning toward Bessie's ear, he reduced his voice to a whisper Heidi could just barely hear. "Don't tell the others. I don't have enough carrots for everyone."

Jacob's gentle way with the cows awakened something in Heidi's heart—the seedling of trust, perhaps. Her mama must have felt it, too, for she presented him an authentically genuine smile before her parting words. "I am apparently leaving our cows in good hands. If you need anything, Jacob, just knock on the front door."

"Thank you, but I think these ladies and I will get along just fine."

Heidi's mother left—left her!—and Heidi, feeling suddenly trapped, gulped away another bout of panic, which was absurd since—What did her mama call him? Jacob?—had no idea anyone was still in the barn with him. Knowing that milking all twenty cows by himself would probably take him three hours, Heidi rolled her eyes heavenward. *When I asked You to help me face my fears, this isn't exactly what I had in mind.* The edge of her mouth crooked upward. *Who says God doesn't have a sense of humor?*

The clomp of Jacob's boots and the scrape of the milking stool on the wood floor as he set it next to Bessie claimed Heidi's attention. The quiet ping of the milk against the sides of the pail was punctuated with calming comments to the cow. Jacob discussed various topics from the weather to his nephew's latest antics. He was a great storyteller, and a few times Heidi had to clamp her hand over her mouth to quell her laughter.

Jacob moved from cow to cow, emptying the raw milk into the five-gallon jugs along the wall just as her mama had instructed. His one-sided banter with the animals continued, and as Heidi listened, she realized what God had given her—a unique opportunity to see the heart and soul of a young man without pretense or façade. He had absolutely no reason to put on airs for a cow. Her mouth quirked in humor. A small part of her felt guilty for eavesdropping, but a greater part just felt thankful.

In her fearful mind, all young men had been repainted to

be like Peter, yet here in her barn was a man who was the exact opposite. Peter was arrogant, selfish, greedy, and lazy. The entire world revolved around him, and he would use anyone to get what he wanted. He didn't care who he hurt along the way. Even his family was only a means to fulfill his greed.

Jacob was respectful and kind, first to her mama, then to the cows, of all things. He worked hard, even when no one was watching. Well, except for her, but he didn't know she was watching. Adding together morning and evening milking, he had volunteered six hours of every day for as long as he was needed. His stories told of a good relationship between him and his family. God had reminded her that there were still good guys in the world—men like Papa. Jacob almost seemed too good to be true.

If he continued his clockwise pattern, Jacob's next cow would be directly below her. Heidi silently reached for her sketchpad and pencils and opened to a blank page. After emptying his milk pail, he positioned the stool, but the cow seemed a bit skittish. With a smooth stride, he strolled to her head so the cow could see him eye-to-eye. "Shh. It's been a while since we've seen each other, but I'm gentle. I'd never hurt you. Just trust me a little bit, and I'll prove that I'm a friend."

*Was he speaking to the cow or to her?* The conversation felt personal and heartfelt. *How strange!*

He stood there a moment until the cow let him rest his hand on her face. As he moved to settle on the milking stool, his hand never left contact with her coat. Then he crooned, "It's still me over here. Are you ready?" When she stood still, the pinging of the milk commenced.

From her clandestine spot above him, Heidi began her sketch where the light hit his left hand and forearm. Knowing she didn't have much time before he moved, she faintly outlined his rolled shirtsleeve, his outstretched legs and boots, and the milk pail between his feet. That done, she quickly added a few details to be enhanced later—the stitching on his boots, the dent in the pail, the wrinkles in his folded shirtsleeve, the raised veins on his arm and the back of his hand.

When he finished, he patted her side with his hand as he stood. "Thank you, girl. You did great."

Heidi's disbelief left her speechless. Of course, she couldn't speak aloud without giving her presence away, but her mouth fell agape in a very unladylike fashion. *Seriously, who thanks a cow? Could anyone truly be that kindhearted?* The next thought rushed in unbidden. *What would it feel like to be the recipient of such a sweet, simple compliment?* Her cheeks warmed at the thought.

While Jacob milked the last three cows, Heidi schooled her wayward thoughts. Sliding a blank piece of paper under her hand to protect the drawing from smudges, she focused on the hand in the center of her sketch—Jacob's hand—changing her pencil for each depth of shading, the softer graphite for the darker areas and the harder graphite for the lighter ones.

Jacob stood and stretched his arms over his head before he returned the milking stool to the corner. "It's been lovely visiting with you ladies. Ruminate well. I'll see you in the morning." He lifted his hat from the wall hook and settled it on his head before he left.

For all the emotional trouble Jacob had unknowingly caused when he first entered the barn, she was saddened to see him go. Jacob had come to milk cows, but God had used him to begin healing her heart.

## CHAPTER 10
## Frederick's New Brother

Shifting her gaze to the transom window, Heidi watched the gray horse and his rider get smaller and disappear from sight. With a deep cleansing breath, she rested her head backwards against the hay and considered her unexpected afternoon, not sure quite what to make of it.

"Heidi!" her mama's nearly frantic voice breaking her from her musings.

"Still up in the loft, Mama."

Ingrid searched for the source of her daughter's voice, but could not spot her concealed location, even knowing approximately where the studio was. "I'm so sorry I forgot to get you after the doctor left. Please forgive me. Are you all right?"

"Yes, I'm fine. Truly. I've been reading and sketching." Heidi studied the drawing of Jacob's hand once more before she closed her sketchpad and collected her Bible and pencils and slid them into her leather bag.

After Heidi descended the ladder, her mama engulfed her in a hug before holding her at arms' length. "Bringing a strange man in here, especially with no warning, must have been so frightening for you." Mama's face was pinched in painful regret, and her eyes searched Heidi's. "Once I realized what I had done, there was no way to get you out without revealing your existence."

"At first, I did panic. Jacob resembled Peter enough to rekindle all the bad memories. And then you left me with him."

"Oh, Heidi!" Ingrid groaned. "I thought my staying in the barn would only raise his suspicions."

"But God had a purpose in it, Mama. While the doctor was here, I reread God's promises about not having to fear because He is always with me. I specifically asked Him for an opportunity to face my fear with courage. Then Jacob arrived. He may look a bit like Peter on the outside, but he is nothing like him on the inside."

"How do you know?" Ingrid's voice was filled with more curiosity than skepticism.

"The entire time he was milking, he talked to the cows." Her mama's brow wrinkled in confusion. "The simple sound of his voice would have soothed them, but he told stories and discussed a myriad of topics as if the cows were his friends."

Ingrid tilted her head, and her eyes narrowed. "Is he daft?"

Laughter spilled from Heidi's mouth. "No, not at all. He just has a lot to say, and I was the unwitting recipient of an interesting conversation."

All of the caution written on Ingrid's face fled in an instant. In its place bloomed a joyful expression. "Heidi, I haven't heard you laugh since we left Pennsylvania."

"I nearly laughed a few times this afternoon, but I clamped my mouth shut in time to stay silent. Jacob is an excellent storyteller, and the anecdotes with his nephew are incredibly funny."

Ingrid had expected her daughter to be utterly distraught after so many hours with a stranger, but the glint in Heidi's eyes hinted at merriment. And to think that a young man had been the source of her laughter! God had indeed orchestrated a small miracle today. The corners of Ingrid's mouth edged upward. "Well, then. Let's bring these cans of milk inside. Since we have additional cheese orders to fill for the general store, I'd like to make a second batch after dinner."

---

The following morning, Jacob arrived promptly at six o'clock. Heidi pushed aside the curtain just enough to see him without being seen. Ingrid opened her mouth to give her daughter a mild reprimand, but held herself in check when she remembered she had stood in that exact spot yesterday. Instead, Ingrid grasped the handles of two of the galvanized containers by the door. "I'll take the clean milk cans to the barn. You stay here." She did not use the word *hidden*, but it was definitely implied.

"I will, Mama."

When Jacob dismounted, he moved toward Ingrid and reached for the cans. "I'll take those." She released them to his hold. Placing them near the barn's interior wall, he realized the others were still missing. "Do you want me to carry the rest of them over? I don't mind."

"No!" Ingrid blurted, then recovered quickly. "Johann and Frederick are still under quarantine, as you know, and I don't want to risk your being exposed to their illness."

Jacob's mind filled with the image of the shrouded form of his brother Buck's body draped over his horse Wind Dancing's back after he had died from influenza. He shook the memory away. "Okay. That's fair. But I'll check in with you after milking. If you need me to do anything else for you before I head home, like chop wood or whatever, just let me know."

"Thank you, Jacob."

Jacob unbuttoned his cuffs and began rolling up his sleeves

as he turned toward the cows shuffling into place. "Good morning, ladies."

Ingrid twirled to face the house in order to hide her burgeoning grin. Jacob had charm, all right, but did he have too much charm to be trusted? Peter had seemed charming—until he wasn't. Only time would tell Jacob's true character.

Nearly three hours later, Jacob's knock sent Heidi skittering to her bedroom like a squirrel being chased up a tree. Ingrid cracked open the door to find him standing several feet away on the porch steps. "Do you have any other chores for me?"

"No, we have everything we need."

"Very well, ma'am." He tipped the brim of his hat. "I'll be back this afternoon."

Ingrid closed the door and faced Heidi as she emerged. "This afternoon . . ." Her smile fell as she scrunched her face in concentration. "Dr. Hamilton said he'd stop by on his way home from the clinic. I'm guessing that will be while Jacob is here for evening milking. How will we hide you? The walls don't mask enough sound for you to stay in your bedroom without being heard."

"I'll just stay in the loft studio like yesterday," Heidi responded with a casual air. Thus, the routine was born. Heidi would stay in the house during Jacob's morning visit and would slip up to the loft around 4:30 and stay until after Jacob left. That way, she was present to help with the morning cheesemaking and still make time for her sketches.

---

One week after his initial visit, Dr. Luke folded his instruments into his medical bag and lowered himself onto the edge of Frederick's bed. "Well, young man, since your rash is completely gone and you haven't been running a fever the last couple of days, I officially clear you to end quarantine." At Frederick's confused expression, Luke leaned over and ruffled the boy's hair. "That means you can go outside and play."

Frederick's grin was instantaneous. "Can I help your brother milk the cows?"

At the nod of permission from Mrs. Müller, Luke replied, "Yes, on one condition. You must promise that you will rest when you get tired. After being in bed for a week, your body will need time to find the energy you had before you became ill. Be patient. If you try to push yourself too hard, your recovery will actually take longer."

"I promise." Frederick tried to put on a serious face, but the excitement in his eyes gave away his eagerness to be free from these four walls.

As soon as the front door clicked behind Luke, Ingrid laid a hand on Frederick's shoulder. "I don't mind your helping Jacob, but be careful not to give any hints about having a sister. Heidi is in the loft, but for her safety, you must not even glance upward in her direction. Do you understand?"

"Yes, Mama. I'm sorry I almost mentioned her that first day when I met Dr. Luke."

Ingrid kissed his forehead. "What's done is done. Just remember that one of your jobs as a brother is to protect her."

By the time Luke had untethered Dakota, Frederick had already dressed and escaped from the house in a beeline for the barn. Luke smiled, remembering what it was like to be an energetic boy, but the doctor in him called a gentle admonition. "Slow down, and take your time. Don't forget your promise."

"Yes, Dr. Luke," Frederick responded just before he ducked into the barn.

Luke chuckled and glanced up at Ingrid. "I think you're going to have your hands full keeping his energy corralled until he's fully recovered." His focus turned toward the barn.

"Would you mind if I poked my head in and asked Jacob not to let Frederick do too much?"

A veil of mixed emotions covered Mrs. Müller's face. Suspicion? Concern? Protectiveness? How could his one simple question have raised such a response?

Just as quickly, she schooled her expression. "I'll walk over with you."

"All right." Luke left Dakota ground tied and joined Ingrid. He had the odd sensation that he was being tested. Ingrid led the way into the barn, but he stayed in the doorway and leaned in with his head and shoulders, careful not to step across the threshold. "Jacob?" With the sudden change in lighting, he could just make out his brother's profile milking a cow on the far side of the barn.

"Hey, Luke. What can I do for you?" Jacob's hands didn't miss a beat of his pinging rhythm.

"As I'm sure you've guessed, I cleared Frederick from quarantine and gave him permission to help you, but please encourage him to take it easy."

"Will do, big brother."

With a nod of farewell to Mrs. Müller and a concise, "Until tomorrow," Luke slipped from the doorway and mounted Dakota. During his short ride home, he kept mulling over Ingrid's reaction. Whatever the Müller family was hiding seemed to be hidden in the barn.

---

Ingrid spoke with Frederick and departed a couple of minutes after Luke left. Jacob lifted an eyebrow in curiosity. *Odd.* Her presence felt more like she was supervising Luke than checking on her son.

The lad had already positioned his short stool and pail and

was busy milking the next cow in line. "So, your name is Frederick?"

"How do you know that?" Frederick asked incredulously.

"I'm smart." Jacob laughed. "Truth is, I just pay attention. Luke mentioned your name when he popped into the barn."

"And your name's Jacob." Frederick hesitated. "Should I call you Mr. Hamilton?"

"Hamilton? No, my last name is Collins, but you can just call me Jacob."

"But Dr. Luke is your brother, right?"

"Yep."

"Then why don't you have the same last name?"

"That, Frederick, is a very astute question." Jacob quieted to a conspiratorial tone. "*Astute* means to be discerning or observant. Luke taught me that one. He loves big words." Frederick's laugh enlarged Jacob's smile. There was no better sound than a child's laughter.

"Now to answer your question, my brothers on the ranch and I are adopted. With the exception of my younger brother Josiah, we were all born in different families but came to live at the ranch after our parents died. When our oldest brother James was offered Daniel and Emma Taylor's last name, he declined, wanting to keep his surname in memory of his first family. The rest of us followed suit."

While Jacob was talking, he noticed the tings of milk into Frederick's pail were slowing down. Pausing next to the boy on his way to pour his milk into the collection can, Jacob could see the fatigue around his eyes. "After I empty this, I'll make sure she's dry, and you can rest for a spell."

With a bit of a whine in his tone, Frederick spoke, "I don't want to rest. I'm tired of resting. I want to do something."

Jacob scratched his chin in thought. "Yeah, I get that. But we don't want the cows to get an infection because of retained milk, either. Besides, I gave my brother my word that I wouldn't let you overdo, and I keep my promises. Tell you what, you can sit with me and keep me company. That's helping, right?"

"Sure, I guess," came Frederick's less than enthusiastic reply.

"Great. I'll be right back." When Jacob returned, he set the stool next to Frederick and wordlessly gestured with his thumb for him to scoot over. Jacob took Frederick's place and squeezed a bit more milk into the pail. The young lad's shoulders were slumped, and his mouth curved downward in a frown. *Lord, show me how to encourage him. Luke and Josiah are the encouragers in the family. What would they say to lift this boy's spirits?* "You did a good job for your first day back."

Frederick dipped his chin. "I didn't even finish one cow."

"But you did milk most of one cow. That's more than you did yesterday. Give yourself a little grace."

The boy lifted one shoulder in a half shrug. At least the deep furrow of his frown began to relax.

"How many did you milk before you came down with the measles?"

"Usually five."

Jacob let out a low whistle of awe. "That many, huh? I was only milking two at your age."

Frederick's expression brightened, and he sat a bit taller. "Papa would milk three, and I'd do the fourth, and we'd leap frog down the line until we finished."

"I know your papa must be grateful to have you helping him."

"I'd much rather be milking than doing math. I'm learning fractions." He said the word *fractions* as if it were the most disgusting word in his vocabulary.

Jacob wrestled with his desire to laugh. "Fractions can be intimidating, to be sure, but they're not that bad once you get to know them."

Frederick looked askance at him, not convinced in the least. "How many cows are there?"

"Twenty."

"And you milk five of them—five out of twenty, right?"

"Right." Frederick drew out the word.

"Five over twenty. That's the fraction of cows you milk each day. Just put the part over the whole."

"Huh. That makes sense. What about reducing fractions?"

"That's just one more step. Is there any number that goes evenly into both five and twenty?"

"Five."

"Right again. Divide both numbers by five. What do you get?"

"One and four."

"One over four, more precisely one-fourth—your reduced fraction."

Frederick's gaze roamed the cows, and Jacob watched his mouth form the words as he silently counted, "One, two, three, four, one, two, three, four . . ." Then Frederick's eyes lit in excitement. "Because I milk one of every four cows."

Jacob beamed. "Exactly." His hands were still busy, so he nudged Frederick with his elbow. "See how smart you are?"

"You made it easy to understand."

"Sometimes all you need to overcome something hard is a new perspective—and maybe a guide to help you find it."

---

In the loft above, Heidi sketched as she listened to the impromptu math lesson and raised a silent cheer when fractions suddenly became a less ominous obstacle to her brother. Jacob's last statement stilled her pencil, and she recited it in her mind. Her "something hard" was her fear, and Jacob had unknowingly become the guide leading her to a new perspective—one of faith and trust.

Her dedicated drawing time these last seven days had been cathartic all on its own, but the addition of Jacob's conversation, albeit mostly one-sided, was a salve to the wounds her fear had created. The crazy thing was that he didn't even know! There was another life lesson: When we are faithful to the work God has called us to do, we can have an influence on others we may never know about on this side of heaven.

Repositioning her pencil, Heidi's focus returned to the sketch in her lap—a conversation between the man and the boy below her drawn from the shoulders up with the faint outline of a cow behind them. The man's face was earnest and attentive, as if imparting some tidbit of wisdom, and the boy's face held a tinge of wonder. She glanced down at the pair below her. Yes, her sketch was an accurate representation of Jacob and Frederick.

The two of them moved on to the next cow, but their conversation still wafted up to the loft. Frederick was warming up to Jacob now. "Do you like having brothers?"

"Sure do. We work together, play together, and always have each other's backs. Big brothers are like cowboys driving cattle. They keep you safe from predators and lasso you in if you stray too far away. Little brothers are like calves. You protect them and train them and watch them grow. They want to follow everything you do, so you have to work extra hard to be the right example."

"Did you ever get in a fight?"

"Sometimes. When we were younger, we used to wrestle quite a bit. At the orphanage, I had to defend Josiah from bullies on occasion." Jacob pointed to his face. "See this crook in my nose?" Frederick nodded. "My oldest brother James punched me and broke my nose."

Frederick's eyes grew wide and his jaw dropped in a look of horror.

"Believe it or not, I deserved it."

"Did you stray too far away?"

Jacob chuckled at Frederick's use of his analogy, "Yes, but he pulled me back into the herd before I could get into any trouble. Not too long after that, my brother Tim confronted me."

"Did he punch you, too?"

"Nope, he beat me in checkers. That seldom happened, by the way. He challenged me to determine whether or not I had a personal relationship with Christ. You see, I had been depending on a prayer, being baptized, and going to church every Sunday, but I had never given my heart to Jesus. That night changed my life forever. Jesus became more than *a* Savior; He became *my* Savior; and I will never be the same again."

Heidi swiped the tear away before it dripped onto her sketch. Jacob had such a strong, yet simple, faith. His story of salvation stirred a chord within her that began a measure of music. Whether that piece of music would become a short chorus, a hymn, a sonata, or a multi-movement orchestral masterpiece remained to be seen. What Heidi did know is that she wanted to continue to learn more about this man.

The intensity in Jacob's eyes right now is exactly what she needed to capture in her sketch. She caught her bottom lip between her teeth in concentration as she made the adjustments with her pencil.

Jacob had just settled in to milk the final cow. "Will you be my big brother?" The innocence in Frederick's voice melted Jacob on the spot.

"Well, I don't know. Brothers come together in one package deal. If you want me, you have to claim all my brothers, too. Are you sure you want that?"

Frederick pressed his lips together in serious concentration. "I don't know. Tell me about them."

"James is the oldest; he can be a little bossy, but he's a great ranch foreman because of it. Tim is impulsive; he tends to jump in with both feet before he thinks things through, but he's kindhearted and would give you the shirt off his back if you needed it; he's now a pastor in Kansas Territory. You've met Luke, the doctor; he reads all the time, and he's really smart; he once had to pull a bullet out of Tim's shoulder when we were in the middle of nowhere—saved his life. Josiah is my younger brother by birth, so he's a Collins, too. He's generally more quiet, like Luke, and he loves building things with his hands. Sam lived with us for a short while, but he's on the building crew for a school down in Texas. You won't get a chance to meet Buck, since he passed away a few years back, but he was one of the bravest men I've ever known."

"Was he old?"

"Buck?" Frederick nodded in the affirmative. "No, he was only five years older than me. Buck was half Kiowa, and when he contracted influenza, his body didn't have the immunity to fight it."

"He was an Indian?"

"Yep. Looked the part, too. Buck was a man I greatly admired. We all did. If you get a chance to meet my nephew, Matthew is Buck's spitting image."

After a moment of serious thought, Frederick decided. "Dr. Luke is really nice. If you like the others, I'm sure I will, too. I'll take all of you."

Jacob grinned and reached over to tousle Frederick's hair. "You got your wish, little brother."

So many happy tears were flowing now that Heidi had to close her sketchpad and put it out of reach so she wouldn't ruin it completely. This man continued to surprise her with his kindness and compassion. The seedling of trust was starting to grow roots in her heart, but part of her still feared an unexpected storm would come and uproot it.

## CHAPTER 11
## *Sketches*

Frederick could barely contain his eagerness to share his news as he stood on the porch and waved to Jacob as he left for home. When Shadow disappeared to the right at the end of the lane, Frederick bolted inside. "Mama, guess what? I've got a brother!"

"Have you now?" A smile tickled the edges of Ingrid's mouth.

"From what I heard, you have more than one." Heidi closed the door behind her. When she turned around, Ingrid's mouth tipped downward.

"You've been crying. What happened?"

Heidi waved off her concern. "I've never seen such kindness. And from a near stranger, nonetheless."

Frederick's words burst from him like a geyser suddenly spewing forth with unstoppable force. "Jacob thanked me for helping him, even though I only milked one cow. He taught me fractions, too. They're really not so hard once you know how they work. And he told me all about having brothers. One of his brothers broke Jacob's nose once, but they're friends now. And brothers are good to have, because they always have your back. So I asked him to be my big brother, but he said I'd have to claim all of his brothers to get him. So I did. Now I have a whole bunch of brothers."

Ingrid blinked, trying to bring all those words into focus.

A low voice emerged from the direction of the bedroom. "What's this about brothers, son? Come talk to me. I'm feeling rather abandoned in here."

"Coming, Papa!" Frederick scurried to the bedroom doorway and regaled him with stories from his time with Jacob. By dinnertime, his energy had waned, and he barely finished eating and made it to his bed before he fell asleep.

Heidi tucked the blanket around him and bent to kiss his forehead. When she had gently closed his door, her papa beckoned from across the hall. "Heidi, how have you been? I've had plenty of time on my hands to pray for you."

Being careful not to enter the quarantine room, she answered from the hallway. "Thank you, Papa. I'm good." Her face held a wistful expression as she quoted Jacob. "Sometimes overcoming a hard thing requires a new perspective and maybe a guide to help you find it."

"Wise words."

"Yes, and when that perspective is grounded in the promises of God's Word, healing can truly begin."

Johann regarded the light in Heidi's eyes—a light he had yearned to see again. An inward change was definitely beginning, but what had been the catalyst for that change? "Have you been drawing?"

Her entire face brightened to match her eyes. "Yes. Would you like to see my sketches?"

"Always, my daughter. I have missed seeing them." Heidi's drawings were more than just artwork; they were a window into her soul.

When Heidi pulled the sketchbook from her bag, Ingrid reached for it. "I'll take it to him. Though he has not been feverish, he is still on quarantine until his rash has disappeared and Dr. Luke releases him."

A teasing gleam danced in Heidi's eyes. "You just called him Dr. Luke instead of Dr. Hamilton." For her mother to break formal protocol was out of character for her.

Ingrid smirked, "Ja, well, if he's going to be one of Frederick's brothers, I suppose I can call him by his first name." She slipped into the bedroom as Johann moved to sit on the side of the bed.

Holding the collection of drawings gently as if he were cradling a baby bird, Johann opened the cover and soaked in every detail.

Leaning against the wall across from her parents' bedroom, Heidi focused on her papa's expressions as he studied each sketch. The fluttery feeling she felt when her papa studied her work was even more intense than usual. She knew what was in that portfolio. How would he react to her drawings of a stranger?

"The contrast between the rough barn wall and the smooth flower petals is incredible. You have an amazing gift." One by one, he considered each page carefully.

When his jaw tensed, Heidi knew which sketch he was viewing. "Heidi, these are not my hands nor Frederick's." His penetrating gaze nearly undid her.

"No, Papa, they are Jacob's."

Sudden worry creased his forehead. "Has he seen you?"

"No, Papa, he has seen only Mama and Frederick."

The tick in his jaw said he still wasn't pleased. "I should have never allowed him to come. This stupid quarantine. I'll resume milking tomorrow and send this boy home where he belongs."

Ingrid planted her hands on her hips. "You will do no such thing." Her eyes bore a fiery determination. "We need him—for milking, for Frederick." She looked briefly at Heidi but did not add *that* thought. "And for you, if you'd be willing to put aside your pride long enough to see what a blessing he has been to us. And he has done it all without asking for one thing in return."

He pursed his lips and exhaled audibly. His frustration ebbed. "You are right, as usual, my wife." He focused on the sketch—calloused, work-worn hands being used to fill *his* milk pails. The next page was of Jacob talking to the skittish cow, his left hand resting on her coat. Calm and patience were written in his body language. Both were qualities he admired in a man.

When he lifted the page to view the final sketch, Johann's breath caught. The sheer wonder on his son's face eased the remainder of Johann's tension. When the image became blurry, he blinked a few times to clear it.

"Papa, are you crying?"

Johann cleared his throat. "No. Just admiring your work." His focus shifted to Jacob. Though the young man smiled, his eyes were fervent with an unnamed passion. "What was Jacob telling Frederick in this portrait?"

"The story of when he gave his heart to Jesus."

Humbled, he nodded and carefully closed her portfolio of sketches before running a reverent hand over the cover. "Thank you for sharing these with me." He returned them via his wife's hand and loosely folded his arms over his chest. "Now tell me more about Jacob—besides the fact that Frederick claims him as family."

Ingrid began praising Jacob's attributes, and Heidi added to the list from her observations. The subtle blush on his daughter's cheeks when she spoke of Jacob did not elude him, and his protective father's instinct flared. Only the best of men would be worthy of his daughter's affections, and that judgement call belonged to him, for from the beginning he had been the only one to see through the veneer of Peter's charm to the devil he truly was.

## CHAPTER 12
### *The Meeting*

On quarantine day fourteen, Ingrid lightly rapped on Heidi's bedroom door and poked her head in when beckoned. "Dr. Luke is going to drop by this morning rather than this afternoon. He is apparently assisting the other doctor with a surgery that may run late. With that in mind, I'd like you to slip up to your studio soon. You'll still be able to help me with the cheese when Jacob leaves. Here, take this breakfast with you to tide you over until after milking." Ingrid laid a wrapped bundle next to Heidi's leather bag.

"Should I wake Frederick?" Heidi asked.

"No, let him sleep. I think he overdid it a bit yesterday; he needs the rest."

"All right. I'll head over now." When she stepped outside, the crisp air bit her cheeks, and she scurried over to the barn. *I'm glad I wore my wool dress today. The air is chilly.* A brief thought to grab her coat flitted through her mind, but she dismissed it, assuming the weather would warm after sunrise.

When Jacob descended the steps of the bunkhouse and hurried to the relative warmth of the barn, he studied the ominous clouds in the predawn sky and buried his hands in his pockets. He saddled Shadow and quickly returned to the bunkhouse for his bedroll with an extra blanket, a couple of sandwiches, a book, and his current whittling project.

While tying his bedroll onto the back of his saddle, Emma approached him in the barn and handed him a wrapped food parcel. "Jacob, if the snow gets heavy, plan to stay sheltered in the Müllers' barn."

Reaching for the proffered food, Jacob gestured to his saddle. "I'm ahead of you."

Emma's mind was flooded with memories of James after he got turned around in a blizzard. If not for the quick thinking of her other boys, he would have died. Pushing those thoughts aside, Emma gave Jacob a side hug and whispered, "Stay safe."

"I will. I promise." Jacob hugged her back and smiled enough to show off his dimples. He mounted smoothly, adjusted his scarf, and nudged Shadow into the cold air.

Light, wafting snow began to fall about midway to the Müllers' farm. When he arrived, rather than hitching Shadow outside, Jacob walked his horse into the barn and prepared the empty stall for him. Shadow shifted his hooves hesitantly, unsure of his new surroundings. Once settled in the stall, he nudged his nose into Jacob's chest, and Jacob rubbed his long face. "Good boy."

Jacob collected the milking pail and stool and sat beside the first cow before he removed his gloves and stuffed them into his pockets. Bringing his uncovered hands to his mouth, he blew warm air on them and rubbed them together briskly. When the cow eyed him suspiciously, he warned her, "Bessie, these hands of mine are cold. Be thankful I'm warming them up for you."

As soon as Jacob's hands thawed out, he began singing and milking, the ping of the milk against the pail serving as his metronome. Jacob knew from his brother Josiah's appraisal that he sang off pitch, but he did not have the ear to tell the difference in intonation. Since the cows did not care and God asked for a joyful noise, Jacob sang his favorite hymns with abandon, not knowing a human pair of ears was listening.

When Jacob finished milking, he poured the last bucket of milk into the galvanized can for that purpose and cracked the barn door open to peer outside. The snowfall had increased to an intensity that partially obscured the farmhouse across the yard. The temperature had dropped, and the gusty wind made the air feel even colder.

Closing the door, Jacob turned toward his horse's stall and slipped inside. "Since the storm has picked up, we'll just stay here until evening milking." Shadow nodded his head and snorted in approval. Jacob grabbed a horse blanket and covered Shadow before he gathered his whittling knife and the small chunk of wood he was fashioning into a tiny replica of James and Emily's puppy Asher for Matthew's birthday. Compared to Josiah, Jacob whittled at the speed of a turtle. Thankfully, he still had a few months before his nephew's special day.

After Jacob latched the stall door closed, he placed the milking stool close enough to the wall that he could lean back against it. He lowered himself onto the short stool and stretched out his legs in front of him. Crossing one ankle over the other, he soaked in the scene around him. He could hear his horse munching hay behind him and the cows lowing and shifting to his left. In spite of the smell that even he would admit was not terribly pleasant, the barn emanated a certain serenity that helped him relax.

Jacob inhaled deeply and released the tension in his shoulders with his exhale. Setting his wood and knife on his thigh, he warmed his hands again. Then he lifted the wood's crude form, turned it slowly in his hands, and bit the inside of his cheek in deep concentration as he planned his cuts. Raising his knife with his right hand, he began to remove tiny flecks of wood.

Whittling tended to make Jacob introspective, and today was no exception. After about an hour, he rested his head back on the stall and closed his eyes. *Lord, carving a piece of wood into something pretty and useful reminds me of how You work in my life. Please remind me that the hard times in life are meant to mold me into someone You can use to glorify You more. The whittling in my life can be painful, but the result will be worth the discomfort.*

*My heart feels lonely, Lord. Even a perfect Adam needed Eve. Do you have a woman chosen for me? James has Emily, Luke has Julie, Tim has Laura, and I have no one. I believe You have given me this desire for a reason. If I have misunderstood and You wish for me to stay unmarried, please take away my desire and my loneliness. If, however, You do plan for me to marry, please help me to be patient as I wait for You to bring her into my life.*

Before Jacob could finish his prayer, he heard a rustling sound inconsistent with the other noises in the barn, and his senses came to instant attention.

---

In the loft, Heidi peeked over the edge just far enough to see Jacob resting against the stall with his whittling tools in hand and realized he was not planning to leave anytime soon. She needed to go to the house, but the only way out was the door near Jacob's position. She had carefully obeyed her papa's command to stay out of sight, but the young man's change in routine left her in a quandary. *Lord, what should I do?*

Heidi's silent assessment of Jacob over the last two weeks made her comfortable in his presence, but she didn't know how he would react when he discovered hers. She shivered again, the cold seeping through her woolen dress and stockings—

another clue that she needed to head home. Resolving to leave her hiding place, even if it meant revealing her existence to the young man downstairs, Heidi fought the unnamed fear at the thought of encountering a strange man in such close proximity without the protection of her papa. *Lord, be my fortress. Keep me safe.* The words of Psalm 56:11 filtered into her soul: *"In God I trust; I shall not be afraid."*

Before she could talk herself out of leaving, Heidi tucked her sketchbook and pencils into her bag and lifted the handle over her head so the strap landed across her body and the bag rested against her back. She moved stealthily toward the ladder and took a deep breath for courage. Jacob's eyes were still closed. Perhaps she could sneak past him. A part of her, albeit a small part, trusted him, and that part of her caused her to distrust her own judgement. Trust must be hard won, not given on a whim.

*Here goes,* Heidi whispered to herself. She swung her leg over the ladder and started down. Behind her, she heard Jacob move, but there were no footsteps toward her.

Jacob was startled at the presence of someone else in the barn, but quickly recovered when he noticed the skirts swishing onto the ladder. "Do you need any help?" Jacob stood but did not move closer, not wanting to stand beneath her for modesty's sake.

Heidi stopped her descent and looked over her shoulder. "No, I'm all right."

When she landed safely on the barn floor, Jacob approached slowly as if she were a figment of his imagination that might vanish if he moved too quickly. The young lady lifted her eyes from the floor to meet his gaze. Those eyes. They were the color of the sky on a sunny day. Her blond hair was pulled back into a braid, but a few wisps curled around her face, softly framing it. Faint freckles dotted her nose and cheeks. He had always disliked his freckles and was grateful they had faded almost completely with age, but on her, freckles were endearing. Suddenly, he realized he was standing there staring like an idiot. Where were his manners? Something kept him from extending his hand. Instead, he stuffed his hands into his pockets and greeted her, "Hi, I'm Jacob."

"Hello," was her simple reply. She could see the curiosity on Jacob's face was piqued when she didn't offer her name, but she turned and walked purposefully toward the barn door.

*Would it be impolite to ask her name?* Jacob wondered. She seemed skittish, like a young fawn who had not yet learned who to trust, and he didn't want to spook her. When he realized she was leaving, he quickly took in her woolen dress with no coat or head covering and called protectively, "Wait!"

She jerked around, startled, with fear in her eyes, and took two more steps backwards toward the door.

Though he was sorry he had scared her, he could not in good conscience neglect her safety. "You cannot go out without a coat. The snow is really coming down and the temperature is well below freezing."

One more step backwards. "I'm only crossing to the house."

Jacob began to shrug out of his coat and took a step toward her. "Here, wear my coat. It's warm."

"No!"

Surprised by her reaction, Jacob instantly stilled. His mouth opened, but no words emerged. Inwardly, he kicked himself. He hadn't wanted to frighten her.

The look of genuine innocence on Jacob's face assured her again of one fundamental truth: This man was not Peter. The veil of fear lifted, and she saw Jacob's offer for what it was—kindness. She shook her head slightly and spoke in a normal tone, "I'm sorry. My father wouldn't understand. He'd be furious."

Still not wanting to let her leave without some sort of

covering, he grabbed his bedroll from the floor and peeled off the outer blanket. He shook it open and extended it to her at arm's length. His feet stayed firmly grounded, allowing her be the one to close the gap. "Here. At least cover your head with this and wrap up in it. To go outside in this storm unprotected would be dangerous. I nearly lost a brother to a snowstorm." His brow furrowed with mild frustration at her stubbornness.

An uncontrollable shiver overcame Heidi, and her teeth began chattering. Despite her conflicting thoughts, she reached for the blanket and twirled it around her with a graceful, dance-like movement until it landed on her head and swallowed the rest of her like a hooded cape.

The howling wind whistled around the outside of the barn, and Jacob stated the obvious. "The wind is quite gusty, and the snow can reduce visibility even over short distances. May I walk with you across to the porch to be sure you find your way?"

Heidi reached for the door handle and looked back at him once more. "No, but thank you for your kind offer."

*Don't push.* Jacob nodded his acceptance of her boundaries. "All right, but I will watch from the barn until you are safely to your door." He donned his hat and gloves while he spoke.

A remark that could have sounded menacing resonated only as genuine concern. Heidi opened the door and a rush of freezing air and snow whirled around her. She fixed her gaze on the front door of her home and walked toward it in as much of a straight line as the gusts would allow. When she reached her goal, her fingers wrapped around the door handle, and she glanced back toward the barn. The barn door was ajar just enough for her to see Jacob watching protectively. She quickly nodded her thanks before she scurried inside.

Jacob watched the young woman's every step with bated breath. Though the front door was still visible in the swirling snow, the woman's steps zigzagged across the yard as the wind pushed her. Twice he nearly bolted from his sheltered position to help her. Both times she regained her footing just as he began to step into the storm. When she disappeared into the house, he latched the the barn door closed and leaned against it.

Jacob now had a new purpose in life: to learn the young woman's name. And he wouldn't mind coaxing a smile from her in the process.

As he walked further inside the barn, the reality of the last few minutes hit him and thoughts swirled around in his head at the speed of the snow outside. *Who was she? She must be part of the Müller family. A daughter perhaps? How long had she been in the loft? She hadn't come in while he was milking, so she had been there since before dawn. Why was she hiding up there? Had she heard him singing?* He cringed at that thought. *What had happened to make her scared of him?* When he replayed the scene again, he could not think of anything he had done that might be perceived as threatening. He had even rested his whittling knife on the floor and had met her empty-handed. *Was she just being shy, or had someone hurt her? Maybe her dad? She did say he'd be furious if she wore his coat, though she didn't qualify if he'd be furious with her or him.* Too many puzzling questions.

Luke's words of caution returned to his mind. *"The Müllers are definitely hiding something, and I think it's in the barn."* "Well, Luke, I think I've found what they've been hiding."

His gaze followed the rungs of the ladder to the loft. A new thought crossed his mind. *Is anyone else hiding up there?* "Hello! Is anyone there?" No answer called back to him.

Jacob hesitated at the foot of the ladder for a few seconds before he climbed up and stood in the loft. Around him were bales of hay piled high with a narrow walkway leading toward the back of the barn. About halfway, the hay had been moved to make enough floorspace for a hay bale chair and short table topped with a couple of books. Crouching down, he picked up the first one and read the spine. *Pride and Prejudice* by Jane Austin. *Wasn't that the book Emma had asked for as a Christmas gift?*

When he glanced down, he realized the one beneath it was a well-worn Bible. An embroidered ribbon marked a place in the middle. The Psalms, maybe? Jacob's calloused fingers lifted the Bible and opened it to the bookmarked passage. Psalm 34. Several verses were underlined, but verse 4 had a heart penned beside it. "I sought the Lord, and he answered me and delivered me from all my fears." The young woman was clearly battling fears, but knowing she recognized them and was going to the Lord with those fears impressed him. She had a relationship with his God, and he knew God would keep His promises.

God had proven Himself trustworthy in his life. *Could God use him to show her how to trust God more? Probably not.* Since he had only seen her once in the two weeks he had been helping here, he would likely not see her again in the next handful of days until he was no longer needed.

He carefully replaced the Bible and the novel and looked toward the edge of the loft. Another little nook had been formed there. When he lowered himself into the space, he could see over the short hay-lined railing into the main room of the barn but remain mostly hidden. There was just enough room to sit with his knees bent, and when he leaned back, he realized the hay had been pushed into a comfortable reclining angle. He relaxed and looked down into the room below. Anyone sitting here would have had an unobstructed view of his milking rounds. The young woman had been spying on him. *Why?*

## CHAPTER 13
## *The Painting Speaks*

Heidi put some weight behind the front door to close it against the wind. Her mother rushed in from the kitchen. "There you are. I was beginning to worry about you. Jacob should have finished milking about an hour ago." Ingrid rubbed Heidi's upper arms and began to guide her toward the flickering flames in the hearth.

"He did. He's staying in the barn until evening milking because of the storm."

Ingrid sensed the situation in the hesitation of Heidi's words. She asked quietly, "Did he see you?"

Heidi nodded slowly and turned to face her mother. No signs of fear were written on her face. "He's nothing like Peter, Mama."

Ingrid made no comment, but one eyebrow quirked upward in understanding. Once Heidi was settled on the chair before the fire, Ingrid returned to the kitchen, a smile tickling the corners of her mouth. She couldn't agree more. Jacob was nothing like Peter.

Such a short walk should not have chilled her so, but the warmth of the fire seemed to thaw her slowly. When Heidi finally warmed up enough to shed the blanket wrapped around her, she was reluctant to part with it, for it belonged to Jacob. She should be too old for schoolgirl flutters over a boy, but perhaps admiring him from afar rather than the affection born of companionable friendship had instigated the feeling.

Heidi needed to help her mother make cheese, but she lingered in the chair for a few more minutes and continued her musings. Jacob worked diligently even when no one was watching—or at least when he thought no one was watching. She had glimpsed his heart of worship as he sang to God while he worked. The gravelly edge of his singing voice was evidence that he didn't sing very often—he must realize that he was off pitch—but she felt honored to be a witness to it, perfect pitch or not.

What she had witnessed in the last hour made her heart want to sing—he possessed thoughtful creativity. When Jacob had studied the block of wood, she could almost see him envisioning the final result. He didn't rush the way Frederick did when he tried to whittle, lopping off big chunks at a time. He carved away the tiniest pieces, taking great care not to remove too much too soon. Even after an hour, the shape was still too formless to accurately guess his subject, but she was fairly sure it was going to be an animal of some kind.

His focus and concentration drew her. She had wondered what it would be like to be the object of his focus. Then she found out. Her initial trepidation should not have been a surprise, for Jacob was indeed a stranger. When she looked up at his face and met his warm gaze, she felt safe—until he called out to wait. The sudden memory of Peter had hit like a large crushing wave pulling her underwater where she couldn't breathe.

Instead of judging her for her panic, Jacob offered a life preserver in the form his jacket and then this blanket. Yes, the blanket had protected her from the elements, but it was the offer of protection that had pulled her from the rushing waves. What had been Papa's words? The right man would cherish and protect. Jacob had already proven that protecting her was almost an instinct. If given the chance, would he know how to cherish her, too?

By the time Heidi joined her mama in the kitchen, Ingrid was separating the cultured curds from the whey. They worked together in companionable silence. When the time-consuming process was finished for the afternoon, Heidi found herself at the front window. Though the amount of snow falling had decreased a bit, the snowflakes were forced into erratic directions at the whim of the angry gusts. The warm glow of Jacob's lantern could be seen through the barn window. Heidi mused, "He's probably started his evening milking."

Ingrid glanced at the mantle clock and joined her at the window. "Yes, it's about that time. The storm looks like it could get ugly again. Did you happen to notice if Jacob brought a bedroll in case he needs to stay overnight?"

Heidi's gaze never left the barn window as she answered, "Yes, he unrolled it to give me his blanket as a coat."

"Knowing him, I'm surprised he didn't offer you *his* coat."

"He did." Heidi's whisper was so soft her mama wondered if she had imagined her daughter's response until she saw the wistful look on Heidi's face. "Mama, we should invite him to sleep in the house. He might freeze in the barn."

"Especially since you took his blanket," Ingrid teased. Sobering, she added, "I don't know how your papa would react to that request."

"Papa doesn't need to protect me from Jacob, but we need to protect him from frostbite. He could sleep on the rug in front of the hearth." Heidi turned to search her mother's face. "Please, Mama."

Ingrid considered her daughter's request for a moment, then nodded. "We might as well invite him for dinner, too."

Heidi smothered her mama in a hug. "Thank you, Mama."
"Frederick!"

The boy appeared in his bedroom doorway. "Yes, Mama?"

"Get bundled up and visit the barn. Invite our helper to come for dinner after milking and ask him to bring his bedroll with him."

"Jacob can come to the house?" Frederick confirmed enthusiastically.

"Just this once," Ingrid reaffirmed.

Frederick quickly disappeared into his room and reemerged a couple of minutes later with several layers of clothing in place. He pulled his winter outerwear off the coat rack and secured his coat, hat, and gloves in place. "I'll be back in a little bit." He was in and out of the door before his mother could change her mind.

Ingrid chuckled and glanced at her daughter. "I think he likes Jacob as much as you do." Heidi didn't say a word. Her blush said it all. "Let me go warn your papa that Jacob will be joining us."

About a half-hour later, Frederick returned. "Jacob said he'd be grateful to come for dinner and a warm place on the floor. He still has about an hour of milking left. I milked a couple of cows to help him, but my hands got tired."

Ingrid could hear the discouragement in his tone. She rested her hand on his shoulder. "Remember what Dr. Luke said. Your strength will return in time. Be patient."

"Yes, Mama."

"Heidi, come help me in the kitchen. We're making schnitzel and spätzle for dinner. Frederick, set the table for four, and put an extra plate at my place for your papa."

Heidi scooped the last of the spätzle noodles from the boiling water and tossed them in melted butter just as the knock sounded on the door. She jolted just enough for her mother to notice. Ingrid leaned in and whispered, "Relax, you will be fine." Ingrid untied her apron and hung it on the wall hook before she opened the door. "Come in, Jacob." Jacob stomped his feet on the porch and scraped his boots on the mat before he entered. "Hang up your coat on the rack and warm yourself by the fire."

"Thank you, ma'am." Jacob leaned his bedroll against the wall and divested himself of his coat and winter wrappings. His hat had made his unruly hair even more so, and he raked his fingers across his scalp in an attempt to tame it. He ambled toward the fire and held his hands out to the warmth, for he had been chilled most of the day. If not for the uncertainty of meeting the beautiful young woman again, he would have felt completely at ease.

Jacob's eyes traveled to the mantel, taking a moment to study the ornately carved clock sitting there. A splash of color moved his gaze upward, and he beheld an intricate painting of birch trees in autumn. The light shone on the white bark and golden leaves, contrasting with the azure blue sky—the same blue as the girl's eyes. This artist understood light and color. The visual details were mesmerizing, and he became so immersed in the scene he could almost hear the leaves rustling.

Jacob was transported to his childhood. About the only thing he could remember about his family home was the walls filled with his mom's paintings. He wasn't old enough to think about asking for them when his parents died. Later he assumed his mother's art was sold with the house. A painting on canvas was more than a material possession; it was infused with the life of the artist. He regretted that he had been unable to keep at least one of his mother's masterpieces.

Frederick broke his reverie. "I'm glad you don't have to sleep in the barn tonight."

"Me, too, buddy."

A moment after Frederick appeared at his elbow, Mrs. Müller called from the kitchen, "Boys, come wash up."

Jacob nodded his head toward the kitchen and spoke to the lad beside him, "I'll follow you." As the pair reached the doorway to the kitchen, the young lady walked through with a steaming bowl of what resembled pasta. If not for his quick reflexes, Jacob would have run right into her. He stepped backwards and flattened himself against the wall just in time to avoid a collision.

Heidi looked up at him, suddenly flustered. "Oh, I'm sorry. Excuse me."

"No harm done." His gaze followed the young lady as she continued toward the table. Jacob did wish that someone would say her name so he could think of her as something other than "young lady." When the doorway cleared, he followed Frederick to the far corner of the kitchen and rolled up his shirtsleeves to wash his hands and forearms.

Frederick handed him the towel. Before Jacob could get his hands completely dry, the boy was dragging him toward the table. "Come on. You can sit by me."

Sitting next to Frederick meant sitting directly across from —Oh, he wanted to know her name! Snapping out of his distraction, he realized that he was the only man at the table. Though he was the guest, he offered, "Would you like me to pray?"

Mrs. Müller seemed pleased. "Yes, thank you." Everyone joined hands, and for a brief second, Jacob wished he were sitting next to—Oh, bother. He needed a name. Frederick was to his left and Mrs. Müller to his right. The blue eyes across from him searched his face before they closed in preparation for his prayer.

"Father, thank you for this meal, for this is far better than what I had planned to eat tonight. Bless this family for their hospitality, and help Mr. Müller to overcome the effects of the measles soon. In my Savior's name, Amen."

"Did you ask that so you wouldn't have to do our milking anymore?" Frederick asked with a hint of disappointment.

"No, I'm happy to help. I just know how hard it is for a man to depend on others to provide for his family when he would rather do the work himself."

"Amen." The unexpected rumble from the hallway startled Jacob.

Mrs. Müller smiled. "Ignore his growling. He's always been a bear when he's sick. Thankfully, it isn't often. Trust me, he agrees with you, Jacob." She finished filling the extra plate and excused herself to take it to the bedroom down the hall.

Jacob reached for the bowl Frederick was passing him. As he added a large spoonful of the pasta—or was it dumplings—to his plate, he commented, "This smells delicious."

There it was. Her smile was even more beautiful than he had been imagining all afternoon. "This is a traditional German meal." She gestured to the plate of meat. "Schnitzel is veal that has been breaded and fried, and the spätzle on your plate is an egg noodle tossed in butter and herbs."

When Jacob had forked one of the schnitzel pieces onto his plate, she handed him a small plate with lemon wedges. "Squirt one of the lemons over your schnitzel before you eat it." Jacob was so lost in her smile—he *really* needed a name—that he nearly forgot to pay attention to her words. He took one of the wedges and imitated her waving hand motion as she sprayed the lemon juice evenly on her meat.

When Mrs. Müller slipped into her chair, Jacob cut his first piece of meat. The schnitzel was an explosion of citrus with the crunch of bread-crusted meat in his mouth. "Mmm. That is good."

Frederick piped up, "Wait until you try the spätzle. It's even better. My sister made it."

His sister. Well, he was right about the family relationship. Still no name. If he weren't certain he would embarrass her, he would risk being impolite and ask her outright. Someone was bound to say it in conversation, right?

The spätzle practically melted like buttery goodness on his tongue. Jacob closed his eyes to savor the flavor.

"I told you it was better."

"Yes, and you were right."

Dinner ended, and apple strudel was served for dessert. Not a soul used her name. Learning her name should not be this difficult. Was it meant to be a secret? What a ludicrous thought! Although she had been hiding in the barn. He stopped the swirling of his thoughts; they were making him dizzy.

When everyone had finished eating, Jacob carried his dishes to the kitchen sink and shaved a bit of soap into the dishpan before reaching for the hot water kettle. "What are you doing?" Heidi asked incredulously.

Jacob looked up and answered matter-of-factly, "Getting ready to wash dishes."

"You're our guest."

He reached for the first plate in the stack. "Okay. Where do you want the food scraps?"

Both of Heidi's hands went to her hips. "You shouldn't wash dishes."

"Why not?"

"Because you're our guest," she repeated as if that one point answered everything.

Jacob tilted his head. "I'm not really a guest. I'm just the milking help. And I do know how to wash dishes. Besides, you cooked dinner, and your family has offered a warm place to sleep tonight. The least I can do is clean up."

"Are you always this stubborn?"

Jacob considered the question. "Probably." He handed her the kitchen towel. "Here. I'll wash. You can dry." The woman now beside him showed no traces of the fear or shyness from their first encounter. On the contrary, she was entirely relaxed with a bit of mischief playing in her eyes.

Frederick teased on his way out of the kitchen, "You had better watch out. Giving her the towel was a bad idea. She can snap that towel on your backside before you even know it's coming."

His sister's blush was instantaneous, and her mouth opened in horror. "Frederick!" She felt surrounded by laughter. Frederick's laughter was coming from one side and Jacob's from the other. When she overcame the humiliation, she tried to glare at the man beside her, but the merriment in her eyes gave away her true feelings. "You shouldn't laugh."

"Why not? Washing dishes practically makes me family for tonight, and your brother was funny."

Instinctively, Heidi turned and quickly pulled the towel through her hand and aimed. Before she could fire, she blinked twice, turned back toward the counter, and blushed again.

Jacob handed her a rinsed plate while he chuckled. "Here. Put that towel to good use. I seem to be wearing armor tonight."

The blue-eyed woman had been teased enough for one night. She carefully grasped each dish and utensil to ensure she would not touch his hand in the transfer, and she remained silent while she dried each item and returned it to its proper place. He needed something neutral to break the silence. "The painting above the fireplace is exquisite." He suddenly had her rapt attention.

"Is it? What captured your eyes?"

"Many people can paint a picture, but only a master artist can capture light so effectively." He dried his left hand on his shirt and lifted it up and back while flaring his fingers forward and right. "The sun was high and behind the artist's left shoulder, and the breeze was gentle."

"How do you know what the wind was doing?"

"Some of the leaves were hanging naturally. Others were fluttering. To be able to show motion on canvas requires perfect details. That kind of talent is a God-given gift."

Her smile had returned. "Do you have that gift?"

"Unfortunately, no, but I know how to appreciate it when I see it."

"Hmm." Her eyes were still smiling as she turned her wistful expression back to the dishes she was drying. Jacob had the distinct feeling that he had just missed something important.

"What do you see in that painting?"

"The promises of God."

Jacob was intrigued by her answer and tilted his head slightly. "How so?"

"Seasons come and go for the birch trees. The gloriously golden autumn leaves in the painting are only two weeks or so from dying and falling off the branches to be crunched underfoot. The promise is that spring will come, and with spring, new life will bloom."

"Our lives come in seasons, too—some sunny and bright—some bleak and dismal—but God's promises never change. He promises that He will never leave us, and He promises that He has a unique plan for us. Just like those birch trees, new life will come after a season of sadness. Joy will come in the morning."

Jacob had stilled and was still holding the final dish in the soapy water. His voice was a soft whisper. "And He promises to answer us and deliver us from our fears."

"Yes, He does." An unspoken understanding passed between them. "The artist faced a season so cloudy the sunlight could not get through but comfort came in remembering the sun is always there beyond the clouds."

"How do you know the artist's struggle?" He rinsed the final piece.

"I know the artist." Heidi placed the last dish in the

cupboard and folded the towel before she slipped quietly behind him and left him alone with his thoughts.

---

Jacob pondered their conversation before he crossed the living area and reverently stood facing the painted canvas. His broadening smile could not be contained. The missing piece of the puzzle had been found. In the lower right-hand corner, the artist's name had been neatly scripted. Heidi Müller. "Heidi." The whisper passed his lips. He knew her name.

At the sound of rustling fabric, Jacob turned his head to find Mrs. Müller coming up beside him. She held out a precisely folded bundle. "Here is the blanket you loaned Heidi. Will you be warm enough, or do you need another one?"

Reaching for the blanket, Jacob answered, "This blanket will be enough. I have a second one in my bedroll."

"I know the rug is not as comfortable as a mattress . . ."

"I will be quite cozy here near the fireplace. I've slept on the floor and on the ground many times. The rug will be a nice cushion."

"Very well, then. Good night, Jacob." She began to turn away, then seemed to change her mind. "Thank you." At Jacob's confused expression, she continued, "In the span of a few hours, you have become Heidi's friend during a time when she desperately needs one. Apparently, God has brought you to us for more reasons than one. For Johann, you faithfully do the milking. For Frederick, you mentor him as a big brother would. For Heidi, you have been the catalyst for the renewal of her trust in God. For me, you have met the needs of my family in ways I could not. Sleep well."

His gaze absently followed Mrs. Müller as she walked away. Once she had entered through her bedroom doorway, a massive figure appeared there. The darkened hallway cast shadows on him, but there was no doubt in Jacob's mind that he was looking at Johann Müller. He might be weak, but his voice still boomed with unquestioning authority. "If you leave that rug tonight, you will answer to me, measles or not."

Jacob understood the declaration of protection underlying the command and nodded, "Yes, sir. I'll stay right here. You have my word." He could feel the man's assessing gaze. Jacob did not cower. He must have passed the test, for Johann nodded to him and closed the bedroom door.

Jacob turned his attention back to the painting for a few minutes before he unrolled his bedding and lay down. He clasped his hands behind his head as thoughts of the day swirled around in his mind and landed squarely on Mrs. Müller's statement. God had used him to be—How did she word it?—"the catalyst for the renewal of Heidi's trust in God."

*Lord, I have no idea what happened to shake Heidi's trust in You, but I'm guessing it was something terrible for her entire family to advocate for her protection. I'm humbled that You are somehow using me in her life. Please make her faith strong and unwavering, grounded in Your promises. You are worthy of our trust, even when the circumstances of life try to tell a different story. Please give me the opportunity to be her friend.* Then, to reduce the likelihood of him snoring, Jacob rolled over onto his side just before he fell sound asleep.

---

In the next room, Heidi replayed the evening as she crawled into bed. When she thought of how close she had come to firing the towel on Jacob's backside, she covered her scarlet face with both hands in mortification. At least she was lying in the dark where no one could see her cheeks burning.

Heidi moved her thoughts to their conversations—much safer ground. Never in her life had she spoken so openly to any male other than her dad and brother. Of course, she had been listening to his side of the conversation for two weeks. Perhaps that had put her more at ease.

Best of all, he had understood her painting—not just the scene itself but the deeper meaning she had shared. Did he know that she had given him a glimpse into her soul? Ugh. What was she thinking? Jacob was still a stranger. Wasn't he? She should be more guarded. Shouldn't she? She wanted to trust Jacob, but could she even trust herself? Her thoughts were such a muddle. *Lord, give me wisdom to know whom to trust and how much to trust.*

## CHAPTER 14
## The Promise

When Johann heard stirring in the family room during the predawn hour, he silently opened his bedroom door until the tiniest ribbon of firelight danced across the threshold. Then he peered out. Jacob's bedroll was already tied, and he was kneeling before the fire, adding more wood and stoking the flames to warm the morning chill away. That done, he donned his coat and his other winter wear, gathered his bedroll, and slipped quietly out the front door.

Ingrid's sleepy voice reached him. "Should I wake Jacob for morning milking?"

"No need. He just left."

"What a responsible young man!" Ingrid stretched and moved to get out of bed.

"Maybe my quarantine will end today."

Ingrid drew near to her husband and lifted his shirt to examine his skin. "Not yet, but soon. The rash is nearly gone." Johann's low growl only made her grin in amusement. "I know you have cabin fever, but you've waited this long. What is another day or two?"

"Torture," he replied. "Maybe the young doctor will have pity on me."

"Maybe, but I doubt it." Ingrid chuckled. "He didn't let Frederick go until the rash was completely healed."

"True. I guess I should resign myself to another day of utter boredom."

"Yes, you should," Ingrid teased.

In a flash, Johann grabbed his shaving towel and snapped it toward her backside. Ingrid giggled and grabbed the end of the towel before it made contact. She knew where Heidi had learned her towel-snapping skills, but her own evasion skills were well-honed after years of practice. "You owe me a kiss—" she proclaimed in triumph. He leaned toward her like a plant bending toward the sunshine. "—after you are cleared from quarantine." Another growl.

---

The winter storm had left freezing temperatures in its wake. Jacob lifted sleepy eyelids as he woke to dying embers struggling to send their heat past the stones of the hearth. Though he was fully dressed and wrapped in two blankets, his exposed nose and cheeks were still cold. If he needed heat lying this close to the fireplace, he could only imagine how cold the rest of the house must be.

The only motivation worth abandoning the cocoon of his blankets to stoke the flames was his desire to generate enough heat to warm Heidi's room. *Why had his initial thought been only of her? He wasn't even completely awake yet.* One side of his mouth edged upward. Though as the thought permeated his brain, he supposed the same heat would probably make the other rooms a bit less frigid, too. Soon, the flames licked the two added logs and the warmth began to billow outward. Jacob lingered just a moment as the first recipient of the renewed heat. Knowing the barn would not feel as toasty, he wanted to be thoroughly warm, even holding the inside of his jacket toward the crackling flames before he pushed his arms into the sleeves and prepared to leave the house.

Jacob made a mental note to check the woodpile after milking in case he needed to chop wood before heading home. His hat and upturned collar did little to protect his neck and face as he crossed to the barn. He entered and quickly closed the door behind him, not wanting to let any unnecessary chill enter the less-than-insulated building. Even within the barn, puffs of breath rose before his face with every exhalation.

After mucking Shadow's stall, he continued down the line and cleaned the other horses' stalls, ensuring they had food and unfrozen water. Then he returned to Shadow and rubbed his face. "Hang in there for a few more hours, and we'll ride home." His horse seemed to understand and nuzzled his nose against Jacob's chest. A wave of reluctance to leave Heidi settled in his mind, but he dismissed the feeling. He just needed coffee.

When Jacob glanced over to the wall near the door, he realized he had forgotten to bring the clean milk cans over with him and rolled his eyes at his omission. Returning to the house would make him look like an idiot, but he needed those cans before he started milking, and the cows were already waking up. Well, he had talked himself out of worse scrapes.

Jacob hurried across to the front porch, noted the lantern light in the window, and knocked softly. Mrs. Müller answered and gestured him inside. "Come in from the cold."

"Thank you. I just finished mucking all of the stalls. All of the horses are set with feed and water. I'll just grab the milk cans and start the milking."

Ingrid noticed his rosy cheeks and pointed him toward the fireplace. "Go, warm up for a few minutes first."

"Yes, ma'am." When Jacob stood before the crackling

flames with his palms extended toward the warmth, he closed his eyes as the chill was slowly expunged from his bones. At the sound of footsteps, Jacob opened his eyes to behold a golden-haired vision approaching. Heidi extended a steaming cup of coffee.

"You're an angel. Thank you." He reached for the cup and sipped, the warm liquid spilling heat inside his thawing body. As his words finally connected with his brain, he blushed, his rosy cheeks becoming a deeper shade of red.

A quick glance at Heidi's blushing face confirmed that he had embarrassed her as well with his comment. He had to make that right before the moment passed. "Forgive me. My brain doesn't kick in until *after* coffee." He winced and gestured with his cup before he took another swallow.

"No apology is necessary."

Her gentle words drew his eyes to hers. Those grayish blue eyes didn't appear either embarrassed or miffed. They looked . . . appreciative? Why could he suddenly feel his heart pounding against his breastbone? *Oh, boy, I really need more coffee.*

Once he drained the last precious drop, Jacob placed the cup in Heidi's outstretched hand. He smiled just enough to outline his dimples. "Thank you. I think I'll live now."

A soft laugh bubbled from the woman beside him, "I'm glad to hear it."

Catching the amused smirk on Mrs. Müller's face across the room as she set the table for breakfast, Jacob cleared his throat. "I'll collect the milk cans now. The ladies are waiting for me." He gathered all of the handles onto his left forearm and reached for the doorknob. He glanced back over his shoulder to where Heidi was still standing with his empty cup in hand and winked at her. "Thanks again."

He winked at her? To his recollection, he had never flirted with a girl. He should be ashamed for flirting with a woman he had just met yesterday, yet nothing in him felt sorry. The grin plastered on his face confirmed quite the opposite, in fact. Maybe he still needed one or two more cups of coffee. One thing was certain—He no longer noticed the cold.

---

The flutters within Heidi were dancing the Viennese waltz, a precise pattern of fast-paced, high-energy movements, not at all like the chaotic frenzy that accompanied anxiety. These flutters were so powerful that she nearly forgot to breathe. Jacob had called her an angel. His blush had proven he had not intended to say the words. He had apologized for embarrassing her, but he had never recanted his statement. The non-premeditated endearment wrapped around her heart like a cozy blanket, warm and—cherished?

Is this what it felt like to be cherished? And all of his gratitude was over a simple cup of coffee, of all things. What she had observed of Jacob confirmed he was a man worth knowing. She craved his friendship—maybe more in time—but his friendship first.

A soft clearing of her mama's throat broke Heidi's reverie. She found herself still standing near the hearth holding Jacob's coffee cup, and a new blush heated her cheeks. Slowly nearing the table, Heidi saw Ingrid's eyes crinkled in merriment. "I gather Jacob likes coffee, then?" In response, Heidi rolled her eyes heavenward, carried the empty cup into the kitchen, and returned with the utensils for the table.

Laying the forks and knives in their respective places, Heidi began to hum, but when she joined her mama in the kitchen to make the breakfast biscuits, her hum transformed into soft singing.

Jacob's knock had brought Johann back to the shadowed doorway of his room, where he witnessed the entire interaction between Jacob and Heidi as well as her reaction after he left. The teasing in his wife's voice lifted one corner of his mouth, but the greatest impact to his father's heart was hearing Heidi sing.

Her fear since that fateful day with Peter had not only stolen her peace and joy; it had stolen her song. Johann lifted his eyes toward heaven with a prayer of praise not only for the inception of healing in his daughter's soul but also for the young man God had sent to milk his cows.

The evidence was piling up in Jacob's favor, but the jury in Johann's mind was still deliberating. His continued investigation would be thorough and patient before he would consider rendering a verdict. His daughter's heart was too precious for anything less.

---

Dressed like a woolen snowman, Frederick bustled into the barn an hour later and pulled the door tightly shut behind him. "Jacob?"

"Over here milking Maisy."

Frederick appeared around the Jersey cow, his face brimming with excitement. "You're amazing!"

Laughter exploded from Jacob's chest. "I've been called many things in my life, but 'amazing' hasn't been one of them."

Nonplussed, the boy asked in wonder, "How did you do it?"

Any other onlooker would have seen the mirth disappear into the confusion etched into the furrows of Jacob's face, but

Frederick was oblivious to the change. *The only thing I'm doing here is milking a cow. That's not very noteworthy. Coffee. I need coffee. Three cups worth might get my brain working.* "Do what?"

"Get Heidi to sing again! She hasn't sung since the day she was hurt, but she starting singing this morning, and Mama said you had something to do with it. How did you get her to sing?"

Jacob's mind screeched to a halt at the words "the day she was hurt," and he could process nothing further. She had been hurt? How? By whom? Was that event the cause of her continued struggle with fear?

"Jacob?"

The rest of the conversation finally filtered through, but he answered with a noncommittal "I'm not sure, but I'm glad she's found her song again."

Frederick jabbered on as he retraced his steps to grab a stool and milk pail and settled beside the next cow to help Jacob with the milking. The war of emotions within Jacob created too much noise to hear anything else—anger toward whoever had hurt Heidi, curiosity mixed with dread about what had happened, awe that God would use him to bring her joy.

Jacob had known Heidi less than one day, yet he felt completely at ease around her, enough to tease and banter with her—even wink at her. The edge of his mouth twitched with the urge to smile again. Though his outgoing personality lent itself to social interaction, his conversations with younger ladies other than family left him feeling awkward and inept. Only his well-practiced jovial air kept him from sounding like an utter idiot. His only amiable female companions were of the bovine variety. Josiah might be more introverted than he, but his brother had a natural grace around females. Nearly every girl in the church grew up having a crush on Josiah, while they practically ignored him in that regard. Not that he minded.

Josiah was always having to tiptoe the fine line between

being friendly and showing interest that could be misconstrued as affection. Jacob never had to worry about that. One thing the brothers did have in common was their desire to guard their hearts. Even as young boys, their mom had taught them to save their emotional attachments for the woman they would marry.

Jacob refused to consider giving his affections to someone he had just met. In truth, he knew very little about her character. *What did he know?* Heidi was pretty and graceful, in addition to being a talented painter, a good cook, and a hospitable hostess. She struggled with fear, presumably over a traumatic event in her past, but sought to overcome it. More importantly, she had a heart for God's Word and a desire to claim His promises. So, maybe their unexpected encounter had taught him more about her than he realized.

He purposed to slow his tumultuous thoughts enough to listen to Frederick's chatter. Now that Jacob had met the Müller family's hidden treasure, Frederick would be free to talk about Heidi. Perhaps if he paid close attention, he might learn even more about his coffee-giving angel. *His angel? Oh, brother. Coffee. I am going to need the whole pot at this point.*

"When I was little," Frederick continued as if Jacob had not missed the last few minutes of his conversation, "Mama would tuck me into bed, and Heidi would read a story and sing a lullaby until I fell asleep. Every night."

"Sounds like you miss it."

"Nah, I'm too old for lullabies now," though the wistfulness in his voice told a different story.

"Mm-hmm. You're not too old. My mom was still tucking me in and reading me stories when I was ten."

"The point is that Heidi always sang while making breakfast, too, so I would go to sleep and wake up to her voice. That I miss."

"Did she sing a lot?"

"All the time, but it was sweet and soothing, not at all like Carla Oaken, who bellowed like a mating cow."

Jacob laughed at Frederick's obvious disgust, despite having no idea who this Carla Oaken was.

"Heidi was always happy, just like the sunshine in her paintings. Even when unhappy days came, she would always look for—What did she call it?—a silver something."

"A silver lining?"

"Yeah, that's it. A silver lining. She always found something good to be grateful for. When we had to leave all but one of her paintings at our other house, I think her silver linings were lost for a while. Waking up to Heidi's singing this morning was like a dream I thought I'd lost forever. Now the world seems right again."

Leaving paintings behind—*that* tangible disappointment Jacob could understand.

With only two cows left to be milked, Ingrid entered the barn and walked directly to Jacob. "When you're finished, would you please come up to the house?" Her expression was neutral, leaving no hint of the reason.

"Yes, ma'am."

With a nod, Ingrid departed.

---

A knot had formed in Jacob's gut. His brain still had not entirely caught up, for after asking Fredrick for the location of the wood pile, he ascended the steps with his arms fully loaded with wood, leaving him no free hand to knock. Frederick scurried past him and burst through the front door. "Jacob's here, Mama."

Ingrid glanced over from where she and Heidi were plating the breakfast dishes in the kitchen. "Good. Jacob, thank you for the load of firewood. You are so thoughtful.

After you drop the wood in the box, come wash up for breakfast."

Her tone brokered no room for argument, yet the thought of food didn't help that knot to unwind. Still, he answered with another, "Yes, ma'am," and did as he was told. When he sat at the table, another steaming cup of coffee was waiting for him, and his mouth lifted in a crooked smile as he spoke a quiet "Thank you" to the pretty blond across from him. He may have thought the angel comment again, but at least he had the presence of mind not to voice it this time.

Breakfast was pleasant, but the niggling sense of foreboding wouldn't go away. Something was off; he just wasn't sure what it was. After Heidi refilled his coffee and he finished his third cup of the day, his brain was in full working order. That's when Ingrid's brow furrowed slightly, and the knot in his gut twisted again.

"Johann and I have something important to discuss with you."

"All right."

The sound of authority boomed from the hallway. "Pastor Kendrick, and now you, are the only ones in town who know that Heidi is here. Due to circumstances I do not wish to discuss, her location needs to remain a secret until we know she is safe. This is an unusual request, I know, but you cannot reveal Heidi's presence to anyone, even your doctor brother. Her pursuers are evil men, and they would do great harm if they found her."

Iron entered Jacob's soul as a surge of protectiveness coursed through him. His determined gaze found Heidi's when she lifted her downcast eyes from her lap to his face. "I will keep your secret. You have my word."

Johann and Heidi spoke in unison. "Thank you, Jacob."

Jacob rose from the table and retreated into the living area just enough to face Heidi's father from across the room to his bedroom doorway. When the visual connection was established, he asked, "Is there anything else I can do?"

"Your silence is enough."

Jacob nodded a solemn acceptance.

"One more thing. Heidi will need to hide in her studio each afternoon while Dr. Luke is here. Now that you know she is in the loft during evening milking, either Frederick or my wife will remain in the barn with you, ensuring you are chaperoned at all times."

"Yes, sir. I understand."

---

While Jacob rode home, he considered the promise he had made. He was resolute in his decision to protect Heidi, yet he knew his greatest challenge, perhaps a nearly impossible one, would be to keep Luke and Josiah from suspecting anything. They were both keen observers and knew how to read his thoughts as if they were printed on the town newspaper's headline. He needed divine help. "Lord, You know I've never been one to keep secrets from my brothers unless it was about an upcoming gift. Give me wisdom to honor my promise and the relationship with my brothers."

When he had released Shadow into the pasture to graze, Jacob turned to find Luke waiting for him at the pasture gate. Jacob sent a quick plea for help heavenward. "Morning, Luke." His brother's eyes studied him.

"You've discovered what the Müllers have been hiding." His comment wasn't a question.

Taking a deep breath to give himself a few more seconds to find the right words, Jacob did not confirm nor deny Luke's supposition. "I have made a promise, Luke, and I intend to keep it."

Not breaking eye contact, Luke nodded his understanding.

His sky blue eyes communicated admiration, not censure. "You are an honorable man, Jacob. Will you be milking there again this afternoon?"

"Yep."

"Good. Perhaps I'll see you there." Luke mounted Dakota. "I'm headed to the clinic. I'll come by the Müllers' farm as usual on my way home."

"Just so you know, I've agreed to be Frederick's big brother under the condition that he include my brothers, too. If you happened to call him your little brother while you're checking on him this afternoon, you would make his day."

"Sure, I'll do that."

"Have a good day." A pause, then, "Thank you, Luke." His brother smiled and waved his farewell.

## CHAPTER 15
## Johann's Approval

That afternoon, Jacob tethered Shadow to the hitching post in front of the Müllers' barn and poked his head inside the barn without stepping in. "Heidi, are you in the loft?"

"Yes," came the distant reply.

"Are either Frederick or your mom in the barn yet?"

"I'm here," Frederick called as he peered out of a horse stall.

"As am I," Ingrid answered from where she was lining up the clean milk cans against the wall. "But I'm heading back to the house for Dr. Luke's visit."

Jacob entered completely and strolled over to the milk pail and stool. "Since my little brother is still here, I'll get to work." He settled beside Bessie and began his rounds.

"See, Mama, I told you I have brothers!" Frederick exclaimed.

Ingrid chuckled. "Yes, so you did. Remember to stay here with Jacob, even if you need a rest, all right?"

"Yes, Mama." As soon as Ingrid slipped out and shut the door, Frederick asked, "What's a chaperone?"

"A chaperone. Hmm. Well, a chaperone is someone who stays with a young man and woman who are not married as a witness that they have done nothing improper. He protects their reputations. It is an important job that should be taken seriously."

Frederick stood a little taller with his shoulders a little straighter. Jacob searched the loft until he found Heidi smiling down at him. Her approval made him sit taller, too.

Wanting to use the next three hours to learn more about the lady in the loft, Jacob included her in the conversation. "Heidi, what do you do to pass the time up there?"

Something inside her melted when Jacob said her name, for his warm baritone gave her name an almost lyrical quality. Never had she loved her name more. "I have a couple of books and my Bible to read, but I spend most of my time drawing."

"Drawing? Like pencil sketches?"

"Yes."

"I'd be honored if you'd show me your work sometime." From their conversation about the painting, Jacob knew how much of herself Heidi put into her artwork. Her sketches would tell him more about her. Besides, he was the son of an artist. He recognized Heidi's skill and wanted to study more of her pieces.

Heat filled Heidi's face when she thought how many of her sketches were of him. She wanted to share her sketchbook with him, but how could she without revealing her interest in him. If she removed some of her non-Jacob drawings, she could show him those. "Certainly."

"You should show him the one of him and me. That's my favorite one in your sketchbook," Frederick proclaimed.

"Frederick!" The name rained down from above.

"So she has a sketch with me in it, huh?" Jacob teased.

"Are you kidding? Most of the sketches in her book are of you. They're really good."

"Frederick!" Heidi buried her flaming face in the arms wrapped around her knees.

"I'm not saying anything that isn't true, Heidi."

"Perhaps not," Jacob intervened, "but I think you have embarrassed your sister."

"How? Even Papa talks about how talented she is."

"If her painting is any indication, Heidi is quite talented; but I think her chagrin has more to do with my being the subject of some of her sketches."

"Why? I think you're great!"

Jacob emptied his pail into the milk can and paused on his way to the next cow. "Heidi?" He waited until her buried face turned enough to see him over her arm. "For the record, I'm honored that you included me in some of your drawings. Frederick doesn't understand how he flustered you, but I do, and you needn't be embarrassed on my account."

"Thank you, Jacob." The reply was muffled by the fabric of her sleeve, but he heard it just the same.

When Jacob's pinging milk rhythm began again, the barn door opened enough for Luke to lean in. "Is Frederick in here?"

"Yes, Dr. Luke."

"How are you feeling?"

"Getting stronger every day. I'm a ch—"

"Great helper." Jacob cut in abruptly. "He's up to three cows each milking session. You should be proud of him."

Luke nodded, "I am proud of you, little brother. Keep up the good work." He glanced over at Jacob and winked.

"Thank you, Dr. Luke!" When Luke slipped away, Frederick grinned. "He called me 'little brother,' too!"

"Yep, he sure did!" Jacob lowered his volume to a stage whisper so Heidi could catch his words to Frederick. "Don't mention the word 'chaperone' to Luke, for it would give him a big clue that there is a girl in the barn. Remember that he doesn't know about Heidi."

"Oh! Is that why you interrupted me?"

"Mm-hmm."

"Thank you, Jacob."

"You're welcome, little brother."

For the rest of the evening milking session, the three of them discussed a myriad of topics from serious to funny, and Jacob shared stories about his family and his life on the ranch next door. Jacob carefully steered the conversation away from Heidi's artwork or "the event" that had created so much fear and disruption for Heidi and her family.

His greatest achievement of the day was winning Heidi's smile when he would recount one funny story or another. A couple of times, he even earned her laughter, light and sweet like a line of music. Boy, he needed to guard his heart, or he was in jeopardy of losing it altogether.

---

Midway through the milking rounds the next evening, the imposing figure of Johann Müller entered the barn. The man was even more massive than he appeared when standing in his bedroom doorway, and his stern expression declared that he was not one to be crossed. "Protective" rather than "dangerous" was written in his stance and demeanor, though Jacob had no doubt Mr. Müller could easily produce a dangerous side if his family were threatened.

Multiple thoughts ran through Jacob's mind at once, the one gaining the most traction was that his time with Heidi was drawing to a close. Something inside him grieved at that thought.

Over the course of the next couple of days, Jacob continued to come promptly at milking time, but Johann's quickly increasing strength made the sessions shorter and shorter. Though he felt awkward at first, Jacob strove to maintain a variety of conversational topics, including Mr. Müller along the way. Heidi's dad, or "Papa," as she called him, began with curt, gruff replies but gradually warmed to Jacob's presence. One time, from her perch in the loft, Heidi even coaxed a smile and a laugh from the man. That single moment transformed him from a determined protector to a loving father.

Throughout their time together, Mr. Müller's scrutinizing gaze seemed to be taking Jacob's measure. Thankfully, he was already used to Seth's penetrating looks; though Mr. Müller's inspection was more intimidating. *Lord, please help me to make the mark on whatever ruler he is using to measure my character. I would dearly love the opportunity to know Heidi more, and this man will either open or shut the door to that possibility.*

At the end of evening milking on the third day, Jacob grabbed the last two full milk cans and followed Mr. Müller to the house. After setting them on the floor in the kitchen, Johann turned to face him. "Thank you for being a blessing to our family, Jacob, but Frederick and I will tend the milking from here."

The suddenness should not have surprised Jacob, but it did, and he blurted, "May I still come to the farm?"

Johann regarded him critically. "Are you not needed at your ranch?"

"This is our slow season. Once spring calving begins, I will be needed around the clock. My chores now can be finished in a few hours, giving me plenty of time to help here."

Johann considered his request for several seconds, then shook his head. "I cannot pay you."

"I'm not asking for payment."

"Then why do you want to come?" Johann's penetrating gaze threatened to dispel Jacob's courage, but he rose to the challenge.

"Two things. First, I have enjoyed helping you these last few weeks. It has given me a purpose beyond my usual responsibilities, and I would like to continue. Surely there jobs on your 'to-do' list that need a man's help." Jacob tried to stand taller. He felt like David next to Goliath, albeit a less menacing version of the giant. "Second, and more importantly, I wish to have more time to build my friendship with Heidi."

A muscle ticked in the giant's jaw. "What are your intentions?" Johann boomed.

Jacob's eyes never strayed from the elder man's gaze. "Initially, to pursue a friendship. We barely know one another, yet we have already found several things we have in common. Truly, I find great delight in finding her smile and making her laugh. I know she has been hurt somehow, and I've learned from personal experience that having a friend in the dark times can make the path back to the light much easier. Even Jesus had a best friend in John. Fear can be a devilishly hard emotion to overcome without having someone walk the journey to faith and trust with you."

Johann's eyes softened ever so slightly. "And after a friendship is established?"

"Then, if feelings of attachment ensue, I'll ask to court her while we consider a more permanent relationship."

"Why is a friendship so important to you?"

"My mom always taught me that having the foundation of a strong friendship before marriage will make a marriage stronger. A true friend is one who looks out for the best interest of the other person, not himself. When the storms of life threaten a marriage, selfless love will enable a husband and wife to weather those storms together and become stronger on the other side. When they both continue to unite their faith and trust in God, their marriage will become unbreakable."

"Wise words. Have you ever courted another woman?"

"No, sir. I believe the right one is worth the wait."

Johann's brow arched. "And you think Heidi is the right one."

"I do hope so, sir." Jacob swallowed as he considered the other alternative. "And if not, I will have gained a friend."

Jacob must have earned satisfactory marks on his evaluation, for Johann extended his hand. "I'll expect you tomorrow after your chores at the ranch are complete. Your family should become your priority again."

Jacob's smile spread, and he shook the man's massive hand with a firm grip. "Thank you, sir. I'll be here."

That was the moment Heidi walked into the house. Her eyes shifted from her papa to Jacob and back and lowered to focus on their clasped hands. When the handshake released, Jacob moved toward the door, pausing to stand a few feet from Heidi. The light dancing in his eyes proclaimed his joy, but all he said was, "Until tomorrow," and he left.

---

Her papa looked like Frederick when he was sneaking a cookie before it cooled. "Papa, what have you done?" Heidi asked the question suspiciously, but her smile held a world of hope.

"Jacob gave me several compelling reasons why you two should develop a friendship, and he offered to continue volunteering here at the farm just so he can spend time with you."

Heidi intertwined her fingers and drew her clasped hands to her chin, trying in vain to contain her delight. "He wants to be *my* friend?" The utter joy on his daughter's face confirmed that he had made the right decision, though a twinge of jealousy reminded him that his little girl was grown up, and he had ceased to be the only source of her smile.

## CHAPTER 16
# A Budding Friendship

The following morning, Jacob woke early, eager to get his ranch chores done for the day. Josiah usually beat him to making their shared pot of coffee in the mornings, but Jacob was determined to do the task this day. Though he tried to work quietly, his inadvertent clattering woke his brother.

"Jacob, why are you already up?"

"I thought I'd get my chores done and head over to the Müllers' farm."

"You said they didn't need you to help with milking anymore."

"True, but Mr. Müller has other two-man jobs that need doing, and Frederick is only eight."

Josiah sat on the side of his bunk and scrubbed his face with his hands to wake up. "If you want to wait for me, I'll go over with you and lighten the load."

"No!"

Josiah's brow rose in surprise.

Gentling his tone, Jacob repeated, "No, thank you. Luke said they don't want any strangers on their farm, remember?"

"But I'm your brother."

"I know, but I'm in a unique position to help since they already know me."

"But I would not be welcome." Josiah's tone was more hurt than critical.

Jacob answered with a slow shake of his head. "It's nothing personal, Josiah. If it were up to me, I'd take you up on your offer."

Pointing to the pot, Josiah commented, "Don't burn the coffee. You definitely need a cup or two. You're not making any sense."

Jacob plunked two empty cups onto the butcher block counter and filled them both. "Here." He handed one to his brother and took a hearty sip from the other. *I've made a muddle of this, Lord. I don't want anything to come between me and my brother.* Straddling a chair, Jacob faced his brother. "Look, I know this seems unorthodox, but I've made a promise I'm not going to break regarding the Müllers' privacy. Their concern is for good reason. I need you to trust me."

The hazel eyes looking back at Jacob narrowed slightly beneath pinched brows in a contemplative expression. How Josiah could process complex thoughts before coffee confounded Jacob entirely. "All right, Jacob, I'll trust you. If you need anything, I'll be here for you."

"Thanks." Jacob reached out and rested his hand on Josiah's shoulder. "You're the best brother ever. Don't tell the others you're my favorite."

A crooked smile lifted to show off his dimple. "I have known you my entire life, so I had a jump start on the whole brother thing. I'll always have your back."

"I know, little brother, I know." Jacob smiled, his own matching dimple making an appearance. He squeezed his brother's shoulder before removed his hand. When he had drained his cup, he stood and poured a second cup.

Josiah stood and stretched. A parchment card on the table caught his eye, and he reached over to nudge the corner of it. In near-perfect calligraphy script was the verse from Isaiah 41:10. *"Fear not, for I am with you; be not dismayed, for I am your God; I will strengthen you, I will help you, I will uphold you with my righteous right hand."* "Is this what you were working on last night with your calligraphy pen?"

"Yes. I've been missing Mom more than usual the past few weeks. Practicing the script she taught me so many years ago made her feel not so far away."

"The flourishes you added around the border are a nice artistic touch."

"Thank you." Jacob finished his coffee and bundled up against the cold. "Meet you in the barn."

Josiah watched his brother leave their bunkhouse then scratched his chin while he focused again on the verse. There was a hidden message here; he just wasn't sure what it was.

---

After chores, Jacob collected the parchment card he had left out to dry overnight and rode Shadow to the farm next door. Mr. Müller met him at the hitching post. Standing next to the man was rather intimidating, but he was already used to being the shortest man in the family. Jacob wasn't short, per se, for he was only a couple of inches shy of six feet tall. All of his brothers were around the six-foot mark, except for Tim, of course, who exceeded that by another six inches. Even Seth and Pastor Kendrick were taller than he was.

A brief memory of him and Heidi washing dishes side-by-side brought a smile. She was about five or six inches shorter—a perfect height difference. Jacob caught Mr. Müller giving him an odd look, and he snapped from his reverie. *Coffee.* He should have had a third cup before heading over here.

Regaining his composure, Jacob greeted Heidi's papa. "Good morning, Mr. Müller. What do you need me to do for you today?"

Johann handed Jacob a sheet of paper. "I have compiled quite a long list. We'll start at the top and work until lunch, which won't be until after Ingrid and Heidi have finished the morning batch of cheese. My wife has invited you to join us. Then you can relax with us for a few minutes before we get back to work until you need to head home."

As Jacob perused the list, his smile grew. There were enough jobs to keep them busy for at least a week or two, maybe more. "Perfect."

They started with sealing the windows in the house and moved from one task to the next. Though Jacob sensed that both he and his work were being evaluated, he still managed to find a camaraderie of sorts with the gruff-around-the-edges man. By lunchtime, Jacob was beginning to read the older man's cues, and they worked together quite well.

For the midday meal, Jacob was placed between Frederick and Mrs. Müller. He wouldn't have minded sitting next to Heidi, but now he understood why Buck usually picked the spot across from Julie before they married. The view was beautiful. *Oh, boy, he was a goner.*

After lunch, Jacob collected the dishes with Heidi with the intention of washing them, but Mrs. Müller shooed him and Heidi away. "I'll take care of the dishes today. You two go sit by the fire." Something about the twinkle in the woman's eyes made Jacob's heart sing. At least he seemed to meet with Mrs. Müller's approval even if he had not yet won over her husband.

Jacob stoked the fire to generate a bit more heat while Heidi settled herself on the sofa. Then he walked over to where his coat was hanging and pulled the parchment card from his coat pocket. Approaching Heidi, he extended the card toward her. "I made this for you last night."

A low-pitched, formidable voice from the side chair bellowed, "You will not give anything to my daughter without my permission."

Without missing a beat, Jacob took two steps toward Mr. Müller and handed him the card. "May I give this to Heidi?"

Without examining the card, Mr. Müller glowered at Jacob. "Why are you giving my daughter gifts?"

"It isn't meant as a gift as much as a reminder of God's promise." Jacob gestured upward at Heidi's birch tree painting over the mantel. "My mother was a painter. She would sketch some, too, but she loved oil paints and watercolors best. When a friend of hers needed encouragement, she would make a folded card with an ornamental painted something on the front and a calligraphy note within. I haven't her gift for painting, but my mom did teach me the artistry of calligraphy."

"When one of my brothers need some support or inspiration, I'll challenge them to checkers or help them with chores, for I prefer to show them a tangible way that I care in addition to words of kindness. I've never had the opportunity to encourage a friend who is a lady, so I thought I'd follow my mom's example." He shifted his weight from one foot to the other. "If I have done something inappropriate in offering this, please forgive me." Jacob's cheeks flushed in humility.

Johann turned his focus to the paper in his hand. A Bible verse was beautifully scripted with an ornate border that reminded him of the illustration work in his parents' family Bible back in Germany. He read and reread the verse from Isaiah, words that spoke encouragement to his own heart, and he knew they would do the same for his daughter's heart. "This is masterfully done." Johann handed the card back to Jacob. "You may give it to Heidi."

"Thank you, sir." Jacob received his card and took a deep

breath before shifting back to Heidi. "This verse was a particular comfort to me after our parents died. As a ten-year-old boy, I was given the responsibility to care for Josiah, and the struggle to keep us together weighed heavily upon me. When I would become afraid or feel abandoned, I would find this verse and read it aloud. I don't know the details of your past, but I sense that you struggle with fear because of it. I hope this verse will give you the courage it gave me."

When Jacob extended the card toward her this time, Heidi reached up and slid it from his hand, careful not to touch him during the transfer. She held it with gentle care and read the verse Jacob had chosen. "Thank you, this is a wonderful promise." Heidi studied the lettering and traced her finger along the decorative border. "Your mother taught you this script?" Jacob nodded. "It's beautiful. This must remind you of her."

"It does," Jacob answered softly. Heidi gestured for him to sit on the sofa near her. He lowered onto the cushion leaving plenty of space between them. "Mom believed that milestone birthdays held extra meaning, and apparently my tenth birthday needed special celebration. For as long as I can remember, I had always loved my mom's calligraphy, but my attempts to recreate it were laughable. My parents saved their extra pennies all year and gave me a dip pen with a calligraphy nib that birthday. Mom explained that I needed the right tool to form the letters correctly. I begged her to start teaching me that very afternoon."

"Before we left for the orphanage, Josiah and I had the opportunity to visit our home one last time and gather small remembrances to take with us. One of the items I packed was my mom's cherished pen in its cherrywood case. On Josiah's tenth birthday, I gave it to him and taught him calligraphy, too, as a way to remember Mom."

Heidi's fingertips glided across the card as if she could feel the letters on the parchment. "Would you be willing to teach me calligraphy?"

Jacob glanced at Mr. Müller and raised a brow in silent question for his permission. Upon receiving a curt nod, he smiled and returned his focus to Heidi. "I would enjoy that very much. I'll borrow Josiah's dip pen and give you your first lesson tomorrow."

A quiet moment stilled the air between them. Then Heidi spoke, "There must have been so many memories you had to leave behind."

Jacob's gaze moved from Heidi's face to the canvas hanging over the mantel. "Looking back, I wish I could have found a way to keep at least one of my mom's paintings. They were more than paint and canvas. Each one held a bit of my mom within the brushstrokes. Though, even if I had thought about it at the time, none of them would have fit in our carpetbag." Jacob could feel Heidi's gaze on him and turned to find her eyes filled with empathy.

Opening up to Jacob, Heidi shared, "When our family moved here, we had limited space and packed only the necessities. Leaving my paintings on the walls of our home was like leaving pieces of myself behind. Every one held a story. Once we arrived, I discovered my birch trees carefully wrapped in one of the crates." Tears brimmed her lower eyelids. "Papa understood."

"I wish I could have studied them all. Your birch trees are exquisite."

Heidi considered him a moment. "Wait here." She slipped away and returned a moment later with her sketchbook in hand.

Frederick appeared from somewhere with a nondescript whittling project and plopped down on the floor near his father's feet. "Ooh, your sketches! Show him my favorite one, Heidi. Please?"

Jacob nudged the lad with his toe and admonished quietly, "An artist should always be allowed to choose when and what to show her audience."

Frederick's shoulders slumped a bit in resignation. "All right."

Compassion for her little brother shone in her eyes. "I had been planning to save that one for a later date, but since Frederick requested it . . ." Her thumb skimmed the edges of the pages until she found the right one. "Here." Heidi opened her sketchbook and passed it to Jacob. Frederick popped up onto his knees to see, too.

Jacob was awestruck. There were sketches; then there were masterful pieces of art created with nothing but pencil. The page in his lap was definitely the latter. He could have been looking at himself in a mirror. How she had captured the wonder in Frederick's face and the intensity in his own astounded him. That she had studied him that closely sent a warming thrill through his chest somewhere near the region of his heart.

Admiration softened his tone. "There are no words, Heidi." The detail was remarkable—the wrinkle in his shirt, the upward curl on the front of his collar, the concave skin around his dimple, the wayward curl lying on his forehead. He absently reached up to his hair and brushed the stubborn curl back, only to have it fall across his forehead again. The shading gave every object depth and every pattern texture. He immersed himself in the scene and remembered living it. He had been telling Frederick about Jesus becoming his Savior. Around him, the only sound was the crackle of the fire.

Minutes must have passed before the sound of Mr. Müller clearing his throat broke Jacob's concentration. He glanced around, and every eye was on him. A slight blush creeped into his cheeks, and he handed the book back to Heidi. "Thank you for sharing your sketch with me."

"My pleasure."

Johann thumped his hands on the arms of his chair. "All right, young man, time to get back to work."

"Yes, sir." Jacob presented Heidi a dimpled smile and followed her father to the coat rack to bundle up and then outside to begin the next job.

---

"So, what do you think about Jacob?" Ingrid asked her husband at bedtime as she sat on the edge of their bed and brushed out her hair.

"I keep trying to find something objectionable about him," Johann answered.

"You haven't found anything, have you?"

"No," he growled. "He's hardworking, respectful, good-natured, genuine, forthright, compassionate, artistic; and from what I can tell, he loves the Lord and desires to please Him."

"That's quite a lengthy list of good qualities. Why are you growling?"

"Because I think Heidi cares for him."

Ingrid laughed, "Oh, she definitely cares for him, and I think he may be growing to care for her just as much."

"At this rate, Jacob will be asking to court Heidi before the week is out."

"And what will you do if he does?"

Johann raised his eyes upward and grumbled, "Probably say yes."

"Good decision." Ingrid stood and drew close before she rested her hand on her husband's chest. "Jacob is not only a fine young man; he is who Heidi needs. Think of how much she has changed since he came—she smiles, laughs, even sings again. To my knowledge, she has never shown any of her sketches to someone other than family, yet she willingly shared a drawing that made her very vulnerable. Her care for both Jacob and Frederick are abundantly evident in that sketch. That alone tells me how she trusts him. For her to trust any man but you after what happened with Peter is nothing short of a miracle of healing in her heart. How did Jacob choose to communicate? A Bible verse written in her heart's language—artistic expression. Tell me that God did not design this man for our daughter."

"The right man will protect and cherish her."

"And Jacob has shown both of those qualities."

Johann lifted an eyebrow in question.

"Think about it. He's obviously close to his family, yet he agreed without hesitation to keep Heidi's secret in order to protect her, and he doesn't even know the whole story of why she needs protecting. As for cherishing her, even today he complimented her, reminded Frederick to let her choose if and when to show her sketches, gave her physical space as if he can sense she needs the barrier, and invested his time and talent to give her a meaningful gift. I think Jacob's protecting and cherishing come nearly as an instinct where Heidi is concerned."

"Hmm. Maybe." His deep voice rumbled.

Ingrid patted the hand resting on his chest. "Keep watching Jacob, and you'll see I'm right."

---

Josiah put the wheelbarrow away in the barn just as Luke rode in and walked Dakota to his stall. Josiah met his brother there and folded his arms on the stall door. "Jacob hasn't stopped smiling since he got home from the Müllers' farm this afternoon."

"Huh. That fits my hypothesis." Luke grinned.

"What?"

"The first day I met Frederick he mentioned that he had

always wanted a brother, but all he had was—" He paused. "That's when his mother interrupted him, but how would you finish that sentence?"

Josiah's grin grew to match Luke's. "A sister."

"I think we know what the Müllers are hiding."

Both brothers answered in unison. "A girl."

"That explains why his protective instincts have flared like an autumn bonfire. He cares for her," Josiah observed.

"We can't let anyone else know we figured it out," Luke cautioned.

Loyalty to Jacob rose in Josiah's chest. "If her protection is that urgent, we should keep their secret, too."

"Agreed."

Josiah returned to the bunkhouse to find Jacob scripting another verse from Isaiah 41. *"For I, the LORD your God, hold your right hand; it is I who say to you, 'Fear not, I am the one who helps you.'"*

When Jacob finished, he cleaned the nib and acknowledged his brother. "Josiah, could I borrow your calligraphy pen for a few days?"

"Mom's pen? Sure, I suppose so."

"Thanks."

That was it. No explanation. Just a single word of gratitude.

## CHAPTER 17
## Calligraphy Lessons

The low, gray clouds portended rain, and rain in these parts could become a gully-washer without warning. Jacob studied the sky and grabbed an oilskin pouch from the tack room. The breeze picked up as he trotted over to the bunkhouse where he collected the parchment verse, paper, both pen cases, and a bottle of ink and slid them into the pouch. Not even a downpour would prevent him from giving Heidi's first calligraphy lesson.

Last night, he had lain in bed for a couple of hours with one hand tucked beneath his head while he stared at the ceiling and tried to remember how his mom had initially taught him to write script. He had been ten years old then, and he had taught Josiah a little more than a year later following his tenth birthday. Mom had started him with basic italic lettering before she taught him the eight fundamental strokes of Copperplate script.

Heidi was—well, he didn't know how old she was—but it was a lot older than ten, and her experience with pencils and brushes gave her an immediate advantage over other beginning calligraphy students. Should he just start with Copperplate since that is what he had used on his verse card? In the end, he decided to do just that.

Now he felt better prepared, albeit a bit short on sleep—nothing an extra cup of coffee wouldn't fix. Jacob filled and drained his coffee cup once more before he reached for the oilskin pouch and headed for Shadow. He wasn't sure whether the jitters he felt were from anticipation or four cups of morning coffee, but he made the trip to the Müllers' in good time and arrived before the clouds released their burden. The gusty wind was whipping Jacob's collar as he dismounted, and Johann ushered him and Shadow into the barn moments before the rain began with a whoosh.

The roar of water against the barn roof forced Jacob to yell at the older man beside him to be heard. "I'm glad we finished replacing the worn shingles yesterday afternoon."

"Ja." Johann nodded in agreement. "Today we will mend harnesses and sharpen tools."

Jacob nodded his assent and followed the big man to the rear of the barn, and the two worked together to make the needed repairs. By lunchtime, the falling rain had decreased from a roar to a steady thrumming. Jacob tucked the oilskin bag beneath the folds of his coat and dashed across to the front porch and into the foyer where he divested himself and hung his coat on the rack to dry. He leaned the pouch against the wall near the hearth, safely away from the dripping outerwear.

Once the midday meal concluded, Jacob spread the contents of the waterproof pouch on the table's surface and moved an extra chair to Heidi's side of the table. From that vantage point, they would be facing the rest of the family during her writing lesson and in full view of Mr. Müller's unrelenting observation. Jacob wanted to show by his actions that he respected and honored Mr. Muller's continued scrutiny. Inwardly, Jacob smiled. If he had a daughter as pretty and sweet as Heidi, he'd be wary of any young man showing her attention, too.

Heidi turned from putting away the final dish and caught sight of what Jacob was doing. A sudden smile lit her face like the glow of sunshine. "You remembered!"

Being the source of that smile elated him as if he had just climbed to the summit of the highest mountain—as if he had accomplished something magnificent and had been rewarded with a breathtaking view and a bit of lightheadedness from oxygen deprivation. *Right. Breathe, buddy.* "Are you kidding? I've been looking forward to this since yesterday afternoon."

Jacob pulled out the chair to his left for Heidi. Once she was settled, he sat beside her, but not too close. In front of each of them lay paper and a pen case, with the bottle of black ink positioned between them to share. Jacob opened his polished walnut pen case, lifted his dip pen handle, inserted the metal nib, and gestured for Heidi to do the same. "Josiah let me borrow his pen."

Heidi opened the cherrywood case and lowered her hand to pick up Josiah's pen, but the cherry blossoms engraved in the handle caused a thought that stopped her fingers a couple of inches from the pen and left them suspended midair. "This was your mother's calligraphy pen." The words were spoken with awe, acknowledging the writing instrument as a treasure she was unworthy to touch.

Jacob sensed her reluctance. "If my mother were here in this room, she would want you to use it."

"Why?"

"Several reasons, the most obvious being your desire to learn. Mom was always a proponent of using the right tool to learn a craft. It's just like using the right hardness of pencil or the right brush. Besides, she would have loved you and your work."

Why had that last sentence come out of his mouth? He

could feel the heat rise from his neck into his face. Sometimes he was as bad as Tim at speaking before thinking.

Her freckled cheeks bore a rosy hue, but she reverently lifted the pen into her hand. In an effort to dispel their embarrassment, Jacob instructed, "At first glance, this pointed nib resembles a standard nib. Notice this seam along the top. When pressure is applied, the seam will separate into tines that will widen proportionally to the amount of pressure. Higher pressures will separate the tines further and produce a thicker line." Jacob demonstrated the design of the tip by resting the dry nib on the paper and applying various amounts of pressure. "That tip flexibility will give you the ability to form both the thin and thick lines that give script its beauty."

"My mom taught me italic lettering first, but I was much younger than you at the time, and I think your adept manual dexterity will lend itself to the Copperplate script more easily."

"Is that the script you used for the Bible verse?"

"Yes."

"Then that's what I'd like to learn."

"Excellent. I had assumed as much." He shifted in his seat. "Speaking of age, I turned twenty-one on October 7th." Jacob lifted an eyebrow in expectation. Heidi softly repeated "October 7th" as if she were committing it to memory. When she glanced up at him, her brow furrowed in uncertainty.

From the sofa, her mom chuckled and prompted, "Heidi, I think Jacob is trying to ask your age and birthday without actually asking."

Her cheeks tinted again to a lovely shade of rose. "Oh, um, I'm seventeen. I'll be eighteen on April 14th."

Jacob's mouth curled into a smile without his consent. Without moving his gaze from Heidi's azure eyes, he projected his voice. "Thank you, Mrs. Müller." Bringing his volume to a whisper, he addressed the young lady beside him. "A gentleman is never supposed to ask a woman her age."

A smile tickled the corners of her mouth.

Jacob disengaged his gaze to find the penetrating glare of her father on him. *Focus, Jacob. Time to begin teaching.* Pointing to the verse he drew the evening before, he began, "Though this script resembles continuous cursive, it is neither continuous nor cursive. Rather, it is drawn with eight independent strokes connected in different patterns to form each letter. As such, the pen will lift after each stroke, even when mid-letter." He glanced at Heidi and found her riveted to his words. She nodded in comprehension while her eyes glinted with excitement.

"To be true Copperplate script, the strokes must be slanted thirty degrees to the right of vertical, or sixty degrees from the baseline, whichever way you prefer to think of it." From the bottom of his stack of paper, Jacob pulled a page with slanted guidelines penned on it. "If you slide this underneath your top page, you can refer to these lines as a guide."

"I'll teach you the eight fundamental strokes one at a time until you are comfortable in your mastery of each one. Then you'll learn which strokes to use for each letter, lowercase before uppercase. Once you are confident joining all of the pieces into words, I'll show you how to form the flourishes that add the flowing decorative touch."

"Before we dip our pens in ink, let me demonstrate how to hold the pen, for the hand position is slightly different from a traditional dip pen. The correct angle is imperative to achieve the right effect." Jacob pointed out the landmarks on his hand where the pen rested, then had Heidi mirror the same technique and rest the dry nib on the paper.

"Very close, but the angle of pen to paper isn't quite right." Jacob started to reach toward her, then stopped. "Heidi." He waited until she made eye contact with him. "I'm going to adjust the angle of the pen in your hand, but I promise that I will not touch you. Do you trust me?"

A beat, then, "Yes," her answer was soft, "I do trust you."

Those few words warmed his chest and thawed a place he hadn't realized was still frozen. Heidi trusted him, and he wanted to be a man worthy of that trust. Jacob reached over slowly with his right hand and pinched the handle end of the pen. "Loosen your grip a bit." He slid the pen forward and down to achieve the correct alignment. "There. Do you feel the difference?"

"Yes, I see what you meant now." Her voice sounded—relieved?—as if she had expected to panic with his hand in her personal space, but her trust in him had prevailed over fear.

"Good. Now you are ready to learn the first stroke—the upstroke." Heidi watched as he slowly formed the line on the paper and explained the light pressure he used to form that thin line. Then she attempted to replicate the stroke on her page. Her first few tries were too thick, but with repeated practice across the paper and with Jacob's encouraging praise, she managed to imitate his stroke consistently by the end of the third row.

"Now the second stroke."

"The downstroke?"

"Brilliant." Jacob grinned. "Yes, the downstroke. I knew you were smart." Heidi released a sound that bubbled suspiciously like a giggle. "The downstroke curves from top to bottom in a thick line like this." He demonstrated and gave minor corrections, and she rehearsed his movements until she had a precisely crafted thick curve on her paper.

"Now that you have learned the first two strokes, you will be able to spot them in this verse." Jacob lifted the card he had penned and used the handle end of his pen to point to a few of the upstrokes and downstrokes.

"Now I understand your comment about the strokes being only part of a letter."

Jacob sensed more than heard her papa shift to rise, and he

knew the lesson for today needed to draw to a close. "Since I need to get back to work, we'll save the third stroke until tomorrow. I'll leave Josiah's pen with you so you can practice the first two strokes if you wish." He cleaned his pen's nib before he wiped the ink smudges on his hands. "Remember to clean the nib every time. Removing dried ink after the fact is a chore."

"That sounds like the voice of experience." He smirked and gave a small nod. "I'll remember." When he scooted his chair backward and prepared to stand, she added, "Thank you, Jacob."

The side of his mouth crooked enough to show off one dimple. "This has been my pleasure. You're a wonderful student."

"Having a wonderful teacher helps." As soon as the words left her mouth, she caught her bottom lip in her teeth as if trying in vain to catch the words that had slipped out.

In an attempt to deflect her chagrin, Jacob addressed her papa. "Mr. Müller, may I give Heidi this verse card?"

Johann read the verse and handed it back to him. "Ja."

Jacob laid the card on the table. "I hope this verse will inspire your courage—and your scripting practice."

"Thank you."

"You are most welcome."

---

The rain had died to a drizzle, so Jacob zigzagged across to the barn in an attempt to avoid mud puddles as much as possible. While he and Mr. Müller were finishing the repairs on the harnesses, Jacob asked, "May I bring a new verse card for Heidi each day and give it to her, or would you prefer that I ask you each time?"

Johann eyed him for a moment before he answered. "Ja,

you may give her your cards." Rather than resuming his repair, he continued to consider the young man with him. "Jacob, the verses you have chosen show that you have correctly guessed Heidi's struggle with fear. That fear originated with a young man with your build and coloring who was not as he seemed. Her mother and I have seen remarkable improvement in the return of her cheerful manner since you have entered her life. Heidi trusts you. I had held great doubt that she would ever trust a man again. If you ever betray that trust and hurt my girl, you will answer to me. Do you understand?"

"Yes, sir. I understand. Heidi knows things about me and my past that I've never told a woman outside of my family. In a way, I'm trusting her, too. And trust is the foundation of friendship, right?"

"Ja."

Jacob cleared his throat, and his face pinched in a pained expression. "Did that young man you mentioned—Did he touch her? Is that why she flinches if I get too close?"

"Ja," Johann said again. "Heidi got away before irreparable harm was done, but not before he left bruises."

Righteous anger flamed in Jacob's eyes, and his hands clenched into tight fists. His mouth flattened into a grim line, and his nostrils flared.

Johann's hand landed on Jacob's shoulder. "Ja, that is how I feel, too." He gathered his thoughts. "That is also why I will ask you to take great care not to touch her, even in accidental contact. Your actions when repositioning her pen just now tell me that you sense that already, but now you know the reason."

His ire only deflating slightly, Jacob asked, "If this man is in Pennsylvania, why is Heidi still hidden?"

"A reasonable question." Johann exhaled audibly. "He is an evil man with wealth and connections who wants Heidi for himself and will not take 'no' for an answer. He and his thugs followed us part of the way here, and I do not want to be foolish by exposing her prematurely. If Peter's men arrive in Prairie Hills, no one will be able to reveal Heidi's presence if they don't know she's here."

Jacob's brow scrunched in concern, his tone thought-provoking, not contentious. "But how long must Heidi stay in hiding until you deem it safe? What if these men never come to Prairie Hills? Will you keep her in seclusion forever?"

"Another good question, but I am unsure of the answer. Jesus Himself was whisked away to Egypt to hide from Herod's murderous plot, but His parents had the advantage of an angel to tell them when it was safe to return. I pray the Lord will give me wisdom to know when the time is right."

The analogy hit Jacob's chest like the kick of a mule's hind leg. "Would he try to kill Heidi?"

"I do not know, but he would certainly want to harm her if she refused him another time. I have underestimated him before. I will not do so again."

"So he has the attitude that if he cannot have her, then no one will."

"Precisely."

"Then I will pray with you for wisdom and protection, and I promise to do everything in my power to keep her safe."

Johann tilted his head and softened his iron-like gaze. "Ingrid was right about you."

"How so?"

"You have an instinctive desire to protect Heidi."

Jacob contemplated the truth of his statement before he voiced his agreement. "Yes, sir. That sounds about right."

---

In the house, Frederick practically skipped up to the table and teased in a sing-song voice. "Heidi's in love with Jacob!"

"Frederick!" Heidi exclaimed.

"And if you marry him, he'll be my brother for real!"

"Frederick!"

Her brother dashed away in the direction of his room to distance himself from any retaliation. Her mama, however, came close to her with a mischievous glint in her eyes and whispered, "He's not wrong, you know." Heidi faced her mama with her jaw agape, and Ingrid just shrugged and laughed. "Jacob would make a good son-in-law, I think."

"Mama!"

"Tell me that thought hasn't crossed your mind at least once," Ingrid challenged with an upraised brow. Only silence ensued. "Mm-hmm. That's what I thought." She settled into the chair beside her daughter and rested her hand on Heidi's forearm. "Jacob has been so good for you, Mein Liebchen."

"When I am with Jacob, I feel brave, protected, safe. Every time he makes me laugh, another ray of sunshine breaks through the clouds and shines all the way to my heart. His unwavering faith in God bolsters mine. He sees the real me—my fears and all—and wants to be my friend anyway. After Peter, my life felt devoid of color, like a painter's preliminary sketch on a blank canvas. Jacob may not characterize himself as an artist, but he thinks like one. He sees not just who I am, but who I can become."

"Would you consider him as a candidate to be your suitor?"

"My heart desires to say yes." Moisture gathered on Heidi's lashes. "Jacob is a good and godly man, not to mention being incredibly handsome, but if our courtship were to lead to a broken heart, I fear my fragile heart would shatter into dust and be scattered in the wind and lost forever."

Ingrid wrapped Heidi's hand in her own. "Though I understand your caution, I think your statement may be a bit melodramatic. Jacob has shown in many ways that he cares for you. If courtship were to end in anything other than marriage, the two of you would find a way to stay friends. Do not shy away from him out of fear. Finding true love is worth the risk."

## CHAPTER 18
## *God's Heritage*

Lifting his fork to his mouth, Luke furrowed his brow in concern. This was the second day in a row that Julie had not touched her breakfast. He quietly studied her while he ate. Her face was paler that usual. She was currently sitting sideways in her chair facing Matthew and trying to coax him to finish his breakfast. Wrinkling her nose, she pushed her own plate further away from her and was attempting to feed Matthew at arm's length. She stopped, buried her face in her upper arm for a moment, then tried to continue. She set down the bowl and spoon with a hurried clatter and fled through the front door. Luke was right behind her. She barely made it to the bushes before she retched.

Symptoms and diagnoses began to zip across his mind. *No fever. No other GI distress. Probably not a stomach infection or influenza. Pale. Maybe anemia. No apparent cause. No food other than what he had eaten. Risk of food poisoning low.* He was a doctor. He should be able to figure this out. No diagnosis fit.

Luke gently held her hair as the retching turned to dry heaves. When she finally straightened and caught her breath, he handed her his handkerchief to wipe her mouth. "Why don't you come with me to the clinic to see Doc?"

Julie waved him off. "No, I'll be fine by lunchtime." Luke was not convinced, but he refused to push—yet.

Each morning, Julie would lose what little breakfast she ate if she ate anything at all. Every time, Julie refused to visit Doc. By dinner, she always seemed fine. Luke became more than a little concerned. What in the world was going on?

After two weeks, Julie showed no signs of improvement. Luke found Doc alone in the clinic between patients and presented her symptoms. Doc listened patiently and nodded. "What does Julie say about it?"

Luke lifted an eyebrow in surprise at his question. "She says she'll be fine, and I shouldn't worry, but I am worrying. She's just miserable, and her symptoms return every morning. Surely something could be done."

Doc chuckled. "Julie is a smart girl. Go home and talk to your wife. If she asks for me, I'll come. Until then, trust her."

A bewildered Luke left Doc's office.

When the door clicked closed, Doc muttered, "For someone who knows as much about medicine as he does, he sure can be clueless when it comes to Julie."

When Luke returned to the ranch, he stopped by the house to visit Julie first and confessed that he had consulted with Doc. He knelt down in front of her chair.

Julie reached over and cupped his face in her hand. "You didn't need to do that."

Luke ran his fingers through his hair in dismay. "But you haven't kept breakfast down in two weeks. You are pale and much more tired than usual. I love you. I can't bear the thought of anything happening to you."

Luke could see the merriment start to dance in Julie's eyes. "All right, I'll let you send for Doc in eight months."

"Eight months?" When the fog of confusion cleared to

understanding, he blurted, "Wait, did you say eight months?" Luke gently wrapped her hand in his. "Are you . . .?" He was afraid to ask for fear his sudden hopes were going to be dashed.

"Expecting a baby? Yes. Only this time it's your fault."

"My fault?" A slow, mischievous grin spread across his face. "Yes, I guess it is."

Luke stood and tugged Julie upward to stand with him. After kissing her gently, he wrapped his arms around his wife and twirled her in a circle until she giggled. Connecting her feet again with the ground, he kissed her again before he touched his forehead to hers. "We're having a baby!"

Julie rested her hands on Luke's chest. "Yes, we are, and somebody needs to study early signs of pregnancy—including morning sickness."

"Somebody does, huh?" Luke laughed. "No wonder Doc was holding in his laughter. We're having a baby!"

"Mm-hmm. Glad you're finally catching on."

The wonder of the moment shone in Luke's sky blue eyes. He spoke in whispered awe. "Julie, God answered our prayers." Still clinging to his wife, Luke began to pray. "Father, our hearts are overflowing with your goodness. Thank you for trusting us with this little life. Keep Julie and our baby safe and healthy, and give us wisdom as we care for this precious little person. Thank you. Thank you." Tears of joy dripped from his cheeks to hers. "We're having a baby!"

"Is that all you can say?" Julie teased.

"You must admit, it's a wonderful thing to say."

"Yes. Yes, it is." She rolled up on her tiptoes and kissed him again.

When they parted, a shadow crossed Julie's face.

"What is it, my love?"

"I have been so eager for you to figure out that we have a baby on the way that I didn't think—How do I tell Emily? I want to share our joy, but I don't want to hurt her further."

Luke considered her question carefully before he answered. "If the roles were reversed, how would you want Emily to tell you?"

"I'd want her to tell us first—after James, of course. I would be happy for her, even though I would grieve in my heart. Hearing the news first would give me time to adjust to the idea before other family started to celebrate for her and James."

"Do you feel up to having them over for dinner? If so, we could tell them together away from the other family."

"That's a great idea. Could you invite them over tomorrow night? I'm afraid if I ask Emily, she'll suspect something."

"Sure. I'll be heading out to the south pasture from here. I'll ask James then."

---

The following evening, when James and Emily arrived at the Hamiltons' home, Emily crossed to the kitchen to help Julie fill the serving bowls for dinner. James remarked to Luke, "That's Emily. She never offers to help; she just jumps right in wherever she's needed."

Working alongside Julie, Emily whispered, "When are you going to tell me your news?"

Julie's eyes widened in surprise. Then she noticed Emily's faltering smile and the brim of tears in her eyes. She knew. But how? "We were planning to tell you both tonight before we shared with the rest of the family. Luke just figured it out yesterday. How did you know?"

"Losing your breakfast two laundry Mondays in a row was a big clue."

"Luke missed that one."

"By the second week, you were glowing, and I knew."

"He missed that, too."

"But he's a doctor. How did he miss such obvious signs?"

Julie laughed at the irony. "He thought I must be showing early signs of some incurable disease. His worry even sent him to consult with Doc, who sent him home to talk to me and figure it out. When I told him he could bring Doc in eight months, the truth finally dawned. It was glorious!" Julie's delight died as guilt stabbed her heart. "Oh, Emily. I'm so sorry."

Emily shushed her with a hug, and she clung to her best friend for a moment. Tears threatened to clog her throat, but she managed, "There is nothing to be sorry about. I am so happy for you I could burst. Yes, your joy is another reminder of my grief, but it doesn't make my joy for you any less. If anything, your baby is another proof that God still answers prayers for little ones."

"Oh, Em, I pray for you and James every day."

"I know, and I'm grateful."

Across the living area, James and Luke sat on the sofa with their gazes fixed on their wives. Luke was incredulous. "Emily knew."

"She had a high suspicion."

Luke turned his face toward his brother. "Then you knew, too."

James nodded and affected a teasing smile. "Sounds like I knew before you did."

Luke wasn't fooled in the least by James' lighthearted attempt, for he saw the pain in his brother's eyes. "Julie has been agonizing all day how to tell Emily without hurting her. I've been feeling the same way about you."

"Emily's words to Julie ring true for me, too. We are happy for you both, and your news gives us hope that God will answer our prayer, too."

## CHAPTER 19
### *Courting*

The weeks of winter gave way to hints of spring. Every day, Jacob would bring Heidi another parchment card with a Bible verse in Copperplate script. With every calligraphy lesson, Heidi's penmanship improved and their friendship deepened. On the first Saturday in March, when Jacob and Mr. Müller finished the repairs slotted for the day, Jacob entreated, "If it's all right with you, I'll come tomorrow after the church service and lunch with my family."

"Ja, that would be fine. We will not do repairs on the Lord's Day, but you are welcome to visit in the afternoon."

The invitation resonated like approval, and Jacob's mouth twitched upward in an attempt to hold his smile captive. "Thank you, sir. I'll be here."

---

The family gathered around Emma's table for Sunday dinner. When James' "Amen" concluded his prayer of thanksgiving, Luke piped up, "We have an announcement." The joy dancing in Luke's expressive eyes left little doubt what his news would be.

"I knew it!" Emma clapped her hands in glee.

"Did everyone know before me?" Luke asked in mock dismay, looking at his wife.

Julie shrugged, enjoying her opportunity to tease him. "There were signs."

"I'm lost," Josiah brows knit together in confusion.

Luke's grin was unstoppable. "We're having a baby!"

"Congratulations!" echoed around the table. Jacob was reminded again of the power of prayer, and when he studied the faces of James and Emily as they shared in Luke and Julie's joyous news while their hearts were still hurting, he renewed his determination to continue praying for them every day.

When the family dispersed for their own homes, Jacob returned to the bunkhouse and examined his reflection in the mirror. He was elated that Luke and Julie were expecting a baby, but his thoughts were distracted by something else entirely. Since work would not be required of him this afternoon, he would be able to wear his Sunday clothes to the Müllers' home. That would give him the perfect opportunity to ask Mr. Müller for permission to court Heidi. The cows would start dropping their calves any day, and he needed an excuse to visit Heidi when he would no longer be available to work at her family's farm. He didn't know much about making such a request, but somehow it seemed more appropriate to be dressed up for this important discussion.

His promise to keep Heidi's secret forbade him from seeking advice from Seth or one of his married brothers, so he conversed with the One who knew everything. "Lord, You have brought Heidi into my life; I'm convinced of it. In the few weeks I have known her, she has become my best friend. I'm already falling in love with her and am having a hard time imagining my life without her in it. She is sweet and kind and creative and beautiful. I am drawn to her in a way I've never experienced before. Is it foolish to take this step before my family has had the opportunity to meet her even though I cannot think of a single objection they might have? Father, I desire Your will most of all. Please guide me."

Josiah walked in as Jacob was straightening the bow of his necktie and regarded him with an upturned brow. "Are you headed to the Müllers' farm then?"

Jacob met Josiah's gaze in the mirror, but his tongue seemed glued to the roof of his mouth as he stood there stiff and silent. Josiah came up behind him and laid his hand on Jacob's shoulder, and a mischievous grin crinkled the corners of his eyes. "Just promise that you'll introduce me to this mysterious young lady before you ask her to marry you."

Jacob's eyes widened, but he remained speechless. *How did he know?*

As if Josiah could read his mind, his brother added, "No, I don't know for sure, but my best guess is that you're protecting a young woman you have grown to care for. If I'm wrong, you can tell me when your promise has been fulfilled, and we can have a good laugh. I will say that I've never seen you so happy, and happy looks good on you." He gave Jacob a couple of good-natured thumps on the back.

Jacob's expression softened, but he gave nothing away. "I'll be home before evening chores." With that, he strolled to the barn for Shadow and rode to the neighboring farm.

"Thank you, Lord, for Josiah's moral support. Please help Mr. Müller to say 'yes.'" Not knowing the answer he might receive had his gut tied in a knot tighter than a half hitch. Jacob had been honest with Heidi's papa about his intentions, and Mr. Müller had been an eyewitness to their interactions and increasingly personal conversations. Surely Jacob's intended question would not catch him by surprise.

He dismounted Shadow and wiped his sweaty palms down his pant legs. "Lord, help me to do this right."

---

Smoothing the fabric of her new dress with one hand, Heidi tried in vain to focus on the words of the book in her other hand. Giving up, she closed her book and laid it on the small table beside the sofa and reached up to ensure her hairpins were secure.

"Heidi, you look lovely." Her mother's voice reeked of teasing, and the sound shot Johann's head up from the newspaper.

Heidi could almost feel her papa taking her measure. "Did you make that dress from the fabric your mama just purchased last week?"

"Yes, Papa." The blue polished cotton with lace trim was modestly tailored yet fitted enough to be feminine. Her mental excuse for dressing up today was that it was Sunday. Though their family's extended devotional time once a week was not a perfect substitute for church, she still tried to give more effort to her appearance on Sundays out of a heart of worship. If she were honest with herself, however, her actions held another motive today, and he should be arriving any minute.

She had been spending time with Jacob every day. Why was her pulse all aflutter today? Maybe because Jacob's reason for coming today had nothing to do with work and everything to do with visiting her family. Was it presumptuous to hope that he was coming to visit her in particular? There was no cause for her hands to be quivering. Well, besides the fact that she was falling for this man—and his dimples were a complete and utter distraction from any rational thought—and he had winked at her before he left for home yesterday. *Oh, her heart was in jeopardy of being crushed if Jacob's thoughts were only friendship.*

Another thought rushed into her mind. He would have

probably changed into casual clothes after dinner, and she would look like a preening dolt. Should she slip into her room and change before he arrived? She didn't want him to think her flirtatious. Just as she made her mind to change, the knock sounded on the door.

Her heart rate ratcheted in response, and she stood to answer the door, but Frederick bounded past her and reached it first. "Hi, Jacob!"

Reaching out to tousle Frederick's hair, Jacob returned the greeting. "Hi, little brother." He stepped into the home but stopped as if his feet were mired in molasses when his gaze landed on Heidi. Her hair was braided into an intricate knot with curls and ribbon to soften the chignon, and the blue of her dress darkened the shade of her irises to a mesmerizing color. She smiled shyly, and a gentle blush in her cheeks tugged him nearer. He stood a pace away from her and handed her another parchment card for her collection before he stuffed his hands into his pockets to prevent himself from reaching up to touch the tendril of curls framing her face. Instead, he simply smiled and complimented her. "Heidi, you look lovely."

Her lashes dipped bashfully. "Thank you." Lifting her eyes only to the level of his necktie, she gestured toward the sofa. "Won't you please join us?"

After Heidi settled on the sofa cushion, he claimed the familiar spot on the next cushion. Heidi's mama, who was deftly clicking a pair of knitting needles, broke the awkward silence by asking, "Jacob, how was your morning?"

"Filled with good news. My brother Luke announced at lunch that he and his wife are expecting a baby. I'll be getting a new niece or nephew before Christmas."

"That is exciting news!" Mrs. Müller agreed.

Mr. Müller folded his newspaper and tucked it beneath a basket on the side table. "How was the church service?"

"Pastor Kendrick's sermon was from John chapter 8. 'You

will know the truth, and the truth will set you free.' Jesus clarifies what 'the truth' is in chapter 14 when he said, 'I am the way, and the truth, and the life.' Not only will knowing Jesus in salvation set us free from eternal sin and death, but knowing the truth of His promises will set us free in this life from the bondage of sin, of fear, of anger, of bitterness. He never promises that our lives will be easy, but He desires for us to experience the freedom of peace and joy even when the tough times come."

"A powerful truth," Johann's gaze became unfocused in a contemplative expression.

*Now, Jacob. Ask him now.* "Mr. Müller, may I speak with you privately?"

His eyes leveled on Jacob. "Whatever you have to say, you can say to all of us."

"Oh, um, all right." Jacob wiped his slick palms on his thighs and tugged at the collar that suddenly seemed too snug around his neck. A glance toward Heidi's papa showed his typical solemn facial expression, but his eyes gleamed with—amusement? Was Mr. Müller entertained by his discomfort? Jacob took a deep intake of air and swallowed hard enough to make his Adam's apple bob.

For an infusion of courage, Jacob glimpsed to his right. Heidi was worth every second of this emotional torture. Before he could wrangle the words in his mind into a cohesive thought, Heidi handed him the card he had presented her mere moments ago. The message in script seeped all the way to his soul like a spring rain on parched soil. The verse was Joshua 1:9. "Have I not commanded you? Be strong and courageous. Do not be frightened, and do not be dismayed, for the LORD your God is with you wherever you go." His eyes flicked to Heidi's, and the intensity of her gaze fueled his courage. Jacob straightened his spine, and just like David, he faced his giant with the faith to trust God for victory.

"Several weeks ago, you asked me my intentions regarding Heidi. At the time, I affirmed that my priority was to develop a friendship first. In these past several weeks, Heidi has become my best friend. In her, I have discovered a long list of endearing qualities, but the most important is her love for God's Word and her desire to claim His promises."

"When we spoke, I honestly confessed to you that I hoped she would be the one I would wish to court, and our growing friendship has confirmed that desire. May I have your permission to ask Heidi if she would accept me as her suitor?"

After a long moment of uncomfortable silence, Mr. Müller responded with a question. "What are some of the 'endearing qualities' you have found in my daughter?"

Jacob's mouth formed a smile of its own accord, and he loosely wove his fingers together in his lap. "Heidi is kind, thoughtful, and creative. She's a talented artist, a gracious hostess, a patient listener, a loyal friend, and a beautiful young lady. Shall I go on?"

The smile Johann was attempting to curtail during Jacob's list threatened to burst forth, but the only hint of it was the lift of one side of his mouth and the crinkles on the outward edges of his gleaming eyes. He moved his focus to his wife. "What do you think, Meine Liebe?"

"I think Jacob has proven himself worthy, and you have tortured him long enough."

A deep chuckle resonated from the big man's chest. "Ja, Jacob. You have my permission to ask Heidi to court you. Before you do, however, I wish to speak to my daughter. Heidi, I have watched Jacob closely for weeks. I have found him to be hard-working, amiable, patient, kindhearted, gentle, strong, trustworthy, and loyal. He keeps his promises, and God has used his servant's heart to be a blessing to our entire family in many ways. Best of all, God has used Jacob to resurrect your smile, your laugh, and your song. Jacob has reached your heart, and the healing of your soul had been nothing short of remarkable. If you choose to accept him as a suitor, I believe he is a man who would protect and cherish you. The choice is yours, Mein Leibchen, but your mother and I heartily approve."

Listening to Mr. Müller's list was both humbling and inspiring. Jacob inhaled his first relaxed breath since he left the ranch and sent a brief "Thank you, Lord" heavenward. God had done the impossible task of bringing the sweetest girl he had ever met into his life. *Now if she only says "yes."* Shifting in his seat on the sofa cushion, Jacob angled himself toward Heidi. When the focus of her blue eyes melded with his, he flashed his dimples at her in a hopeful smile. "Heidi, would you do me the honor of allowing me to court you?"

---

Heidi had never met a man more protective than her papa. Hearing him list Jacob's character qualities revealed nothing she had not already discovered on her own, but coming from Papa's lips, the descriptives felt certain, like the confidence born of achieving the same result from thorough repeated investigations. All of her doubts regarding her own evaluation skills vanished like the vapor of exhalation on a cold day. In its place resonated assurance. If Papa found Jacob worthy, she could trust the man beside her. The seedling of trust had just blossomed with the flowers of spring, and its roots had burrowed deep and sure.

When Jacob moved to face her and their gazes met, she studied the tiny gold flecks in his chocolate brown eyes. The slight hesitation in his smile whispered his apprehension. Though her own stomach fluttered in kind, she could think of no higher privilege than being courted by this man. He asked his question, and his eyes seemed to plead for an affirmative answer. "You have become a dear friend to me as well, and you are everything Papa has discerned about you. When you are with me, I do feel safe and cherished. I would be blessed to have you as my suitor."

"So that's a 'yes'?"

Joy overflowed from her heart and bubbled out as laughter. "Yes."

---

Everything within Jacob wanted to jump up and cheer. Despite the rushing tide of emotions, he kept himself seated, but his enthusiasm burst forth unfettered in his grin and the delight in his eyes.

Johann smiled. The simple movement completely altered his visage. No longer did he resemble a formidable fortress. Indeed, his countenance had transformed into that of an ally. Once Jacob had been accepted by Heidi, he had earned a place as a part of this family.

"Now that that has been decided, I have another question to discuss," Johann stated as if the previous question had not just altered the course of Jacob's life forever. "What do you think about rejoining the world beyond the farm to attend church next Sunday?"

Jacob's gaze never left Heidi's face, which had suddenly become the pallor of flour. Her hands were folded in her lap, her fingers clasped so tightly that her knuckles were as pale as her face. When her breathing quickened, she closed her eyes, presumably in concentration. In an effort to advocate for her, Jacob inquired, "May I offer an alternative to your suggestion?"

"An alternative to attending church?" The hint of disapproval colored Johann's tone.

"No, just an alternative to having that be Heidi's first

outing." Turning his focus to the woman beside him, he soothed, "Breathe, Heidi. You are safe." He waited patiently until Heidi's color returned and her clasped hands relaxed before he continued, "You have not left the farm since you moved here several months ago. Rather than having your first outing be an unfamiliar town and a church building full of strangers, consider traveling to my family's ranch for a picnic. Our land is just beyond the line of fir trees, so you would not need to travel far; and other than a wave from Emma on her porch or one of my brothers across the pasture, you would not have to encounter strangers." When Heidi began to regain her composure, he asked, "What do you think?"

Embarrassment shrouded Heidi like a hooded shawl. Rather than answering his question, she admitted, "I just wish these irrational attacks of panic would cease tormenting me. I am sorry."

"Heidi, you have absolutely nothing to apologize for. These attacks are not irrational for they have a cause. Not knowing when something will trigger them must indeed be frustrating. Crippling fear must be defeated in baby steps. The crawling infant cannot win a foot race. Give yourself a little grace."

Pretending to be affronted, Heidi smirked at him with a mischievous glint in her eyes. "Did you just compare me to a crawling infant?"

"Um . . ." Jacob scratched his temple with his forefinger as he felt the heat creep up his neck. "Okay, that was a bad metaphor, but the principle is still true."

"Hmm." Heidi took a deep breath and donned a countenance of determination. "You're right. I'd like to accept your invitation for a picnic."

"Excellent." Jacob beamed and included the rest present in his visual scan. "You'll have me and your family there to surround you with familiar faces." He lowered his voice for her hearing only, "And don't be anxious about having a panic attack. If one happens, we will be there to help you through it."

"Thank you, Jacob. You truly are a remarkable man."

Finding approval written on Mr. Müller's face, Jacob invited, "Would your family be available for a picnic one afternoon this week?"

"Since you and I finished our list of repairs yesterday, how about tomorrow?"

Nodding his assent, Jacob replied, "Tomorrow it is. Am I correct in assuming that I may tell my family about Heidi now?"

'Yes, it is time." Johann studied him. "Who will you speak to first?"

"Josiah." The reply came without hesitation. "Keeping Heidi's secret from him has been the hardest part of my promise."

"Thank you for being a promise keeper."

---

That afternoon, Jacob barged into the bunkhouse with inexhaustible enthusiasm. Josiah's head popped up from the book he was reading, and Jacob plopped on the bench seat across the table from his brother. Without preamble, Jacob blurted, "You were right! The Müllers have a seventeen-year-old daughter named Heidi. I've never met anyone so sweet and kind. She's a gifted artist like Mom, and she's beautiful—blond hair, blue eyes, and freckles sprinkled on her nose. This afternoon she accepted me as her suitor."

Josiah closed his book and smiled. "When will I get to meet her?"

"Soon." Jacob's exuberance faded just a tad, and he hurried to explain. "Heidi has experienced something horrific, and she still struggles with fear because of it."

"Hence the verses you have been choosing for her."

"Right. I've invited her family for a picnic here on the ranch tomorrow. It will be her first time leaving the farm since they moved here—her first step toward 'rejoining the world' as her father put it."

"And you don't want me to ambush her with a bear hug, is that it?"

Jacob winced. "Please don't. Even I have never touched her. I've never stuffed my hands into my pockets so much in all my life."

Josiah's smile turned downward. He knew Jacob would never do anything improper, but was his protection for this girl duping him into thinking his well-honed protective instinct was the same as affection? "You've never touched her at all? Don't you want to?"

"Sure, I want to, but a man's touch fuels her nightmares. At least she no longer flinches if I get too close."

Understanding eased Josiah's qualms. Jacob held deep affections for this girl—enough to put her needs first. "Will I get a chance to meet her tomorrow?"

"Maybe more of a distant wave of greeting?" Jacob shrugged apologetically. "If tomorrow goes well, I'm hoping to officially introduce her to you and the rest of the family soon."

"All right. I'll be patient. Just don't forget that I was right!"

Laughter rang from Jacob before he exhaled audibly. "You don't know how hard it was not to tell you from the beginning. Now I feel like a one hundred pound bag of feed has been lifted from my shoulders." His features became more fervent. "Josiah, Heidi is the one I've been waiting my whole life for, and I truly am looking forward to introducing you to her."

Josiah grinned. "Well, there's been all kinds of good news today—a new niece or nephew and a new sister-in-law on the way!"

"Don't rush things, but yeah, that's what I'm hoping for,

too." Jacob slapped his palms onto the table and stood. "Now I need to tell the rest of the family what's going on before they think I'm crazy."

Jacob made it partway to the door before Josiah's chuckle caught him. "Too late."

## CHAPTER 20
## The Picnic

On the morrow, Jacob drove the buggy laden with two large picnic baskets to the Müllers' farm, planning to time his arrival with the conclusion of the morning batch of cheeses. The sun provided the kiss of warmth to this glorious spring day. God's blessings seemed to surround him, and while Jacob was thankful, something quietly gnawed at the back of his mind, a foreboding that maybe all of this was too good to be true. Pushing the pessimistic thought away, Jacob latched on to optimism and prayed, "Thank you, Lord, for this beautiful day. Please use our outing as a time of healing for Heidi and her family."

Frederick answered Jacob's rap on the front door and invited him inside. Heidi and her mama were just setting up the final pressure on the Gouda rounds, and he knew they would be finished shortly. "So, how many cows did you milk this morning?"

"All five!"

"Really? Good work, little brother!" He glanced over to the kitchen, and somehow in that brief exchange with Frederick, Heidi had disappeared. Moments later, she emerged from the hall wearing a soft-flowing blue gingham dress with ruffled sleeves and a fitted bodice. *Boy, she's pretty.* Frederick waved his hand in front of Jacob's face to regain his attention. "Sorry, Frederick, I was distracted by a beautiful lady."

The boy rolled his eyes heavenward. "I'll say. Your mind has turned to mush."

When Jacob glanced back at Heidi, she was trying in vain to stifle a grin. Ingrid hung her apron on its hook and diffused the moment. "Frederick, go let your papa know we're about ready to leave."

Heidi's brother gave Jacob a sad shake of his head, as if he were beyond hope of restoration, before he slipped out to find his father.

Mrs. Müller waved the courting pair outside, too. "You two get settled in the buggy. I'm just going to grab my hat."

For the first time, Jacob noticed a piece of millinery in Heidi's hand. He held the front door open for her to slide through, and once they were on the porch, she lifted her head covering and pinned it into place. The blue flowers on her hat perfectly complemented her dress. *What a beauty!*

Now was the time to voice the puzzle he had been working on during his drive over. "Heidi, I'm in a bit of a quandary." The woman beside him glanced his way. "A gentleman will always lend his hand to help a lady into a buggy, for it would be very rude to leave her to flounder on her own, but I know you do not wish to be touched. If I wore a thick work glove, would you allow me to assist you, or would you prefer that I just stand nearby in case you need assistance?"

Heidi held his gaze and blinked a few times in contemplation, and Jacob worried that he had pushed too far. "Whichever you decide is fine with me. I didn't mean to put you on the spot. I just didn't know what you would prefer, and I want today to be perfect." He squeezed his eyes shut. "And now I'm rambling."

"Jacob, yours was an honest question." He opened his eyes and searched hers. "For today, would it be all right if Papa helped me up?"

"Of course."

"I'll think about your glove suggestion for next time. That is an ingenious idea." Heidi lowered her voice to a conspiratorial tone. "Just so you know, since this is my first courting outing, I'm also hoping today will be perfect, and I fear I will do or say something embarrassing."

"Today is a first for both of us. I've never courted before either." At that revelation, Heidi visibly relaxed. *Finally, I said the right thing.*

Mr. Müller finished harnessing his team to their wagon and approached the couple still standing on the porch. "Since you are officially courting now, I thought you'd appreciate traveling together without the rest of us. We'll follow in our wagon."

"Thank you, Papa."

Speaking to Jacob, he added, "I've got my eyes on you, young man."

A short laugh escaped Jacob. "Of that I have no doubt." When Heidi's father turned back toward his wagon, Jacob's voice stopped him. 'Sir, Heidi would like you to give her a hand up into the buggy." Wordlessly, Johann nodded and waited at the side of Jacob's buggy while they descended the porch steps and came to meet him. He assisted his daughter while Jacob climbed up the driver's side.

Despite the wagon following behind them, Jacob was delighted to have Heidi riding alone with him. Something about having her all to himself made this next step in their relationship feel real, and after spending all of their time together on her family farm, he was excited to show her his family's ranch. *Oh, he wanted to be worthy enough to be her husband. Woah, there, partner. This is only your first date. Slow down and enjoy your time together. Build your relationship carefully.*

Nearing the end of the Müllers' lane, Jacob observed Heidi. She seemed relaxed enough. "Are you all right so far?"

"Yes. You've told me so many stories from your life on the ranch that I'm eager to see it." Heidi smiled, and Jacob mirrored her expression.

When they turned right onto the main road, Jacob began pointing out landmarks. "This first quarter mile or so on our right is still your land, and the fir trees mark the beginning of ours. This large stand of fir trees is where we choose our Christmas tree every year. In the spring, we plant a new one to take its place, ensuring there will be enough Christmas trees for generations to come."

"This three-rail fence borders our north pasture. In the next few days, we'll begin rounding up the cattle from the outlying pastures to have them close by for calving season." He turned the buggy to the right, and they passed underneath the engraved timber sign for the Rugged Cross Ranch. "If you look way back to your left, you can just catch the front porch of James and Emily's house. The ranch house ahead on the left is where Emma lives, and the bunkhouse across from Emma's is where Josiah and I live. Beyond the bunkhouse is the corral and our barn, of course. The fence beyond the barn frames the south pasture."

Heidi's attention was focused on the bunkhouse—Jacob's home. Sitting on her porch swing holding a glass of lemonade, Emma smiled and raised a hand in greeting. Jacob nodded and whispered, "Emma is on the porch," and Heidi shifted her gaze and lifted her hand to wave back. When they had passed by, Heidi admitted, "I had pictured Emma a bit older. She's looks about Mama's age."

"That's probably close. Emma is only twelve years older than James." At Heidi's puzzled expression, Jacob explained, "She was twenty-six when she and Daniel adopted James as a fourteen-year-old." Jacob slowed the buggy as they neared the south pasture and pointed. "Josiah is checking the herd." Josiah spotted them and waved, and Heidi returned his gesture. "When I told Josiah about you yesterday, he was thrilled for us and is eager to meet you."

Jacob turned the buggy down the lane to the southeast and indicated the hill behind the ranch house. "I don't know if you can see it from here, but there is a bench under the oak tree on the crest. That is where Daniel taught us to get alone with God." A little further along the road, Jacob motioned toward the tree line. "That house is Luke and Julie's. If you look to the right of it through the low branches, you can glimpse the teepee where Buck and Julie lived when they married."

The buggy entered the tree line and a moment later exited near the river. "This is usually our swimming hole, but today, it's our picnic spot." Jacob pulled to a stop before a grassy glade that led to the water. The river tumbled over a few rocks, making a waterfall about three feet high. Below the waterfall, a long flat log spanned the river before the banks widened, making a perfect pool for swimming.

"When I was younger, all of us brothers would come here to swim and play. Now I come because I find the sound of the waterfall soothing and peaceful. If I need some time alone with God, I will still go to the hill." Jacob gestured toward the high rise now behind them. "When I want a quiet place to read or think, I come here."

After Heidi's family pulled in behind them and her papa helped her down, Jacob passed him one basket and grasped the other. He wandered to his favorite spot closer to the waterfall, placed the picnic basket on the ground, and tugged the blanket from its place within the handle. When he began to unfold it, Heidi offered, "Let me help. Toss me the other edge." Together they laid the blanket on the grass.

Looking over his shoulder, Jacob was grateful that Heidi's family was setting up their picnic about one hundred feet further away from the river and giving them at least some modicum of privacy. The edge of his mouth twitched upward in a smile.

Jacob knelt on one corner of the blanket, and Heidi settled herself on the opposite corner, ensuring her feet were tucked under her skirt. Once their basket's contents were displayed between them, Jacob stretched one leg out straight and tented the other one to rest his forearm on his knee. He started to reach toward her to pray but caught himself partway across and returned his hand to his lap.

"Dear Father, thank you for this basket of food and the beautiful day You have provided for us. Thank you for bringing Heidi into my life. Please show me how I can help her overcome her battle with fear. Help the truth to set her free. In my Savior's name, Amen."

Heidi had noticed the movement of Jacob's hand. That he had wanted to hold her hand in prayer emphasized that he thought of her as more than a friend. That he had pulled it back reminded her that he was worthy of her trust.

She took a sip of her lemonade and absorbed her surroundings. "This is a relaxing place. The sound of the water is quite soothing."

"The sound of that waterfall used to be terrifying."

Having the distinct feeling Jacob was going to reveal something personal, Heidi inquired, "How so?"

"After I witnessed my parents swept away to their deaths by a flash flood, I was petrified of rivers. When Josiah and I moved to the ranch, our brothers would come here to cool off, but I could come no closer than where the buggy is parked without hyperventilating. Tim wanted to tease me about it, not realizing the cause, but Buck and Luke would admonish him every time he tried. The only reason I came at all was to keep an eye on Josiah, but day after day, watching them horsing around and having fun, I was drawn closer to the water. More than two months later, I finally put my feet in. The next day, I joined their games."

"This place is now a reminder of my victory over fear. God has done the impossible in my life, and I know He will do the same in yours."

Moisture gathered on her lashes, but Heidi blinked to keep the tears at bay. *This man. Could she be more blessed?* Jacob had opened up to her, she needed to return the favor. Now was the time to explain her past to Jacob.

"I'm not sure how much Papa has told you, but I was attacked by a young man who is determined to find me and has the resources to do so. Peter was handsome and acted like a gentleman, but there was something about him that unsettled me. Besides, Papa didn't trust him, and you know his keen discernment firsthand."

"When Peter asked to court me, I politely declined. His charming smile turned threatening in an instant. I felt justified in my decision, but I thought his reaction was simply disappointment and hurt. Then his father the mayor began to threaten my papa, but the threats felt empty, not anything he would actually act upon."

"One day, I went into town to deliver cheeses to the general store. On my way home, Peter jumped from an alley and ambushed me. God gave me the clarity of mind to fight him and get away, but he was furious and vengeful. So much so that we had to leave under the cover of night in order to escape him and his father."

"My nightmares started the night of his ambush, and random words or thoughts began to trigger overwhelming bouts of panic. The painting over the fireplace drew me from a dark place and helped me find the sunshine again, but it wasn't until you came that I found hope and joy."

"Listening to your conversations with the cows healed the

inward part of me that Peter had left raw and wounded. Even your singing lifted by spirits."

Jacob groaned, "I can't sing."

"Nonsense. You sang from your heart. It was glorious." Jacob raised an eyebrow in skepticism, but Heidi chuckled. "Truly. You might not ever win a solo competition, but your heart of worship shone that day."

When they had finished their meal and packed the dishes into the basket, Jacob excused himself. "I'll be right back." Heidi's gaze followed him as he crossed the river on the log's flat edge and knelt to pick a handful of wildflowers. *How sweet!* What amazed her most was watching him stride across the log as if he were strolling down a wide thoroughfare—not a hint of hesitation or thought of wobbling.

Procuring their empty lemonade bottle, he added some river water and slid the wildflower stems inside and placed the makeshift vase in the middle of their blanket table.

"Thank you, Jacob. They're beautiful!"

"Not as beautiful as you."

Heidi felt suddenly shy and needed to deflect her attention. "How did you walk across the river so easily?"

Jacob shrugged. "I have exceptionally good balance. Josiah planed that log, so it is perfectly flat and level. One of the games we would play was to climb on the log and use long sticks to try to push the other person off balance and into the water. I'm the reigning champion. I've never lost a match."

Glancing wistfully at the log, Heidi divulged, "I'd like to cross that log someday."

"How about today? I'll help you. Do you trust me?"

The side of her mouth quirked upward. "Yes, but how?"

Jacob rummaged under the trees until he found a sturdy branch about five feet in length. Then he carried it to the edge of the log and removed his boots and socks. Heidi approached with her face scrunched in a question. "I can feel the log better barefooted. Since I'll be walking backwards with precious cargo, I'm taking extra precautions."

Jacob stepped up onto the log and half-pirouetted to face Heidi. Holding the branch horizontally, he instructed. "Step up and hold the branch with your arms extended at a comfortable length. The further apart you grab, the more stable you will feel. I won't let you fall."

Heidi took the first step, and her heart started pounding against her ribs. Her hands clutched the branch.

"Now walk with me. Are you ready?" At Heidi's nod, he took a step backward, and she followed. With each footfall, her smile grew. Soon they were across, and she found herself in a small meadow filled with flowers. A few bees and butterflies were busy visiting the colorful blooms, and Heidi stopped to admire them.

"Pretty, isn't it?" Heidi nodded in reply. "Our land extends for about another quarter mile, so this meadow is part of the ranch, too." Jacob made a point not to stand too close, knowing her father was likely watching him with an eagle eye. "Let me know when you're ready to cross back."

Heidi twirled to face him, her skirt swishing the wildflowers and giving her the semblance of a fairy. "This scene would be perfect on canvas." She twisted slightly and crouched to study the details of the butterfly dancing near her. When Heidi slowly extended her hand, the monarch alighted on her fingers for a few seconds and gently waved his wings back and forth a couple of times before fluttering to a flower close by. "This place is almost magical."

"Then I dub this spot 'Heidi's Meadow' in your honor." Jacob bowed to complete the effect. Heidi laughed in pure delight.

"'Heidi's Meadow'—That will be the title of my painting." In her peripheral vision, Heidi found her papa staring at them. "I guess we should head back before we upset Papa."

Jacob's dimples winked at her. "Good idea. We'll cross the same way. Ready?" Though Jacob stepped backwards, his sure-footed stance kept Heidi from stumbling even when her shoe slipped once on the smooth wood. He paused until Heidi found a stable position then continued the rest of the way.

"That was amazing. Thank you for taking me across."

"How could I not take you to your namesake?" His teasing eyes made her wish she had a dish towel nearby. He could use a good flick to his backside.

"Having some towel-snapping thoughts, are you?" Jacob grinned. Heidi blushed beyond rosy to bright red.

---

Deftly changing the subject away from Jacob's teasing, Heidi decided to share another thought on her mind. "Your family has been so kind to give me my space today, but I would like to meet them."

Jacob's smile remained, but it transformed from mischievous to gentle. "They all want to meet you, too. I'd thought about inviting your family for Sunday dinner, but having all of us together at once might be a bit overwhelming for your first meeting." He rubbed his chin in thought. "What if we took the scenic route back to your home and visited each of them individually for a short introduction?"

"Yes, that sounds lovely." One or two at a time she could handle. They weren't truly strangers, for Jacob had told her so many stories she felt as if she knew them already. Still, the gentle stirring of nerves made her grateful to be next to Jacob, for his presence made her feel safe.

Their first stop was Luke and Julie's home. Heidi tried to stifle the butterflies now swarming in her belly. Luke was still at the clinic, and Matthew was napping, but the sound of the buggy brought Julie outside. She all but bounded down the front steps to greet them. "You must be Heidi. I'm Julie, Luke's wife. You certainly have this brother of mine smiling a lot more." In the short conversation that followed, Julie made Heidi feel welcomed and loved. That was Julie's way.

On the way to the ranch house, they waved at a man in the south pasture. When he approached the fence on horseback, Heidi's butterflies started their barrel rolls again. Though his demeanor held authority, Heidi never felt threatened. His eyes held a teasing glint for Jacob, but he gave Heidi a crooked smile and tipped the brim of his hat. "Ma'am."

This man had dark hair and brown eyes, but he didn't look like Jacob. This must be James.

Jacob confirmed her suspicion when he introduced them. "Heidi, this is James, my oldest brother. He's the ranch foreman and Emily's husband."

"You're the one that broke Jacob's nose." A blush crept into her cheeks for her abrupt comment. *Of all the first words to come out of my mouth!*

A deep rumble of a laugh emerged from James' throat, setting Heidi at ease. "Yeah, but in all fairness—"

"I deserved it," Jacob finished.

James shrugged. "I can't argue with the man. It's a pleasure to meet you, Heidi." A high-pitched whistle brought his head around. "That's Josiah. Please excuse me." He tipped his brim once more before he turned his horse and cantered toward the other side of the pasture.

From there, they stopped by Emma's. She and Emily were pinning clothes to the line, so Heidi was able to meet them both at once. "Heidi, this is Emma, our mama here on the ranch, and Emily, James' wife."

"I'm delighted to meet you both." A rustling sound from the bushes preceded a gray blur bolting toward the buggy. The pup stretched his front paws as high as he could reach on the wheel's spokes. His lolling tongue and wagging tail announced his desire to be included. "And you must be Asher." Heidi reached out her hand to let him sniff her and received enthusiastic puppy kisses in return.

"Jacob was telling us all about you last night," Emma greeted, "and I'm happy to meet the source of his unabated cheerfulness. You have made quite an impression on my son—a son that I'm very proud of. You are courting a wonderful young man." Wanting an excuse to keep her conversation brief for Heidi's sake, Emma looked back toward the wagon behind them. "I'm going to introduce myself to your family."

Emily stepped up and shyly tucked a wayward strand of hair behind her ear. "Jacob has such a kind heart. You are truly blessed to hold his affections, Heidi."

Heidi glanced toward the man beside her and back at Emily. "Yes, I couldn't agree more." She bit her lip trying to remember Jacob's descriptions. "Are you the teacher in Prairie Hills?"

"Yes, the church becomes the schoolhouse during the week."

"Mama is planning to turn Frederick's education over to you in the fall. You may have your hands full with his energy."

Emily laughed, the sound almost musical. "No more so than with the other boys his age. They are energetic, but properly engaged, they can learn more than they intend to."

"He's a good kid," Jacob commented. "He just likes milking more than math."

"Don't they all." Emily's eyes twinkled, and Heidi knew she would be the perfect teacher for her little brother.

## CHAPTER 21
## *Back to Church*

When they left the ranch house and pulled alongside the north pasture, a rider cantered toward the fence near the passing buggy and stopped to greet them. This brother looked like Jacob. "So sorry to interrupt your outing, miss. I'm Josiah, and I'm very pleased to meet you." He lowered his voice to a confidential whisper. "When we have time to talk, I've got stories." Josiah waggled his brows at Heidi and earned her giggle in return. Then he turned his focus to his brother. "Jacob, the first cow just dropped her calf. James needs you to help us round up the ranging cows and bring them into the fenced pastures."

"Sure. I'll be back soon." Josiah tipped his hat to Heidi in farewell and rode back toward the gathering herd.

Johann pulled his wagon up beside them. "You are needed here. Heidi can ride home with us."

"With spring calving starting, my time with Heidi will be limited. Please allow me to drive her home. I'll be back in plenty of time to help James and Josiah. Luke should be home soon, too." With a nod of approval, Johann waited for Jacob to pull ahead of him.

Now that they were somewhat alone again, Jacob verbalized his thoughts. "I'm so glad we were able to enjoy one outing before calving. These next couple of months are our busiest time on the ranch. With calving, branding, and driving the one-year-old steers to market and the rail line in Kansas City, I may only be able to visit you once a week or so. You and your family, however, are more than welcome to visit here anytime you wish."

"Thank you, Jacob, for the lovely picnic. I'll admit that I'm going to miss not seeing you every day, but I understand your ranch needs you here, and I promise to be patient."

"Heidi, I am honored to be your suitor, and I am hoping and praying that I will only ever court one woman." The blush in Heidi's cheeks confirmed that she received his message. "Something Josiah said last night has been bugging me, and I wanted to make sure you understood." The sudden constriction in his throat forced him to clear it, and heat wound its way up his neck into his face. "The reason that I never hold your hand or touch the soft curls around your face isn't that I don't want to. I'm just honoring the boundaries you have given me. I didn't want you to think I'm not attracted to you in that way because I am. You are beautiful inside and out, and one day I hope you will be mine."

The soft upturn of Heidi's lips as she considered his words washed away his unease. "I would never have accepted your suit if I did not feel the same way. The reason for 'my boundaries,' as you put it, is twofold. Peter's touch was not romantic; it was aggressive and painful, and while the trauma of that day is lessening, I don't want to recoil from your touch when it happens. I want to enjoy it. The second reason is that many years ago, I decided that I would not touch a man unless he was the one I would marry. That may sound silly, but to me, even holding hands in prayer seems an intimate gesture. I want to give my heart to only one man."

Jacob's smile unleashed his dimples. He heard her veiled declaration of "when" and not "if" his touch would happen as if he were the one man she had chosen. "I promise I will come visit as often as I'm able."

"I'll be waiting."

---

After a busy afternoon and evening of cow herding, all of the expectant cows were nestled in the two large pastures nearest the barn. Jacob flopped on his bunk, the fatigue of the day catching up to him. "Josiah, in all your free time,"—Josiah crooked an incredulous eyebrow at him—"would you build a small box for me to give Heidi for her birthday the middle of April?"

"What size box are you thinking?"

"Just big enough to hold the parchment cards I've been scripting for her. If she had a box to hold her collection, she would have them handy when she needs some courage."

Josiah rubbed his chin between his thumb and forefinger in thought. "I have a couple small pieces of oak that would be lovely when stained. Are you thinking a box with a hinged lid?"

"Yes, that would be perfect. Just let me know how much I owe you."

"I have what—a little over four weeks? That should be enough time."

---

Despite the fact he was no longer visiting Heidi as often, Jacob still found the time to script a Bible verse every evening before retiring for bed. When Jacob could slip away from the ranch, he would gift Heidi the stack of cards since his last visit, and the two of them would sit on the front porch and talk. Since the swing was too narrow for two people and a space between them, Heidi would sit in the middle of the swing, and Jacob would occupy the nearest chair.

They would tell stories and laugh and discuss more serious topics. All the while, the stitches of their hearts were binding them closer together.

On the evening of Heidi's eighteenth birthday, Jacob presented her with the lidded box Josiah had fashioned for him. The oak had been sanded to perfection and stained a rich mahogany color. Josiah had even carved Heidi's name into the lid with a circle of tiny flowers surrounding it. When Jacob had asked why he had carved her name rather than her initials, Josiah answered plainly, "I fully expect her initials to change soon."

Spring blended into summer. One evening, while they were courting on the porch, Heidi mentioned, "Jacob, Papa hasn't pushed again about attending church, but I know he misses it. We all do. From what you have told us about Pastor Kendrick and the congregation there, I'm sure we would feel welcome. I think I'm finally ready to go. What are your thoughts?"

"You might want to ask your papa to drive you into town once or twice first, just to get a feel for how your emotions will react. When you feel confident enough to come to church, I might suggest sitting on the back pew for the first few weeks. That way you could slip out for fresh air without disturbing anyone or drawing attention to yourself."

"Would you sit with me—um, my family?"

Jacob's eyes twinkled, "I'd be honored, my lady."

The first time to town was just short of a disaster. Heidi gave a valiant effort to keep her fears in check, but when she spied an alley next to the milliner shop, all hope of restraint was lost. Her nightmare returned that night.

"Jacob! Jacob!" Heidi was running from Peter, reliving that horrible day, her lungs heaving in their effort to inhale more air. She rounded the end of the fence line and fell into Jacob's arms.

"Heidi! I'm here, sweetheart." Heidi woke abruptly and attempted to focus on the anguished face near hers. It wasn't Jacob's.

"Papa?" She absorbed her surroundings, the realization that she was in her bedroom bringing clarity to what had happened.

"Was that another nightmare?"

"Yes." Her pounding heart was evidence of the intensity of her dream.

"You were calling Jacob's name. Was he chasing you?"

"No, Peter was chasing me." Heidi rubbed her forehead. "But this time, when I arrived at the homestead, the one running to protect me wasn't you. It was Jacob."

Johann shifted his gaze to his wife, who merely gave him a small smile of understanding. The earthly object of Heidi's trust was changing from him to Jacob. A twinge of growing pains seared his heart.

---

Determined not to give up, Heidi asked her papa to drive her back to town a few days later, and other than an uptick in her breathing and heart rate, the trip was a success. On her third trip, she had even allowed Papa to stop and encourage her to browse the general store for a few minutes, never straying from his shadow.

The following Sunday, the Müller family climbed into their wagon and lumbered through town to the church yard. Heidi spotted Shadow tied to the hitching post and found great comfort in knowing Jacob was already there.

The Müllers ascended the front steps of the church, and Johann introduced his family to Pastor Kendrick, a middle-aged amiable man who welcomed them warmly. Per Jacob's suggestion, they filed into the back pew for the service.

Jacob was leaning over the pew in front of him in a deep conversation with four-year-old Matthew when Josiah elbowed his ribs to get his attention. Jacob glanced at his brother, who grinned mischievously and gestured to the back of the church with his head. "I think someone's family is visiting for the first time."

Jacob's head swiveled the other direction and his gaze landed on the Müllers in the back row. Heidi was looking right at him with a plastered smile in place. He could see the tension behind her expression even from where he was sitting, but he was so proud of her for getting this far. "Excuse me, Josiah. I'm going to sit in the last pew today."

"Yeah, I thought you might."

Gathering his Bible, Jacob strode down the aisle and behind the back pew to where Heidi was sitting on the outer aisle. "May I sit with you this morning?"

"I'd be delighted."

Jacob brought his volume down to a whisper. "I can sense your tension. How are you doing?"

"Okay so far. My mind keeps borrowing trouble." Her periphery caught a small movement, and she shifted her attention to a little bronze-skinned boy with black hair who was waving at her. She couldn't help but smile back and wave at him in return. "That little boy is adorable."

"That's Matthew, my nephew. He's too cute for his own good." Hoping his smile would give her some courage, Jacob shared, "I'm proud of you for being here. I know this is a big step."

With a teasing smirk, Heidi asked, "Have I graduated from a crawling infant to a toddler yet?"

Jacob raised an expressive eyebrow, "Hmm. I don't know. This is an auspicious occasion. You might have even graduated to four-year-old status."

Her laughter seemed to dispel her tension, and Jacob relaxed into the pew just before the service started. When the hymns began, Jacob stood silently and listened to Heidi sing. No wonder Frederick loved to hear Heidi sing him to sleep. Her voice was soft, but it held an ethereal, almost angelic tone. *His angel.* No wonder the moniker kept leaping into his mind. It fit.

Pastor Kendrick began his sermon, but Jacob's peripheral focus was on the woman beside him. At first, she seemed relaxed enough, then all at once, her hands began shaking and her breathing escalated. He moved to step out into the aisle just as she was moving to climb over him, and they nearly collided in her haste to retreat out the back door.

Jacob was right behind her, and he motioned for Frederick to join them. Mr. Müller eyed him, but Jacob held up a hand to stay his departure. The trio slipped out the rear of the building, and Heidi gripped the railing in all-out panic. Her widened eyes seemed to sense danger all around her. Jacob needed to get her to a quiet place, and quickly.

"Frederick, take your sister's hand and come with me." He ducked behind the parsonage to the tree swing. Since they were, in fact, on the edge of town, the parsonage's back yard held an undisturbed air that seemed secluded enough for his purposes. "Lead her to the swing." Frederick complied.

When Heidi had lowered herself onto the seat of the swing, Jacob knelt on the ground in front of her. "Breathe, Heidi. You are safe here. Close your eyes and feel the breeze on your cheek. Slow your breathing down. I'm right here, and I'm not leaving you."

Heidi's mouth formed a grim line of concentration as she complied. In a few minutes, her features relaxed. Though her eyes were still closed, a single tear dripped from the lashes of her left eye and landed on her cheek.

"Will this never end?"

"Are you kidding? You have come so far! Not only have you made several trips to town, but you made it through half of the church service." Heidi looked unconvinced. "Give yourself grace."

"Did you pick up on a sound, or a thought, or a feeling that triggered your panic attack?"

Heidi winced. "A man cleared his throat. The sound was deep and loud and abrupt; it startled me, and my breaths started coming too fast, and I couldn't stop them. Then I felt trapped, and the panic intensified." Surely Jacob would think she was weak and not worthy of his affection, yet his gentle spirit calmed her and accepted her fear as a real, not an imagined, enemy.

"Would sitting on the outer edge of the pew help you feel less trapped?"

"Maybe. As long as you're sitting next to me."

He bowed his head, "Father, thank You for Heidi's courage today. Please don't let her disappointment cloud today's triumph. Continue to encourage her heart with Your promises. You are the God of love, and where love is, no fear can take permanent root. Help me to know what to do and say to be the comfort Heidi needs. In Jesus' name, Amen."

"Thank you, Jacob."

"Frederick, stand at the corner of the parsonage so you can see us and the front of the church building." A few minutes later, Johann and Ingrid rounded the pastor's home to find

Jacob still kneeling in front of Heidi, who had regained her composure.

Johann's words resonated with concern. "Did we try to come too soon?"

Heidi gazed into Jacob's eyes for courage. "No, I'll be ready to come again next Sunday."

*That's my girl,* Jacob thought.

One week later, the Müller family occupied the back pew again, and besides a couple of white-knuckled grips on her Bible, Heidi made it through the entire service unscathed. The joy on her face after the conclusion of the service rivaled Jacob's own.

Jacob's family meandered to the rear of the church and formed a cocoon around Heidi. She fellowshipped with them while they blocked any strangers from getting through. Jacob stood next to her and beamed his admiration of the woman who had stolen his heart.

## CHAPTER 22
## The Empty Cradle

With a heart full of prayer for his wife, James dismounted Trigger and took his front steps two at a time and unlatched the front door. He remembered her conflicted tears when the telegram arrived announcing the birth of Kathryn O'Brien, Tim and Laura's baby girl. "Emily?"

She was drying a dish and turned to face him. "Yes?"

James held up the envelope and closed the gap between them as Asher bounded up to him for his attention. He scratched the pup behind his ears and extended his other hand toward his wife. "You received a letter from Laura."

Emily's chin trembled, revealing the truth behind her smile. After setting the clean dish in the cupboard, she reached for the missive, examined the address, then flipped it over to carefully open the envelope's flap. James rested his hands on her upper arms and studied her face as she unfolded the pages and read.

Her smile wobbled as the first tear fell. Emily closed her eyes, determined to regain her composure. Asher whimpered softly and pushed gently against Emily's legs in a puppy hug as if he could sense the turmoil within his favorite person. A couple of minutes later, Emily lifted her gaze to James' dark brown eyes. "Tim and Laura are planning to visit this fall. They want to bring Katie to meet her family, and Tim wants to help with harvest. We should invite them to stay with us."

James' brows knit in concern. "Are you sure?"

"Yes. The parsonage doesn't have enough room. I know Emma has room in her house, but Laura is my sister, and we have two rooms for them. One is already set up as a nursery. We can ask Josiah to finish the cradle he has reserved in his workshop for us."

The furrow in James' brows deepened. "That cradle is for our baby."

Emily laid her hand on James' chest over his heart. The thrumming beat under her fingers infused her with courage. This amazing man loved her. "That doesn't seem to be God's plan for us. Withholding our cradle when we have a precious niece to share it with feels selfish. Besides, having them here will give me more opportunities to cuddle and spoil that little girl as much as I can. It isn't Laura's fault God blessed them with a baby before us."

James pulled his wife into his embrace and buried the side of his face in her hair. "I love you. Whatever you decide is fine with me."

"I'll write a letter tomorrow inviting them to stay with us. I miss Laura and Tim, too."

"Katie doesn't know how blessed she is to have an Aunt Emily."

---

A couple of weeks later, James arrived home to find the dinner table set for two and a pot of something that smelled delicious on the stove. Asher was curled on his bed by the hearth and followed James with his big brown eyes. He knelt down and petted Asher's furry coat. No Emily. He noticed her journal still opened for the ink to dry on the page and walked over to read it. Emily had written a poem she titled "The Empty Cradle."

### The Empty Cradle

*Lord, why do you deny the desire of our hearts?*
*The heritage you promised—we yearn to have a part.*
*We love You, Lord, and understand that children are a treasure.*
*Our baby, Lord, would grow to know your love is without measure.*

*Our home, though not quite perfect, is full of love and praise.*
*We want a chance to share our love in many different ways.*
*To teach a song, or give a hug, or help them tie a shoe—*
*So many memories to be made, so many things to do!*

*We enjoy our lives together now, as husband and wife alone,*
*But long to hold a little one who is our very own.*
*The hopes and heartaches come and go as each month passes by,*
*And draw our hearts together, as he comforts while I cry.*

*Remind me, Lord, to trust in You and grow in faith each day;*
*And use me please to share Your love and grace along life's way.*
*Help us to keep our eyes on You, for You will never fail.*

*Please make our dreams come true, we pray, to fill our empty cradle.*

Moisture gathered on his lashes, and he lifted his arm to rub his eyes with his sleeve before the tears could fall. Emily had captured the cry of their hearts so eloquently. Where was she? A soft rustle of fabric pulled his attention toward the second bedroom—the nursery—and he caught a glimpse of pale green skirt fabric. He strolled to the doorway and leaned his shoulder against the frame. Emily swiped her hands across her cheeks and sniffed softly. Before them sat an ornately carved and stained cradle.

"Did Josiah deliver the cradle today?"

His wife nodded, "A couple of hours ago."

James reached for her, but when she stiffened under his touch, he released her. Dinner was quiet, almost somber. Neither felt comfortable enough to break the awkward silence so not a word was spoken. Emily tidied up the kitchen, and they both readied for bed. James lay mere inches from the woman he loved more than anyone else on earth, but she might as well have been half a world away. They were both hurting, yet a barrier seemed fixed between them. He didn't understand it enough to break it down, but he grieved its existence.

---

Noticing that James was not himself during their interactions before and after church on Sunday, Seth prayed for an opportunity to speak with him privately. Sometimes a man needed advice from a father-figure, and Seth was fulfilling that role more often in the lives of Emma's sons, especially with James.

The next morning, James ambled up to the entrance of the

forge with Trigger's reins in his hands. Seth acknowledged him. "Did Trigger throw another shoe?"

"No." James hesitated. "Could you spare a few minutes?"

Seth waved at his Uncle Caleb to get his attention. When Caleb paused the hammering of the iron on the anvil, Seth informed him, "I'm going to step away for a little bit."

The older blacksmith saw James standing there and nodded. "Go ahead. I'll handle the customers."

"Thanks, Uncle Caleb." Seth gestured for James to follow him outside around the back of the forge where they had both shade and privacy. He folded his arms across his chest and casually leaned against the wooden rear wall of the building. "James, what is it that's bothering you?"

Raising an eyebrow, James asked in return, "Is it that obvious?"

"Probably only to me. Tell me about it. What's going on?"

Shifting his weight uneasily, James finally replied, "I love Emily more than I ever thought possible, but I haven't been able to give her the one thing she wants more than anything else. I feel inadequate, like I have failed her, and our disappointment is stealing our joy and pulling us apart."

"A baby," Seth nodded in understanding. "Don't forget that Emily knows how much you want to be a dad, too. I guarantee she feels just as inadequate about not giving you your heart's desire. More than that, she probably thinks she is losing your love because she hasn't given you a child. Loneliness is destructive."

"Why, Seth? Why is having babies so easy for some, but so difficult for us?"

"I wish I knew the answer to that question, but I don't. What I do know is that you need to be careful, James, or Satan will destroy your marriage."

James sniffed, and Seth could see the moisture in his eyes. "I feel guilty, Seth. When I hug Emily, she involuntarily tenses up, so I find myself not hugging her when I want to because I don't want to hurt her further. Mealtimes are quiet. In our effort not to talk about what is truly on our hearts, we don't say much at all. This isn't what I want. I want Emily back. What do I do?"

"Have you suggested that Emily talk to Emma about it? She would empathize with what Emily is going through."

James took a deep breath. "Yes, but with tears streaming down her face, she said, 'I'm not ready to give up yet,' as if going to Emma meant admitting defeat."

"James, this is what you need to do. Go to the Hill and wrestle with God until you can honestly say you will be content even if His plan is for you to remain a family of two. Plan to stay there a while. Only then can the rift between you and Emily begin to heal from the inside out."

Running his hand through his hair, James replied honestly, "I don't know that I can. I've wanted to be a dad for as long as I can remember."

"Do you trust God?" Seth confronted him.

"Sure," James answered.

"Do you? Do you trust Him enough to hold your dreams?"

James hesitated and his brow crinkled. "What if He says no?"

Lifting his hand to James' shoulder, Seth responded, "You and Emily should know from experience that God's perfect answer is worth the wait. God answered your prayer to have Emily as your wife. Will He give you children? He might. He might not. You must trust Him either way. Your marriage depends on it. God knows your heart's desire. You have to leave that desire with Him and be willing to wait for His timing. Ground your faith in what you know to be true about God's character and trust the promises in His Word."

Seth could read the inward turmoil on James' face and saw the moment of submission. "Okay," James nodded thoughtfully, "I'll go straight to the Hill from here. What should I do after that?"

"Share your heart with Emily. You both need the support of someone who understands exactly what you are going through, and there is no one better than each other. Make sure she knows that your love for her is unconditional, that it will not change whether God grants your desire for children or not."

"She knows I love her," James replied with pain in his voice.

"Tell her again anyway. Hug her often. She needs your strength and reassurance more than ever right now." Seth tapped James' chest with his pointed index finger. "If you hear someone sling a barb at Emily for not having children, be the knight in shining armor who deflects the blow and protects her. Listen to her when she grieves. Wrap her in your arms and grieve with her. Then consume your thoughts with what you are thankful for and overcome the grief together."

James' soul responded to Seth's words, "I will. I promise."

"One more thing. After you have your heart-to-heart conversation with God and start the healing process with Emily, recapture the bliss of your wedding day. Take Emily for a romantic walk or a picnic and bring her back home to a trail of rose petals that end scattered on your bed quilt. Children are wonderful, but they will change your life dramatically. Choose to cherish this time together as husband and wife. Once your first baby is born, you won't be alone again for many years." Seth paused, thoughts of Susanna filling his heart. "You have no promise of ever having time alone together again."

The realization of Seth's words hit James with a jolt that immediately put his pain in proper perspective. "I'm sorry, Seth."

"Trust God. Cherish your wife."

James reached out and hugged Seth fiercely as he would have hugged Daniel. "Thank you." The simple phrase spoke volumes to both men, for it conveyed James' heartfelt gratitude and the impact of Seth's influence in his life.

"You're welcome. Go." Seth waited while James mounted Trigger and waved farewell before heading to the ranch and the Hill.

James rode home and unsaddled Trigger. He stepped up onto his front porch and took a deep calming breath before opening the door and entering their home. Noticing that Emily was not there, he remembered that since today was Monday, she would be at Emma's doing laundry. He was both sad and relieved. He strode to the bedroom and retrieved his Bible from the small table by his pillow. On his way out, he walked around to the other side of the bed and rested his hand on Emily's empty pillow. "I love you, Emily, and I will fight this battle within so I can fight Satan for our marriage. He will not win."

James remembered Seth's words, "Plan to stay there a while." Though the time was still mid-morning, he lifted the lantern and a box of matches from the mantle, pulled the door closed behind him, and made his way to the Hill.

---

In the mid-afternoon, Emily returned home from laundry day with Emma and Julie. Asher mostly stayed with her, though he would go bounding off after any squirrel or rabbit that caught his eye. Emily tried to let his puppy antics lift her spirits, for spending time with Matthew was bittersweet. She loved her nephew, and he adored her, but he was yet another reminder that her arms would be empty after they parted.

So far, Emily had succeeded in not letting bitterness take root in her heart, but she was hurting. When she noticed Trigger in his stall, she was surprised not to find James in the house. Out of routine, she put the clean laundry away and started dinner preparations. Routine dulled the pain within, and James' absence meant not seeing his eyes mirroring the same pain she felt and made it easier to go through the motions.

Dinnertime came and went. James didn't come. At first, she was a bit perturbed, but after another hour passed, she began to worry. After sliding the dinner plates in the warming oven, she walked over to the hearth to retrieve the lantern, but it was missing. For a reason she could not explain, Emily felt alone and abandoned. Asher lifted his head from his paws, and Emily sat next to him and ran her fingers through his thick fur. Her spirit felt drawn outside. With a soft command to Asher to stay, she stepped onto the porch to gaze at the stars in the night sky. Something about seeing God's handiwork in the heavens always calmed her soul. Emily rubbed her upper arms for an extra bit of warmth in the cool evening air and took a deep cleansing breath. When she turned toward the Hill, her eyes spotted a pinpoint of light on the crest where the bench welcomed all who climbed there.

"Lord, that must be James. Should I stay or go to him?" *"Go. He needs you."* Emily reached just inside the door to grab her shawl and wrapped it around her shoulders as she descended the front steps. A few moments later, she first glimpsed her husband. He was sitting on the bench, leaning forward, with his head in his hands. His Bible was open on the bench beside him. She approached slowly. When she heard him crying, the sound nearly broke her heart. Emily stopped, not wanting to disturb him. A rising fear whispered that she was the cause of those tears. Suddenly, she wasn't sure whether she would be accepted or refused. She started to turn and quietly retrace her steps, but the soft voice came again to her soul, *"Go, he needs you."*

With trembling hands, she came close and laid a gentle

hand on his shoulder. James slowly lowered his hands from his face and looked up at his bride. The flickering lantern light made her beautiful face glow. Without words, he pulled her onto his lap and wrapped his arms around her. The tears continued to flow while he held her. Rather than tensing, her body melted into his embrace.

A few moments later, James found his voice. "I love *you*. I married *you*. I've missed you. You are more important to me than a dozen children. I want you in my now. I want you in my future. I want you in my arms for always. I don't know why God is asking us to wait for our dearest dream, but I placed our dreams in His hands tonight, and I trust Him to do with them as He wishes." James brushed his thumb on Emily's cheek. "If God gives us children, they will be treasured. If He chooses not to bless our family with children, you are still the most precious thing in the world to me, for you hold my heart."

Now Emily was in tears, too, but they were healing tears. She cupped the sides of James' face in her hands. With a quivering chin, she finally spoke, "I love you."

James raised his forearm to wipe his face with his sleeve. Emily wiped her tears with the other side of his sleeve. Then they did something they had not dared to do in quite a while. They laughed. Laughter truly was good medicine. Once the tension had abated, both James and Emily were able to share their most inward thoughts and struggles.

By the time they left the Hill, the moon was high in the sky. Though their longing for little ones was still present, the burden of their sorrow had been lifted. When they stood, James pulled her close and kissed her. He partially released her and reached for his Bible and the lantern with his left hand and tucked her under his right arm. "Let's go home."

## CHAPTER 23
## *Kathryn O'Brien*

During one of Jacob's courting visits to the Müllers' front porch, he inquired, "Now that you're venturing further from the farm without your papa, would you join Frederick and me on a tour of the ranch?"

"I'd enjoy riding with you, but haven't I already seen the ranch?"

"Not all of it, and not for my reason." His mouth twitched with mischief.

"Which is?" Heidi prompted.

"I was hoping you might help me choose a plot of land for our house."

Heidi's hand flew to her mouth, and her eyes glistened with tears of joy. "Our house," she repeated, still trying to grasp the phrase. "Oh, Jacob! Yes, I'd be happy to join you!"

"I've already saved most of what I need for the building supplies. With the sale of the hay and alfalfa harvesting soon, I should have enough to finish the house. Start thinking about the layout you want."

"Layout?"

"Mm-hmm. The number of rooms, where you want the

kitchen and living area situated, one story or two. James can help us with rudimentary blueprints when we get that far. He drew the ones for his home."

"Our house." Heidi tried the phrase again, the reality of the meaning fully sinking in. Her face fairly glowed with her joy.

"Two simple words that hint at the promise they represent."

The next morning, Jacob donned his work gloves and offered his hand to Heidi as she climbed into the buggy. Frederick scrambled up the other side and stationed himself on the bench between the courting couple.

Jacob showed Heidi several tracts of land and explained the pros and cons of each one. Fully invested, she asked a myriad of questions and compared the views from each location. They stopped by the ranch house for lunch with Emma and discussed Heidi's notes.

After the midday meal, Jacob and Heidi returned to the plot they both had ranked first. The land lay on a rise just south of the river road. An opening in the tree line along the river would provide a beautiful view of the waterfall and Heidi's Meadow from the back porch.

The trees to the left of the plot would provide privacy from the other homes and buildings on the ranch, but the proximity of the river road provided convenient access to the ranch. The path that formed the extension of the river road led to a natural break in the stand of fir trees, an area they could clear to create a shortcut path to her family's farm, should Heidi wish to continue helping her mama with the cheesemaking.

Heidi and Jacob walked the perimeter of the plot and discussed where they would position the house. Heidi extended her arms and twirled in a slow circle. "This is perfect!"

Jacob grinned, "I couldn't agree more."

A week before Jacob's birthday, the entire family in addition to the Kendricks, Carters, and Heidi and Frederick gathered on the boardwalk in Prairie Hills to meet the afternoon stage. Jacob stepped forward to assist Laura as she disembarked. As soon as her feet hit the ground, Emily swallowed her and Katie in a welcoming hug.

Tim followed and seemed to unfold his tall frame when he landed on solid dirt. He grabbed Jacob in a man hug, and they thumped each other on the back. "Man, I've missed you," Jacob declared.

"At least you've had a pretty lady to fill in for me," Tim teased. He took one loping stride toward the only blond he didn't recognize. "You must be Heidi." At her nod, he thumbed over his shoulder, "And you like this clown?"

Heidi smiled, "I do."

Jacob shoved Tim with his shoulder, and Tim laughed. Looking down at his brother, he winked. "Well, I can't say much for her intelligence in choosing you, but she is pretty."

"Heidi, this is Tim," Jacob introduced.

Laughter bubbled from Heidi, "Yes, I had gathered as much."

"I am very pleased to meet you. All teasing aside, Jacob is a great guy. You couldn't do better." He winked at her. "Only a real man can be sheriff."

Heidi scrunched her brows in puzzlement, and Jacob chuckled. "Remind me, and I'll explain that comment later. There's a story there." By the time Jacob turned to face his family, Katie was already in Emily's arms. "Let's go meet our niece."

"She isn't my niece," Heidi reminded him.

Jacob waved her comment away as if it were of no consequence and flashed his dimples her way. "Nothing that time won't cure."

Little Miss Kathryn O'Brien had a beautiful ivory complexion and a shock of red hair. Her big emerald green eyes were fixed on Emily's face, and her chubby hands were reaching for a dangling tendril of her aunt's golden hair.

Jacob and Heidi greeted the little bundle. Jacob placed his forefinger within her grasp to intercept her from pulling Emily's hair, and Katie wrapped her tiny fingers around it. The simple touch wound around his heart, and he grinned at Heidi. "I'll bet Katie already has Tim wrapped around her little finger."

She scrunched her face and sneezed. Jacob dipped his brow slightly. "Maybe we should get her away from these dusty streets."

"That's a good idea," Emma agreed, and she began herding everyone toward the wagons. They all congregated again at the ranch house for dinner. With a full-length extension added to the table, everyone was able to eat together. Jacob's eyes roamed to all the friends and family gathered there and landed on the beautiful blond beside him. His heart was full, completely full.

When everyone held hands to pray, Jacob and Heidi rested their hands on the table an inch apart, and he crooked his mouth in a lopsided grin complete with its corresponding dimple. They might not be physically touching, but in his heart, he was holding her hand just the same.

---

Dinner was nearly finished when Kathryn started crying—not a whimper, but a loud lusty demand for attention. Laura fed Kathryn and changed her diaper, but she wouldn't stop wailing.

Tim reached for his daughter and tucked her against his chest. The rich, warm sound of his thick Irish brogue surrounded her like a soft blanket. "Ah, mi beautiful little Katie O'Brien, why are you crying, mi love? Missing your Daddy too much, are ye?"

Katie's emerald green eyes blinked up at her Daddy's, and she fell silent. Tim's heart was overflowing. How could a man have so much love for such a little person? "There's a good lass. Only when ye stop crying can I see those beautiful eyes the color of the pastures of Ireland."

Laura stepped up beside him and laid her head against his shoulder. "She loves her Daddy."

"Aye, she's a Daddy's girl, for sure. She's a smart lass, this one." Tim winked at his wife. "Smart like her mum."

Finally looking toward the rest of the gathering, Tim viewed the expressions of surprise. "What? Haven't you ever seen a grown man holding a wee babe before?"

Jacob blurted, "Where did you get that accent?"

"Mi mum's Irish accent was smooth and lilting, and mine copied hers until I began working with the logging teams. By the time Daniel found me, mi brogue was almost lost. When this little one would get her lusty cries going, I remembered that dad always said only mi mum's brogue could soothe me as a baby. When I gave it a try with Katie, she loved it."

Still holding his daughter snug against him, Tim joined his brothers and sat on the sofa. "Now that this little lass has quieted down a bit, let's discuss harvest. James, what are your plans?"

## CHAPTER 24
## *Nathan's Reaper*

Nathan Lange had been buzzing about the arrival of his mechanical reaper for months. Thanks to Cyrus McCormick's invention, Nathan would be able to reap his harvest in a fraction of the time and need only himself and a couple of men to do the entire job. In anticipation of a much more efficient yield, Nathan had even sown an additional two acres of wheat during spring planting. Now his fields had ripened for harvest two weeks earlier than the previous year, providing an opportunity for his neighbors to witness the reaper's demonstration without neglecting their own crops.

Thad, Nathan's seven-year-old boy, was nearly as enthusiastic as his dad. When Nathan announced to the other farmers at church that he was going to begin harvest the next day, several of the men decided to come and see the new contraption in action. Tim and Jacob were among them.

Not wanting to be left out of the excitement on Monday morning, Thad begged to join them. "Dad, I can come and watch, too, right?"

"Honey," Molly Lange cut in, "I don't think that's a good idea, Those long cutting blades are sharp and dangerous."

"But I'm not made of wheat; the blades won't hurt me.'

"Sharp metal will cut whatever it touches, wheat or not."

Trying desperately to make his case without whining, Thad pleaded, "I've been looking forward to this forever! May I go out and watch? I'll be really careful. Please?"

Molly rested her hands on her hips and considered her son. Those puppy-dog eyes of Thad's could melt Molly's motherly resolve in an instant if she didn't fortify her mind. She didn't doubt this would be a wonderful learning opportunity; she was just concerned for his safety.

In that moment, Nathan bridged the gap to his son and beamed at Thad. "He'll be all right, Molly. I'll keep and eye on him. New advancements like this don't come along every day."

"I guess you're right," Molly conceded.

"Yippee!" Thad jumped up and down before running full force into his mom and flinging his arms around her waist.

"Just promise me that you'll keep your distance and listen to Daddy's instructions."

"I will. I promise!" With that, he bounded outside to follow on Nathan's heels.

"That boy," Molly smiled and shook her head, peeking out the window at his retreating back. "Lord, keep my boy safe during today's adventure."

Over the next hour, nearly a dozen men arrived to see how well this reaper performed. Nathan harnessed his Belgian workhorse to the machine and climbed into the elevated metal seat before he guided his gelding to the first row of wheat. With the release of the blade assembly handle and the command for the horse to pull, the long blades began spinning slowly and gradually gained speed with the forward motion of the rig.

One blade after another sliced the stalks and laid them flat. The two men actually helping with the harvest followed behind and bundled the wheat into sheaves. The others examined the process from all angles and discussed the merits and drawbacks of owning a reaper of their own.

Thad stayed close to the wandering group of men, and Jacob checked on him from time to time knowing Nathan was preoccupied with managing his rig. Jacob commented to Tim beside him, "This thing is quite impressive. He's already finished four rows. If if weren't for the expense, I'd consider getting one for cutting hay."

"Maybe Nathan would rent his machine to you. If you planted an extra acre of hayseed, the yield would more than cover the cost of the rental fee and give you additional profit with a shorter harvest time."

"Not a bad idea, I'll discuss the possibility with Nath—" Jacob's peripheral vision caught Thad chasing a large dragonfly directly toward the rotating blades. Without a second thought, Jacob sprinted to intercept the boy while screaming, "Stop! Thad, stop! Nathan, stop! Stop! Stop!"

Nathan reacted, but the weight and momentum made slowing the rig difficult. Thad froze in fear, his eyes glued to the massive blades bearing down on him. Jacob reached him, grabbed him around the waist, and flung him out of harm's way, but the angle of attack left no room for Jacob to correct and maneuver away himself. He fell, left arm extended to brace his impact with the ground, but the blades reached him before the ground did.

## CHAPTER 25
## *Jacob*

Luke heard galloping hooves and ran to the door of the barn, arriving just as Tim pulled his mount to a stop.

"Luke! Grab your bag! Jacob is hurt! His arm— Hurry! Take my horse! I'll saddle Dakota and meet you at the Langes' farm! Go!" Tim quickly swung his leg over and leaped onto the ground.

Luke hung the handle of his medical bag on the saddle horn and hoisted himself into the saddle. The stirrups were too long, but he wasn't about to take the time to adjust them. He leaned low over the horse's neck and sped off toward Nathan Lange's farm, praying as he rode.

Arriving at the farm, Molly Lange was standing near her home to direct him with her outstretched arm. With her other hand, she wiped her tears with her apron. Luke looked to the indicated direction and saw a cluster of men and the harvest wagon behind the reaper. He nodded to Molly but never slowed his pace. Nearing the harvesters, he could hear Jacob screaming. *Oh, God, help me know what to do.*

In one smooth motion, Luke grasped the handle of his medical bag and dismounted before the horse had even come to a complete stop. Before he could reach Jacob, the screaming suddenly ceased. The men parted, and Luke saw Jacob for the first time.

Jacob was lying on his back, his face pale and pinched into a grimace. He looked whole other than the arm that was shrouded in a canvas. Nathan Lange was trying to hold pressure to Jacob's arm; he looked nearly as pale as Jacob.

"Nathan, what happened?" Luke asked as he closed the gap to his brother.

With tears in his eyes, Nathan replied, "He saved Thad's life but lost his balance and fell arm first into the reaper blades. He's lost a lot of blood, Luke. He's not dead, is he?"

Luke was already feeling for the pulse in Jacob's neck. "No, his heart is still beating. He may have passed out from the pain." He reached over and uncovered the injured arm. The sight of the mangled limb before him made him ill, but he had to stay alert. Jacob's very life depended upon it. Luke took a deep breath to quell the queasiness building within him.

He looked up and gestured to one of the other men, "Give me your bandana." With a quick motion, Luke rolled it and slid it underneath Jacob's forearm before securing it with a tight knot. He addressed Nathan, "This tourniquet will abate the bleeding. You can let go."

Once Nathan moved, Luke could see more of Jacob's left arm. He needed to get Jacob to the surgery in Doc's office immediately. "We need a wagon to get him to town now."

"Tom Wilson already left for one. He should be here any minute." As if on cue, the rumbling of the wagon grew louder as it approached them.

Tim arrived on Dakota as the wagon pulled to a stop. "Luke, what can I do?"

"Help us lift Jacob into the wagon bed. On the count of three. One, two, three." They lifted Jacob's body simultaneously and laid him down as gently, but as quickly, as possible.

"I'll ride in the wagon and protect his arm from too much jostling. Ride back and ask Laura and Julie to meet us at Doc's office, then ride into town and tell Doc to get the surgery ready."

Without a word, Tim turned, mounted, and sped away on his mission. Luke knew that Tim was the most skilled at riding as fast as possible while staying mindful of his horse's safety. He would get everyone assembled in time.

"All right, Tom, let's go." Tom Wilson slapped the reins and the team of horses started toward town. Luke used both hands on the free edges of the canvas wrap to lift Jacob's arm off the wagon bed and hold it at a slight angle to minimize additional trauma and use gravity to prevent the pooling of more blood in the arm.

The jarring of the wagon brought Jacob back to consciousness, but he lacked the strength to scream again. Jacob saw Luke kneeling beside him. He trusted Luke. Even though he was starting to drift back into semi-consciousness, he was aware enough to see the pain and concern written on Luke's face. Jacob winced and groaned, "How bad is it?"

"Your arm doesn't look good," Luke replied honestly.

Jacob reached over with his right hand and grabbed his brother's arm and pleaded, "Please don't take my arm. Promise me you won't take my arm."

With compassion in his eyes, Luke responded, "I cannot promise you that. We will do our best, but if I have to choose between your arm and your life, I will choose you."

Jacob swallowed hard. In a brief moment of more alertness, he asked, "How is Thad?"

"He's pretty shaken, but unhurt. You saved his life, Jacob."

With this knowledge, Jacob's right arm released its grip and fell limp to his side, and he slipped back into darkness. Luke vigilantly observed his brother's chest, but the rhythmic rise and fall continued, assuring him that Jacob had merely fainted again.

When the wagon finally pulled to a stop in front of the clinic, Tim and Doc quickly approached. Doc made eye contact with Luke and simply asked, "Luke?"

Luke looked up at him and shook his head. "He's unconscious. His hand and wrist are unrecognizable."

Doc nodded, "All right, men, let's get Jacob inside." After getting him moved to the surgery table, Luke unwrapped the canvas again. Doc examined the arm gravely. "Amputation is his only option."

Laura and Julie entered the clinic together. Doc delegated, "Julie, I need you to administer anesthesia." She immediately washed her hands and opened the glass doors of the cabinet to collect the gauze and the bottle of chloroform she would need.

"Laura, grab the shears from the table and cut off Jacob's shirt. I also need you to sterilize the instruments." She quickly removed the shirt that was already torn from the accident, forcing herself not to think about the large blood stains covering most of the left side of the garment. After that task, she removed his boots, praying silently as she worked. Laura gathered the surgical instruments and soaked them in carbolic acid.

"Luke, I'm going to need an extra set of hands. Performing amputation surgery on a loved one is not an easy task. Would you be willing to assist me?"

Luke responded without hesitation, "Yes, I'll do whatever you need."

"Good man. Get the bucket and the warm water. We need to get this arm as clean as possible to prevent infection." They worked together to remove as much dirt and debris as possible. "Pull up the narrow table and cover it with clean towels." Doc removed the dirty canvas completely and cleaned the underside of Jacob's arm, then held the arm outstretched for Luke to position the table beneath it. This arrangement would allow Doc and Luke to stand on either side of the arm and both have access to the instrument tray at the end of the table near what was once Jacob's hand.

Laura added the sterilized instruments to the surgical tray while Luke washed his hands and donned a surgical gown; then Doc did the same. Laura then gathered the canvas and the dirty bucket and took them from the room.

Julie refused to look at Jacob's arm. She could see the severity of the injury when she read Luke's eyes. She wiped the sweat and dirt from Jacob's face before she gently laid an unfolded square of gauze over his nose and mouth. She sat on a stool at Jacob's head, checked his pulse and breathing, and waited for the signal from Doc.

Doc and Luke faced each other with Jacob's arm between them. Doc asked, "Julie, how is Jacob?"

"His heart rate is rapid, but steady; his breathing is even, and his lips are still pink, showing no signs of respiratory distress."

"Good. You may begin. Ordinarily, I would say he would need more anesthesia than Susanna did during her surgery, but in his weakened condition, he may not. Just keep a close eye on him."

Julie dropped a couple of drops of chloroform onto the gauze. He looked so pale. *Oh, God, don't let him die.*

Doc made eye contact with Luke before he bowed his head in prayer, "Dear Father, You are the Great Physician. Please use our hands to perform Your healing. Give us alertness and skill. Give Jacob strength to endure this surgery and help him to heal without complications or infection. In Jesus' holy name, Amen."

To Luke, he instructed, "We need to clamp off the blood vessels first so we can remove the tourniquet." They worked precisely, but quickly.

"How much of his forearm can we save?" Luke asked.

"More than I had originally thought. We only need to get above the damaged bone with enough tissue to stabilize and pad the end of his arm."

Luke pointed to a transradial line about an inch above the wrist. Doc nodded.

"Julie, is Jacob still doing all right?"

"Yes, Doc."

"Be ready to give him a bit more chloroform. If anything will wake him up, this will."

"Laura, ask Tim to come in, please." She went to the door to get her husband, and Tim entered with his eyes never leaving the floor.

Doc directed, "Tim, put your hands on Jacob's shoulders with enough force to hold him down if necessary." He leaned over his brother and pushed his hands firmly against Jacob's shoulders until he was pressing with all of his weight. Tim's height gave him additional leverage, just in case. He closed his eyes and turned his head away from the faint smell of the chloroform that was keeping his brother asleep and the stronger metallic smell of Jacob's blood.

Addressing the man facing him, Doc instructed, "Luke, be sure his arm is lying straight and hold it tight against the table. When I saw the bones in his forearm, they need to be perfectly even."

"Julie, Laura, cover your ears. This sound is not pleasant." The quiet room accentuated the abrasive sawing strokes. Doc and Luke's entire focus was on Jacob's forearm, but Laura's gaze was on her husband's face. Tim's features were scrunched into a grimace, and the color was draining from his cheeks.

Laura stepped forward in case she had to try to catch him. The absurdity of that thought almost brought a smile. She would never be able to support Tim's weight if he fainted. The best she could do was cushion the floor when he fell on top of her. At least she could keep him from disturbing the surgical field if the worst should happen.

When the bones had been severed, Doc said, "Thank you, Tim, you may go."

Tim didn't need to be told twice. He immediately turned and left on legs that were as weak as a newborn calf, sinking to the boardwalk out front and gasping for fresh air. Soon Laura was beside him. She laid a comforting hand on his shoulder, and quietly instructed, "Put your head between your knees for a few minutes until the lightheadedness passes."

When Laura looked up, she realized James and Josiah were standing there with the men who had been harvesting at the Langes' farm. Emma and Heidi were sitting on the bench against the clinic wall, and Frederick was sitting on the edge of the boardwalk with his legs dangled over the edge.

Laura announced to those gathered, "The amputation part of the surgery is finished. Now Doc and Luke need to reconstruct Jacob's arm. Keep praying." She swept back inside and closed the door.

When the reconstruction was finally complete, Doc asked Luke, "Would you please close the incision? Your suturing skills are better than mine. You would leave less of a scar."

Wordlessly, Luke picked up the needle and suture thread. While Doc approximated the skin, Luke meticulously sewed with even stitches.

When the surgery was over, Julie lifted the medicated gauze from Jacob's face and procured the clean bandages for Doc and Luke to wrap Jacob's arm. They moved Jacob into a private infirmary room simply furnished with a bed, washstand, and chair.

What remained of Jacob's forearm was heavily wrapped in white bandages. Luke bent Jacob's arm at the elbow, tucked a pillow beneath it, and rested his elevated forearm against his chest to reduce pain and swelling. Julie bathed Jacob's face and torso, removing the last of the dried blood from the accident. She and Luke pulled the blanket up to Jacob's chest so only his shoulders and arms were exposed.

While Luke and Julie tended to Jacob, Doc and Laura cleaned the surgery room. When they had finished, Doc exited the clinic door to address those waiting. "Jacob made it through surgery, though he has not woken from anesthesia yet. We have moved him to a quiet room, but I must limit visitors to family. Emma, you may stay as long as you wish." Emma took that as her cue and slipped past Doc to enter the clinic.

Doc continued, "Pray that his arm will heal without infection." Noticing Heidi, he reached over and laid a fatherly hand on her shoulder and added quietly, "Jacob would consider you family. You are also welcome to visit him."

Heidi responded softly, "Thank you, Doc."

James asked politely, "Heidi, would it be all right if the three of us saw him before you do? We need to get home for evening chores."

"Of course," was her sweet reply.

James nodded and turned to his brother, "Josiah, why don't you go first."

Josiah stood and hesitated before he followed Doc to Jacob's room.

---

When she heard footsteps, Emma looked up to see Josiah standing in the doorway, his eyes glued to his brother's bandaged limb. His eyes filled with unshed tears. Emma stood and gestured to the chair. "Have a seat and talk to him. He's still asleep from the anesthesia, but the tone of your voice would soothe him as it begins to wear off." When he sat, she slipped to the corner of the room.

"Jacob, I don't care how many hands you have, you are my

brother, and I love you. Please don't die. I couldn't bear to lose you, too." Jacob did not respond. Other than the movement of his chest when he breathed, he was motionless. Josiah all but fled from the room.

When Josiah exited the clinic, James offered, "If you want to stay, Tim and I can cover chores."

"No." Josiah's harsh answer was immediate and adamant. Then he gentled his tone. "Thank you, but I can't stand to see him this way. I've got work to do." Not the chores James probably thought he was referring to, but ways to help Jacob adapt. His mind began thinking through all of the everyday movements that had now become daunting. A bit of ingenuity and creativity would be required—talents that Josiah had in abundance.

After Tim and James had each taken their turn, Julie slipped into Jacob's room and reached for the blanket. She pulled it up and over Jacob's shoulders and tucked it in. Only his head and arms were visible. Seeing Emma's quizzical expression, Julie explained, "Heidi is coming in next." Emma nodded her understanding and stood once again to vacate the chair.

---

When James appeared in the clinic front doorway, Heidi stood, knowing her turn was next. She was grateful her shaking legs were covered by the fabric of her floor-length skirt. James settled his hat on his head and tipped the brim to her. "Thank you, Heidi."

Heidi splayed her fingers across her abdomen in an attempt to quell the surge of nerves as she stepped toward the infirmary room. When she neared the doorway, her first glimpse encompassed Jacob's pale features. She stilled. Surely one of his brothers would have told her if he had passed.

Then she saw it: the rise and fall of his chest as he breathed. That simple breath seemed to breathe courage into her soul. Heidi stepped forward, her indecision about what to say vanishing more with each footfall.

The deep recesses of her mind reminded her that Emma was in the room with her, but in that moment, her heart melded with Jacob's, though he remained unconscious. Until now, Heidi had been fairly confident Jacob was God's chosen man for her. This moment changed everything. She was now as certain of her heart's pledge to Jacob as the dawn breaking the darkness each morning.

Heidi bent near Jacob's face and spoke softly. "You are so brave. If you hadn't been there, Thad would have died. You are a hero. I'm so proud of you." She lowered herself into the chair beside him. Heidi had never touched a man who was not her family, but she did not hesitate as she gently lifted Jacob's hand enough to encompass it with both of hers and began to pray.

"Dear Heavenly Father, thank you for protecting Jacob's life and for bringing him into my life. If it be Your will, please keep him in my life forever. You are the Great Physician, and I pray that you would heal Jacob's arm. Heal the incision quickly and without any infection. Help the scar to be minimal. More importantly, though, please heal his heart. For a man who works with his hands, losing one must be a terrible burden."

Heidi stifled a startled gasp when she felt Jacob's hand move. Her first impulse was to remove her hand, but before she could fully form the thought, his fingers curled around her hand. How could the touch of an unconscious man make her feel so loved, so protected? The idea defied logic. She refocused her thoughts and continued her prayer.

"Please comfort Jacob as he relearns how to do everything with one hand instead of two. Guard him from frustration. Help him adjust quickly and keep his heart from bitterness or resentment. Help him to know that the wonderful man he is hasn't changed because he has lost a hand. Help him realize that I do not see him any differently. Maybe I even care for him a bit more for his bravery. Show me how to encourage him. In the name of my Savior, Amen."

---

Emma stood discretely in the far corner and watched Heidi and Jacob while Heidi prayed. About halfway through her prayer, Jacob's fingers curled around Heidi's hand. Emma's attention quickly shifted to his face, but not even an eyelash fluttered. He was still asleep. Subconsciously, his heart must have known who was holding his hand.

When she heard footsteps, Emma looked over and saw Heidi's father standing in the doorway. She caught his eye and put a finger to her lips before he could say anything.

Johann Müller was relieved to see Emma standing against the wall. His daughter had not been unchaperoned. When she motioned for him to remain silent, he realized Heidi was praying. His eyes were drawn to the bandages on Jacob's arm, and he swallowed hard before returning his gaze to Heidi. When he noticed she was holding Jacob's hand, he clenched his jaw but held his peace.

When Heidi closed her prayer, she lifted her head and studied Jacob's face. In her heart, she thought the words, *I love you, Jacob,* and willed him to hear her heart.

From the doorway, her father spoke firmly but not unkindly, "Heidi, it's time to go."

"Yes, Papa." Heidi slid her hands from Jacob's so they straightened his fingers against the blanket. She did not want her father to know Jacob's fingers had embraced her hand.

Heidi rose and followed her father out of the clinic where Frederick was waiting. Johann remained silent until they were riding home. "When you did not return home, I feared the worst."

Realizing her father's perspective, Heidi was immediately contrite, "I'm so sorry, Papa. The wagon carrying Jacob arrived as Frederick and I were leaving the general store. After the men rushed Jacob into the clinic, his brother Tim came outside to sit on the boardwalk. He told me about the accident and Jacob's need for emergency surgery. I couldn't leave Jacob."

Johann nodded his head in understanding. "You did give me quite a scare, though. I don't think I've ever pushed the team that hard. James flagged me down and told me where to find you." Another minute passed. "Why were you holding that man's hand?"

His daughter met his gaze and answered, "I was not holding hands with Jacob; I was praying with him. Does our family not always join hands when we pray together?"

He knew she had a valid argument. "True, but he is not family."

Heidi almost added *"Yet,"* but thought better of it and kept quiet.

Johann cleared his throat, "I plan to tell Jacob he can no longer court you."

A look of dismay clouded Heidi's face, "Why?"

Though the answer seemed obvious to him, he patiently explained, "You do know where courting usually leads, right?"

"Yes, to marriage, and I would be truly blessed if he chose me to be his wife," Heidi replied.

"Heidi, think about what you are saying. Jacob . . ." He couldn't find the right words to complete his thought.

Heidi understood, and she wasn't about to back down. "When you approved Jacob to be my suitor, you listed all the admirable qualities you found in him. Which of those qualities has now changed because he risked his own safety to save a boy's life?"

Johann opened his mouth to deliver his rebuttal, but found he had nothing to say.

After letting him sit in silence for a moment, Heidi continued, "I am not a child, Papa. I am well aware of the challenges Jacob may face in these upcoming weeks and months, but I am also convinced that he will face them with valor. Jacob is no less a man with one hand than he was with two."

## CHAPTER 26
## *Fighting Self-Pity*

The sun had set when Jacob finally aroused from the anesthesia to find Emma sitting next to his bed. With a look of concern, she leaned forward and rested her hand on his shoulder, "You are finally awake. How are you feeling?"

He was groggy, and the pain in his left arm was intense, but he mentally pushed those aside to ask the burning question on his mind. "Did they amputate my arm?"

Emma answered honestly, "Your hand and wrist are gone, but they kept as much of your forearm as they could."

Jacob's bottom lip quivered, and he reached his good hand to his face. "I want to be alone."

"Go ahead and cry, Jacob. Grieving is part of the healing process, but I will not leave you."

He turned his head away from Emma, and the tears began to fall. Soon the tears turned to gut-wrenching sobs. He wouldn't lift his left arm, for he did not want to see what was no longer there.

He thought of what he had lost. More than just a hand. He had lost his ability to do ranching jobs—to do any two-handed tasks. What hurt him the most was that he surely had forever lost any hope of continuing to court Heidi.

When he had finally drained himself of all his tears, he fell into a fitful sleep.

---

In the next room, Luke leaned both hands on the counter before him and hung his head as he listened to Jacob cry. Julie stepped up beside him and wrapped her arm around his waist. He turned his head, and his sky blue eyes searched her warm chocolate brown ones. Julie spoke softly, "I know how much you are hurting for Jacob, but you and Doc saved his life today."

With a voice made gravelly with emotion, Luke replied, "Julie, on our way here in the wagon, he begged me not to take his arm. I know Doc and I made the right decision, but will Jacob hate me for it?"

"Jacob is a changed man since he gave his heart to God. He will grieve, and he may lash out at you in anger, but he will heal. We must pray that God will transform any anger into determination." Luke nodded solemnly, and Julie assured him, "No matter how he responds, I will never stop loving you."

Luke released the counter and pulled Julie to his chest. He clung to her with desperation, thankful that she understood his heart and loved him completely.

---

When Jacob awoke, Emma was there, putting a cool cloth on his forehead. With a scratchy voice, Jacob said, "Thank you, Mama." That single word pulled at Emma's heartstrings. James was the only one of her boys who still consistently called her "Mama." To hear this endearment from Jacob held special meaning, especially during this time when he seemed so vulnerable and in need of motherly love.

Julie came to the doorway after hearing Jacob's voice. "How much are you hurting right now? Do you need some pain medicine?"

He winced and pinched his eyebrows together. "I'm all right."

Responding to his body language rather than his words, she replied, "I'll be right back with your medicine." Julie put a few drops of laudanum in a cup of water and returned to Jacob's room, placing the cup in Emma's outstretched hand.

Emma slipped her arm under Jacob's pillow to lift his head a bit. "Here, drink this." With her other hand, she supported the cup as Jacob brought the vessel to his lips and sipped the foul-tasting liquid. When he had finished, she took the cup and handed it back to Julie, who quietly slipped out of the room.

Emma settled back into her chair. "I think half the town was waiting out front during your surgery. Doc and Luke only let a few in to see you—James, Tim, Josiah, and Heidi."

"Heidi was here?" Jacob asked in surprise.

"Yes, she prayed the sweetest prayer while she held your hand. She prayed that God would heal your arm and your heart as you adjusted to doing things in a new way."

"Heidi wasn't repulsed by my arm?"

"Of all who came to see you, she was the least affected by it. She loves you, Jacob."

Jacob lifted his right hand and stared at it as the complete truth of Emma's words sank into his mind. *Heidi held my hand. I wish I could still feel her hand in mine.* Recalling her promise that she would never touch a man unless he was the one she intended to marry, he blinked away the tears that stung his eyes. The tiniest glimmer of hope had just been fanned into a faintly glowing ember. If Heidi truly loved him, he could overcome anything.

The next morning, Jacob woke to find Luke sitting beside him with his right ankle crossed on his left knee and a large open volume resting on his leg. Luke absently scratched the days' worth of stubble on his normally clean-shaven face before he turned the page, obviously lost in whatever he was reading.

Jacob reached up to rub his chin, realizing that he, too, needed to shave. His movement caught Luke's eye.

"Good morning. How did you sleep?" Luke inquired.

"Better than you, I'm guessing." Jacob stifled a yawn. He grimaced in pain as he tried to shift his weight in the bed. "Have you been sitting there all night?"

Luke nodded. "Yes, I sent Julie and Emma home after you fell asleep so they could rest. Doc had been up late the night before delivering a baby, so I told him I'd stay. Not that I would have left you anyway."

There was an awkward silence between them until Jacob finally remarked, "Emma told me you had to take my hand and wrist."

Luke swallowed hard, and his eyes mirrored the pain he felt for his brother. "I am so sorry, Jacob. The damage was too extensive. Amputation was the only option to save your life." He could see the muscles tighten in Jacob's jaw as he struggled to control his emotions.

With a voice tinged with sorrow rather than anger, Jacob declared, "You may have saved my life, but it will never be the same again."

"No, not entirely. Part of your body is now gone, and you can and should grieve that loss. The next few months will be tough, both emotionally and physically. However, if you would be willing to transform your frustration into determination, you can relearn how to perform your everyday tasks and be able to do everything you could before the accident."

Wanting to believe that might be true, Jacob asked, "How do you know that?" He glanced over at the thick book in his brother's lap. "What are you reading, anyway?"

Luke tipped up the book so Jacob could read the title on the front cover.

"*A Comprehensive Treatise on the Post-Operative Recovery and Strengthening Therapy for the Upper Extremity Amputee Patient*. Where did you find that bit of light reading?"

The tension in the room seemed to dissipate, and the corner of Luke's mouth curled upward in a smile from Jacob's attempt at humor. "From Doc's library."

Jacob took a deep breath and let it out slowly. "I trusted you before my accident, and I choose to trust you now. Where do we begin?"

Luke had not missed the "we" in Jacob's question, and he was certainly willing to be his teammate in the healing process, no matter how long it took. "Initially, our primary goal is to prevent infection. We'll change your dressing regularly, and we'll be sure you eat plenty of protein to speed tissue healing."

"When the incision begins to heal, we will begin strengthening exercises with your left arm to keep both arms equal and balanced. Until then, we will do gentle motion therapy to keep your joints and muscles flexible."

"When can we start? How soon will I be able to ride again?"

"I appreciate your eagerness, but progress will happen one small step at a time." The front door of the clinic opened, and Luke leaned back in his chair to peer through the doorway into the main clinic room to see who entered. "Speaking of small steps, I believe our breakfast has just arrived."

Luke marked his place in the textbook and set it on the corner of the washstand table before he stood and stretched. "Let's see if you can tolerate a sitting position in bed for a few minutes. Roll toward your right side and push up with that arm."

Luke patiently waited while Jacob slowly lifted his upper body. Jacob was nearly out of breath from that simple exercise. Luke rearranged the pillows against the headboard. "Push your hips back so you can rest against the pillows."

Jacob tried, but his right arm was trembling. Luke grasped Jacob's torso and lifted him up and backward until he was resting comfortably. "Do you feel lightheaded at all?"

"Maybe a little, but I'm all right."

Luke could hear disappointment in Jacob's tone. "Keep in mind that you lost a lot of blood yesterday. Until your body makes up for what you have lost, you will feel much weaker and will tire more easily than usual. The weakness will gradually disappear."

"I must admit that it is rather humiliating to need help to sit up in bed."

"Enjoy my help while it lasts. You will always have my coaching and encouragement, but when your strength returns, you will no longer have my physical help. Progress will happen much more quickly without it."

Emma and Julie entered Jacob's room each carrying a plate of bacon, eggs, and toast. Jacob could not help but notice his plate was piled higher than Luke's. He remembered Luke's comment that he needed to eat more protein and realized this was Emma's effort to help him heal.

Emma smiled, "Look who's sitting up this morning. Are you hungry?"

Right on cue, Jacob's stomach growled. "Yes, I guess I am." Emma handed him his plate first, which he balanced on his lap. Then she handed him his fork. "Thank you, Mama."

"You're welcome." She noticed that his left forearm was carefully hidden beneath the blanket. With it obscured from view, he looked perfectly whole, though still a bit paler than usual. Silently, she prayed, *Lord, help me always to see him as whole. As humans, we are so often swayed by outward appearances, but inwardly, he is the same Jacob he was yesterday morning. Like Heidi prayed, help me know how to encourage him.*

Luke accepted his plate from Julie and gave her a quick kiss as a "thank you." Julie scrunched up her face.

"What is that expression for?" Luke asked.

"Your whiskers are prickly."

With a teasing twinkle in his eyes, Luke rubbed his chin and replied, "Oh, I'm thinking about growing a beard." When Julie dipped her chin and lifted her eyebrows, he laughed, "Then again, maybe not."

Julie gestured toward their patient. "Jacob would look ruggedly handsome with a beard. You would just look scruffy."

"And prickly," Luke added.

"Yes, and prickly."

"Jacob, did you hear that? You're ruggedly handsome, and I'm scruffy. What do you think about that?"

Jacob gave half a smile and answered between bites, "I'm staying out of this one."

"Wise man," Julie approved.

"Where is Matthew?" Luke asked.

"Emily is watching him for a bit. He's enamored with Katie, and with our little one on the way, spending time with an infant will help him know what to expect. Besides, I thought you might want my help for Jacob's dressing change."

"Yes, I will need you. Thank you for coming." After a few more mouthfuls of food, Luke mused, "Emily is so good with Matthew; he just adores her."

"Emily is good with children of all ages. She will be a wonderful mother."

"Is there news I don't know about?" Luke asked hopefully.

"No, not yet, but I keep hoping there will be soon."

Luke reached up and rested his hand on Julie's growing womb. "How is my other son?"

"Kicking and being generally rambunctious." Julie moved his hand over to the side of her belly just in time for the baby to kick it.

"Good and strong."

"So, you think the baby is a boy, do you?" Emma asked.

Luke winked at Julie before turning his gaze to Emma. "Actually, the Kiowa culture presumes every unborn baby is a boy until proven otherwise at birth. I'll be happy either way." He lowered his voice to a whisper, "If I had my choice, I think I'd choose a girl, though if she's as pretty as her mom, I'd have to improve my marksmanship skills to keep the boys away."

Jacob remarked dryly, "If you want lessons on how to be a protective father, just ask Mr. Müller." As soon as the words were out of his mouth, he regretted saying them. That protectiveness might just forbid Jacob from courting Heidi again.

Emma placed a gentle hand on Jacob's shoulder. She seemed to read his thoughts. "Johann Müller may be protective, but he loves Heidi and will want what is best for her. If he has any doubts about what is best, Heidi won't hesitate to let him know."

After the men had finished eating, Julie mixed some pain medicine for Jacob. When he had downed the liquid, Luke and Emma helped him back into a recumbent position. The four of them chatted while waiting for the analgesic to take effect.

About half an hour later, Luke spoke to Jacob. "Julie and I are going to remove and replace your bandages. This first dressing change may hurt some, but as long as we can keep infection away, each change to follow will get progressively easier." Jacob's only answer was a nod.

Julie slipped out to procure the supplies they would need, and Luke walked to the other side of the bed and uncovered Jacob's left arm. Emma sat in the vacant chair and held Jacob's hand. When Julie reentered the room, Jacob turned his head toward Emma and closed his eyes.

He had still not looked at his injured limb. Subconsciously, perhaps he thought that looking at his arm would be admitting that the amputation had indeed happened, and the loss of his hand was real and irreparable. If he could deny it long enough, maybe the truth wouldn't seem so overwhelming.

Thanks to his voracious reading, Luke understood Jacob's reaction. He and Julie worked gently but efficiently to remove the surgical bandage. Luke examined Jacob's arm closely. Though bruised and swollen, the arm showed no signs of infection. The incision was cleaned and dried, and a new dressing was applied.

"Jacob, you do not need to watch, but listen as I describe these movement exercises to Emma." He had Emma's full attention. "Every couple of hours, have Jacob straighten and bend his elbow a few times slowly like this." He held his brother's upper arm and forearm and demonstrated the motion. "Is that painful at all, Jacob?"

"No, just stiff."

"Good. Then move his entire arm from the shoulder in a circle." Luke held Jacob's left shoulder with his right hand and rotated Jacob's arm in a smooth circular pattern. "Start with about five repetitions of each exercise." He addressed Jacob, "The goal is for you to do these exercises independently, but for now, let Emma guide your arm." Looking back at Emma, he asked, "Do you have any questions?"

"No, take Julie home and get some sleep."

Luke searched Julie's face and responded when he received her approving nod, "Actually, I'm going to sleep in the other infirmary room next door. If you need anything, come get me."

"Wouldn't you sleep better at home?" Emma asked. "Doc should be here soon."

Julie responded for him, "No, he will rest much better knowing he's close by if you need him. Since we brought lunch with us this morning, I'll come back with dinner." She looked over at Luke and added, "And a shaving kit."

The effect of the pain medicine was causing Jacob's eyelids to droop. Luke told him, "You get some rest, too."

Luke followed Julie out of the room and wrapped his arms around her. "Thank you for letting me stay. I love you." He leaned in to kiss her, and she giggled quietly and pulled away. He smiled and reached up a hand to hold the back of her head. "Come back here. Prickles or no prickles, I need a kiss." Julie granted his wish before they parted.

When Julie arrived later that afternoon, Emma excused herself to heat up the dinner on Doc's stove and Luke once again positioned himself in the chair beside Jacob's bed. Jacob was sleeping, brought into a sedative state by the pain medicine Luke had given him after lunch. Luke took this opportunity to enter the throne room of heaven on his brother's behalf. As he finished his prayer, Jacob began stirring.

Jacob rolled toward his right side and pushed up with his right arm to a semi-sitting position. When he moved, his left arm left its hiding place beneath the blanket. His eyes were drawn to the stark white bandages. He wanted to avert his gaze, but it locked onto the shortened appendage, and he could not turn his eyes away. For a long moment, Jacob just stared at the end of his left arm, flooded with emotions.

Always observant, Luke witnessed the changes in his brother's expression, inferring the turmoil that must be going on within his soul. Luke was not about to shatter the silence with words.

Within Jacob wrestled anger, sadness, and self-pity; but he could no longer deny the absence of his left hand. His eyes shone with tears that he refused to shed. Pulling his focus from his arm, Jacob sought his brother's face, finding compassion in Luke's blue eyes.

Luke reached out and laid a hand on Jacob's shoulder. He gently asked, "Was that the first time you have looked at your arm since the accident?"

Unable to find his voice, Jacob simply nodded slowly, clenching his jaw in his attempt to control his turbulent emotions. He closed his eyes and leaned his head back against the headboard. Two tears escaped and spilled onto his cheeks, and he turned his face away from Luke.

Luke's hand remained on Jacob's shoulder, speaking volumes without saying a word. Luke understood that no words were the right ones. Jacob needed love and support, not empty platitudes.

After several minutes, Jacob's scratchy voice asked, "Luke, how do I fight the self-pity that wants to overwhelm me?"

Luke paused, unsure how to respond. Then, as if Someone had whispered in his ear, Luke suddenly had the answer he needed to give. "Focus on all the other blessings in your life and choose to be thankful for them. Self-pity and gratitude cannot abide each other's company."

## CHAPTER 27
## *Recovery*

"God, I'm struggling. Help me find the good. I don't want to be angry."

A knock on the doorframe interrupted Jacob's silent prayer. He lifted his eyes to find Luke leaning in. "Are you up for visitors? Nathan and Thad are here asking to see you."

Jacob scraped his hand down his face and felt the scruff of his three-day-old beard. "Do I look too scary?"

"I don't know," Luke teased. "Your hair is a little wild."

Running his splayed fingers across his scalp to tame his wayward tresses, Jacob rebutted, "My hair is amazing; this style took me all night." He shifted his weight and used his right hand against the mattress to boost his hips toward the headboard. That he could accomplish this feat independently seemed like little consolation compared to the mountain of adjustments ahead of him, but it was still something to be grateful for. He'd add that to his mental list.

Luke motioned to Nathan, who held Thad's hand and paused in the doorway. Thad looked up at Jacob with big eyes, and giant tears dripped onto his cheeks. "I'm so sorry you lost your hand because of me. Thank you for saving my life."

Jacob's heart melted for the little boy. He beckoned Thad with his hand. "Come here." Thad approached hesitantly, fear etched in his features, but Jacob pulled him up into his lap with his right arm and hugged him. "I'm just glad you are all right." Thad wrapped his arms around Jacob's neck and sobbed. Jacob wept with him.

When Thad's tears turned to hiccoughs, he managed, "Th-thank you for n-not being m-mad at m-me."

Jacob closed his eyes and clenched his eyelids. The ugly thought that Thad's recklessness was the cause of the tragedy had crossed his mind several times. He determined to stuff that thought away and bury it deep. Thad was just being a curious boy; he never meant to cause any harm. He certainly didn't need to carry the weight of Jacob's grief on his little shoulders.

Nathan stood a few paces away trying to hide the tears that overflowed his lashes. Undoubtedly, he was feeling the weight of guilt, too. Jacob struggled to find some words of comfort. "Sometimes, hard and unexpected things happen in our lives—things that leave us sad and broken. We just have to trust that God is powerful enough to make something beautiful out of the broken pieces."

Glancing up at Nathan, Jacob heard him whisper the words, "Thank you for saving my son."

A few minutes after they left, Luke stepped in. "You gave them words of hope and comfort when you are hurting. That took courage."

"My hand is gone, and there is nothing they can do to get it back. To allow them to carry the guilt of my amputation would just be cruel."

"Remember your words, Jacob. Let them encourage your heart, too. God is the Master Potter; He will take your broken pieces and make a masterpiece."

James entered the barn just in time to hear a clatter and a grunt. Following the sound, he found Josiah flat on his back with beads of sweat on his forehead. On his left arm was a thick wool sock. With a smirk, James extended his arm to pull him up. "What are you doing?"

"Trying to figure out how to saddle and mount a horse with one hand."

"Your plan needs more finesse," James teased.

Josiah's ever-present smile was conspicuously absent. "Very funny. This is serious. Jacob will be lost if he cannot ride horseback. I have to find a way for him to mount independently."

James considered him more closely and noticed his reddened eyes and disheveled hair. "Have you had any sleep these last few days?"

"Not much, but I have to figure this out." The fabric of his steady composure was beginning to fray.

Putting his hand on Josiah's shoulder, James took a sobering breath. "You are a loyal brother, but you are not alone. Let me help you. What can I do?"

A sheen of moisture on Josiah's lashes was a visible testimony of the tumble of emotions in the midst of his fatigue. He nodded and turned back to his horse. "Help me think. If you couldn't use your left hand, how would you grab the horn to mount? Using the right hand doesn't work because all the weight ends up on the left side with not enough momentum to get the right leg over before you fall on your back."

"That sounds like personal experience." James planted his hands on his hips and studied the horse for a couple of minutes. "Why would you have to hold the horn?" Josiah stared blankly at him. "Hand me the sock." Josiah pulled it off, and James slid it over his left hand. "Okay, Jacob is shorter than I am, but he's strong. If we can get his weight over the saddle, he should be able to swing his leg around."

James used his right hand to hold the stirrup until his left foot was secure within it. Then he twisted toward the horse's body and grabbed the cantle with his right hand and used his left arm to anchor between the pommel and the horn. When he pushed off the ground with his right foot, he stood on his left foot and leaned his torso over the saddle while simultaneously shifting his right hand to the right side of the pommel and swinging his right leg over the horse's hindquarters.

Seeing James sitting tall in the saddle lifted the heavy burden of grief from Josiah's shoulders in an instant. Throwing his hands in the air, he cheered. "Yes! You did it!"

"We're not done yet. Hand me the reins." Josiah complied, and James struggled to manage Gawain with only one hand. "We need to get Julie involved. She can train Shadow to neck rein. He's a smart horse; he can do it. Then Shadow will be much easier to control with just one hand."

"Jacob won't want knotted reins," Josiah contended.

"If it means he can ride and let the horn anchor his reins to free his right hand to lasso steer, he'll learn to love knotted reins."

---

With the threat of imminent infection now minimal, Doc and Luke released Jacob from the clinic. Doc let him borrow his bathing tub for a good wash, and Josiah brought him a clean pair of pants and one of James' flannel shirts, since his wider sleeves would better accommodate the bandages on his left arm.

Josiah hadn't visited him much at the clinic, but he had obviously been busy thinking about him, for he was able to walk Jacob through getting dressed with one hand. Managing buttons was frustrating, but he'd get the hang of it.

What would have taken him five minutes took him over twenty, and having his little brother teaching him how to dress didn't help his growing frustration. *Breathe, Jacob. Learning new things takes time and patience.* Even climbing into the buggy took several tries, and his attempts were awkward at best, but he made it, and landing his backside on the seat felt like a small triumph.

When he and Josiah arrived at the ranch, everyone was at the Emma's house to meet them. As soon as his feet landed on solid ground, cheers of "Happy Birthday!" surrounded him.

Jacob turned to Josiah. "What day is it?"

"October 8th, but Emma didn't think you'd mind waiting an extra day so we could all have the party here."

*His birthday.* With his life turned upside down, he had completely forgotten. All of his family, the Carters, and the Müllers were there to celebrate with him. They loved him just the way he was. Jacob felt the sting of accruing moisture in his eyes, but he fervently willed it away.

At the table, though Heidi usually sat to his left, today she took the chair to his right. The significance of that change was made evident when everyone held hands to pray. Once again, their palms were a handbreadth apart, but she had made a point to sit next to his hand, a hand that would one day be able to hold hers if his dreams came true.

Emma filled the table with meatloaf, mashed potatoes, and green beans—with apple pie for dessert, of course—all foods easily managed with one hand. With his left arm tucked under the table, he could pretend he was whole for a little while, and Emma's compassion had given him this gift.

His favorite gift was the square canvas Heidi presented him. *Heidi's Meadow* was a poignant reminder of their first picnic and the hope of the view from their home to come. The field of wildflowers wafting softly in the breeze included a pair of fluttering Monarch butterflies chasing each other from flower to flower. "This is your *Birch Trees*, Jacob. A reminder that after the winters of life, spring will come—and spring will be glorious."

"Thank you, Heidi. This is a perfect gift." He lifted his gaze from the canvas to her eyes. "I will treasure it forever."

"And just like that, all of our gifts pale in comparison," moaned Tim in mock dejection. "I could paint a picture."

"Your stick figures are so lovely," Laura laughed.

"At least someone recognizes my talent." Tim gestured to his wife like she was the only smart one at the table.

Jacob grinned and winked at Heidi. "Don't mind Tim. He's just jealous."

With a dramatic sigh, Tim admitted, "I have been officially replaced as the family's best artist."

Leaning toward Heidi's ear, Jacob whispered, "You know Tim likes you when he teases you and claims you as a part of the family."

"I know how much you admire him, so I'm relieved that he approves of me."

"How could he not?"

## CHAPTER 28
## *Anger*

The pendulum of Jacob's emotions swung from the cheerfulness of the birthday celebration to the frustration of evening chores. Milking time doubled. Using a shovel to muck stalls required him to tuck the handle under his armpit for leverage; even then, the simple task left him huffing and sweating.

When Luke met him near the tack room, Jacob knew his brother could see the fire in his eyes. With his brows pinched in concern, Luke laid a hand on Jacob's upper back. "Hey, take it easy. Remember that your body is still recovering from the blood loss. Do what you can, but don't be discouraged. Every task will get easier as your strength returns."

Not trusting the words that might escape his mouth if he opened it, Jacob just grunted his acknowledgment. He reached for the wheelbarrow, but hunching over to grab the left handle with the bend of his elbow made maneuvering it unwieldy at best.

All of the chores he used to accomplish so easily had now become challenging. *Give yourself grace. Give yourself time.* Jacob tried to empower himself for the adjustments ahead, but his frustration was escalating rapidly.

---

Josiah entered the bunkhouse an hour after chores ended with a gleam in his eyes. "Your wheelbarrow problem is solved."

"Oh?"

"I attached a leather loop to the left handle. If you slip your forearm in, you'll be able to stand straight and control it more easily."

Jacob knew he should be grateful for Josiah's effort on his behalf, but the need for modifications at all grated his emotions like sandpaper on an open wound. He slammed the copy of *The Cattleman's Magazine* down onto the table and stood abruptly. "I'm going for a walk."

Jacob stomped around the barnyard, trying in vain to release the building tension in his heart. When he tried to pray, he felt as if his words were landing on the dirt in front of him and getting ground into bits by his boots. His feet carried him to James and Emily's house, and he knocked softly, not wanting to wake Katie. When Emily answered the door, he asked, "Is Tim here?"

A moment later, Tim joined him on the front porch. Jacob stared down at Tim's sock-covered feet. "I'm struggling, Tim."

"I'd be surprised if you weren't."

"That's not very encouraging."

"Jacob," Tim blew an audible stream of air, "you have endured a life-changing trauma. You cannot ignore it, but you must rise above it. You didn't ask for this challenge, and the road ahead will be challenging, but God will be with you every day, every step of the way. He has not forgotten you or forsaken you. He will give you the strength you need, and he will give you joy."

Jacob leaned back against the porch railing, and Tim moved beside him. "Enduring this trial will tempt you to to feel alone and abandoned. You must remind yourself constantly that you have an army of support in us your family, your lady and her family, and Seth, not to mention Pastor Kendrick and your church family."

"Don't let Satan lie to you. You are loved. You are whole. You have been and will continue to be used by God as His beloved son for His purpose."

"I love you, Jacob. You are my brother, and I will always support you." Tim reached for Jacob and pulled him into a bear hug. "You will get through this, and you will become a better man for it."

"We're heading home to the Rafter C in the morning, but I will keep praying for you, and I'll only be a letter away."

---

By the time Jacob returned to the bunkhouse, he was able to genuinely thank Josiah for his creative help, but the next morning's chores only provided more fodder for his growing infuriation.

Jacob's anger was a powder keg ready to explode. All it needed was the right spark, and the unlikely spark came in the shape of a pitchfork.

Jacob battled with the pitchfork, all attempts to toss hay into Shadow's stall landing more hay at his feet than in its intended target. He growled as one forkful after another proved how incapable he was. As the struggle continued, his mounting frustration strangled him until the force of it spewed out of him. "Where is that brother who cut off my hand? Luke! Where are you?"

Luke entered the barn and stood silently, even when Jacob marched up to him and stood toe to toe, yelling in indignation.

"You did this to me! You crippled me! I can't even pitch hay! You have ruined my life!"

Jacob's anger so clouded his vision that he could not see the speechless anguish on Luke's face or the tears that dripped onto his cheeks and off his chin. Luke just stood there and absorbed the brunt of Jacob's tirade, taking the responsibility for his surgical decision while his heart broke for the brother he loved.

Jacob turned away from Luke and threw the pitchfork against the wall with all his might. James stepped up to Jacob and reached to grasp his shoulder, but Jacob twisted away from him. James pleaded, "Tell us how we can help."

With fire still raging in his eyes, Jacob faced his oldest brother, his voice still at full volume. "I don't want your help! I don't want your sympathy! I don't want your pity! I want my hand back!" When Jacob turned to exit the barn, he deliberately rammed his shoulder into Luke, who was still standing where Jacob had left him.

James' ire flared, and he started to follow, but Luke grabbed his arm to stop him. "Let him go. His worst enemy is himself. Give him some time to fight this battle. We need to pray that Jacob will allow God to fight on his side, for only then will he be victorious."

James leveled his gaze to Luke's. "What Jacob said to you wasn't true."

"Yes, it was. I'm the one who performed the amputation with Doc. The surgery saved his life, but I have to live with the consequences of my decision. I just pray he will one day forgive me." Luke wiped his sleeve across his face. "I'll ask Julie to do his dressing change tonight."

Jacob found himself trampling the grass near the swimming hole as his anger had his feet stamping a forceful step. When his pace slowed to a stop, his right hand was clenched in a fist, his brows were drawn together and low over his eyes, and his tight jaw pulled his frown into something hideous.

When he neared the edge of the river, he caught his reflection in the smooth water of the swimming hole, the ugliness of his anger a dreadful shock. All at once, an arrow of shame pierced his heart, and he collapsed to his knees.

Jacob was angry. The kind of angry that simmered in his bones as a frustration gradually building into a rolling boil that overflowed and burned himself and anyone nearby. He knew he was angry. He knew he didn't want to be angry. And that made him even more angry. Jacob growled at the irony.

"God, help me!" Jacob instinctively moved to clasp his hands in prayer. When even that simple act failed, he clenched his fist again and pounded it onto his thigh. "God, I can't even pray!" The tears fell then and turned to sobs.

When his tears ran dry, Jacob lifted his eyes and spied Heidi's Meadow across the river. *Heidi.* Invisible fingers pulled him to that special place, one shared with the woman he loved, the woman who filled him with courage and hope.

He stepped onto the log bridge as he had so many hundreds of times before and started across. When his balance shifted, he extended his arms for stability, but the few missing pounds on his left arm worked against him. He bobbled and tried to regain his footing, but he fell to his right side and splashed into the river.

Jacob stood, the water only chest deep, and stared at the wooden span as if it had betrayed him. Could he do nothing right? Was he to be a complete failure?

After he trudged though the water and up the grassy bank to where he started, Jacob plopped onto the ground, utterly spent. As he stared across to the meadow, the hope of Heidi felt just as unreachable.

## CHAPTER 29
## *Selfless Love*

Jacob loved Heidi with everything in him. The longer he stared at the unattainable meadow named in her honor, the more convinced he became that she deserved better than an angry man. Letting her go would mean losing his heart in addition to his hand. His body was already broken; how much more could he hurt with a broken heart, too?

Heidi deserved a man who was whole, both in body and in spirit, and he loved her too much to let her settle for him. His heart was already ripping in twain with the thought of it, but releasing her from their courtship was the right thing to do.

The sun was setting, the colors brushed across the sky like a grand canvas. Even the heavens reminded him that the artist he loved would no longer be his.

---

First, Jacob needed to find Luke and beg his forgiveness. He stopped by the barn, but its only occupants were the animals who called the barn home. Making up his mind to visit Luke at home, Jacob pointed his feet that direction but stopped short when he identified Julie riding toward him on Cinnamon.

"Hey." Jacob lifted his hand in greeting. Julie pulled her mount to a stop near him. Cinnamon nudged her nose against Jacob's chest, and he rubbed her face.

"Luke asked me to do your dressing change tonight." When she had dismounted and grasped her bag of supplies, she gestured toward the bunkhouse. "Shall we?"

Nodding his assent, Jacob led the way to his living quarters and opened the door for Julie. He lowered himself onto the bench and laid his left arm on the table.

Julie's brow furrowed. "What happened?"

"I fell into the river." The words were simple, but the meaning behind them resonated deeply. Both Julie and Josiah understood their significance.

"Then let's clean your incision and get your arm rewrapped." Julie gathered her supplies and made quick work of her task.

When she finished, Jacob asked, "Is Luke mad at me?"

"No, Jacob. He loves you, and he's grieving for you. The decision to amputate your hand weighs heavily on him. I was there, Jacob. Your hand was mangled and mostly severed. The amputation saved your life. He sent me tonight because he did not want to hurt you further."

"Please tell Luke—Tell him that I'm sorry for my vindictive rant, and that I love him, too. I'll tell him again when I see him face-to-face."

"He already knows, but I'll tell him anyway." Julie gave him a smile and slipped outside.

---

Jacob had hoped to see Luke during chores the following morning, but he had been called away early for a medical emergency. His conversation with his doctor brother would have to wait.

Determining to be more patient with his clumsy efforts, Jacob listened to Josiah's suggestions, and he realized his little brother had put a lot of time and ingenuity into finding alternative ways to accomplish his manual tasks.

Julie entered the barn as the brothers were finishing up and nodded at Josiah, whose face broke into a grin. Josiah's excitement bubbled out in words. "Jacob, Luke says we can tell you about a project we've all been working on."

"What is it?"

"We've figured out how you can bridle, saddle, mount, and ride Shadow independently. You'll even be able to wrangle cattle."

Jacob's curious expression transformed into a hopeful one. "How?"

Josiah and Julie walked him through the one-handed steps to bridle and saddle his horse. "When James mounted, he was able to wedge his left forearm between the pommel and saddle horn, but mine always slips. So, I added this loop hanging from the horn at the right length to support your elbow if you need it." Then Josiah demonstrated how to mount.

With his balance still off, Jacob tried a few times before he was successful, but once he settled in his saddle, his smile erupted.

Julie stepped forward and handed him the reins, her hand covering the knot. "Jacob, hear me out. I know you don't like knotted reins, but they will give you complete freedom. I have trained Shadow to neck rein, and only a slight pressure of the rein against his neck will turn him. When you need to wrangle, your saddle horn will hold your reins for you, thereby freeing up your hand to use your lariat."

Though Jacob was tempted to frown over the knotted reins,

the rest of her monologue restored the stolen hope that he would one day work the ranch on horseback again.

"When you ride Shadow, start with a walk until you get the feel of the new steering technique. At first, you'll have to consciously think about it so you don't fall into old habits."

"Got it. May I go for a ride now?"

Julie stepped backward and extended her hand in a gesture toward the wide open door of the barn. "Off you go. Be careful."

"Yes, Mom." Julie's laughter followed him out into the sunlight. Hope had been reborn.

---

Later that afternoon, Jacob prayed and agonized over what to say to Heidi to make his mission hurt her less. In the end, he decided a concise explanation would be best. Heidi answered his knock and stepped onto the porch to meet him.

Heidi smiled, and his resolve nearly melted into a puddle at his feet. Jacob inwardly reminded himself that this decision was for her best. He loved her too much to desire anything less for her.

Jacob plunged ahead. "You deserve a man like your father. One who can protect you and provide for you. Not someone who has become half a man."

Her smile vanished. Fire gleamed in Heidi's eyes as she pointed her finger at his chest. She reached out but stopped an inch shy of touching his flannel shirt. Strangely, Jacob could feel the pressure on his chest just the same.

"You, Jacob Collins, are not half a man. Yes, you are missing a hand, but who you truly are is found within. You are strong and brave. You are selfless and loyal. Somehow you have tricked yourself into thinking I would be better off without you. You are wrong. You will not get rid of me that easily, for I'm not going anywhere."

The demure response Jacob had been expecting was nowhere in sight. The frustration he probably should be feeling after agonizing over this conversation had been replaced by a growing admiration for the woman standing before him. That Heidi was willing to stand up to him had him biting back a smile, but he wasn't willing to concede the argument just yet.

The brief glimpse of humor in Jacob's eyes vanished, leaving a look of pain in its wake. Heidi softened her tone. "Jacob, what is it? Please tell me what is really troubling you."

Heidi deserved honesty. Being open about his flaws had never been Jacob's strong suit. The only person he had ever been able to bare his soul to was his mother. When she and his dad died, Jacob had become Josiah's protector, and protectors should never show their weaknesses to anyone. Right? Now he wasn't so sure. His greatest desire was to become Heidi's husband, her protector, but he also craved the trust that only came through complete transparency.

Jacob stuffed his hand into his pants pocket to curtail the temptation to reach for Heidi's hand, for his desire for a physical connection was strong. When Jacob spoke, his voice was quiet but intense. "Heidi, before I gave my heart to God, anger was my first response in almost every situation. Anger defined me." Heidi did not avert her gaze, encouraging him to continue. "God changed me—made me a new creation."

"Since the accident, I have been battling with anger constantly. Quite frankly, that scares me. I don't want you to be bound to an angry man, even in courtship. I refuse to say the words my heart wants to tell you, for this is neither the right time or place, but I do care for you—deeply. Please grant me time for the Lord to work on this heart of mine. I want to be the man worthy of your trust—perhaps even your love—but right now I am not he."

Jacob's words soaked into Heidi's heart like a steady rain on a spring flower garden. The roots of her love and respect for Jacob anchored more deeply. Instead of gray clouds, she saw blossoming color. He had said he was battling with anger; the battle itself was evidence of the Holy Spirit's presence in his heart.

She knew the words he refrained from saying, words that sang in her own heart. If there had been any doubt, he had openly declared he wanted to be *the* man worthy of her trust, not *a* man worthy of her trust. Beyond that, she had not missed the gift of his trust in her. The man always brimming with confidence had allowed himself to become completely vulnerable, a side of Jacob she guessed very few had seen.

"When you are ready to be my suitor again, I will be here waiting. Until then, I am still your friend. Don't be a stranger."

"Thank you for understanding. Pray for me," Jacob requested, his eyes pleading.

"Ardently, I promise."

Jacob lifted the corner of his mouth enough to show off the dimple in his cheek before he turned and mounted his horse. Heidi remained planted where she stood until Jacob had ridden out of sight. The front door opened and closed behind her, and heavy footsteps stopped beside her. She glanced up at her papa.

"Do you still think Jacob is God's chosen man for you?"

"More than ever."

Johann's stoic expression softened. "Good."

---

Jacob woke abruptly, not sure in the lingering haze of sleep if it had been his scream or the intense pain in his left hand that had launched him from sound sleep to sitting upright clenching his left forearm with his right hand.

Josiah landed immediately beside him, his face whiter than his nightshirt. "What is it?"

"My hand is cramping! It hurts! Make it stop!" Whether the cause of his nonsensical words was the insanity caused by the searing pain or his lack of coffee at such an early hour mattered not.

Josiah jumped into his pants and scurried for the door. "I'll get Luke! Hang in there!" He diverted to the ranch house and woke Emma before he ran full out for Luke's house. Emma fired two rifle shots as a signal, and Luke already had Dakota saddled when he arrived.

"What's going on?" Luke demanded.

"Jacob is screaming that his left hand is cramping. But that cannot be, can it?"

"Phantom pain is very real. Let's go." Josiah mounted behind Luke, and Dakota carried the brothers back to the bunkhouse.

Jacob's vain attempt to cover his anguish had Emma standing bewildered in her robe. Luke burst through the door, disheveled but alert, with Josiah on his heels. Luke delegated, "Jacob, sit at the table and lay both arms on it. Emma, grab a towel. Josiah, pull the mirror off the wall."

Emma handed Luke the towel, and he covered Jacob's left arm. "Jacob, breathe."

"My hand hurts!" Jacob's face was scrunched in agony and unwanted tears squeezed from the outer corners of his eyes.

"I know it does, but I need you to breathe. Emma, heat some water for willow bark tea. Josiah, hand me the mirror." Luke set the bottom of the mirror on the table between Jacob's arms and leaned it so Jacob could see the reflection of his right arm in the mirror.

"Jacob, I need you to trust me. Focus all of your attention on the reflection of your arm in the mirror." Jacob complied. "Do not move your eyes from that reflection, but I want you to clench your right hand into a tight fist, as tight as you can. Good. Watch the reflection. Slowly release your fist. Good. Straighten your hand and wiggle and stretch your fingers."

Sometime during those bizarre instructions, Jacob's scream stopped. Beads of sweat covered his forehead, and his breaths were short panting respirations. "Keep your eyes on the reflection, and slow down your breathing. Inhale. Exhale. That's it."

Several minutes later, Jacob looked up at Luke in bewilderment. "What just happened?"

Luke settled across the table from him. "You were born with two hands, and your unconscious brain still thinks your left one is there. The pain you felt is called phantom pain, sensory impulses sending messages from a hand that is no longer there. It will come without warning, but it will rarely be this intense. Sometimes the feeling may be more of an itch."

"What did you do with the mirror?"

"What did you see in the reflection?"

Jacob's voice was tinged with incredulity as the realization hit him. "My left hand."

"Exactly. Your eyes needed to focus on your left hand and see it unclenching in order to communicate with your brain. Only then was the cramp broken."

"Thank you, Luke. I'm so sorry for earlier. I was so angry I couldn't even see straight. I should never have lashed out at you. I was wrong. Please forgive me."

"I do forgive you, Jacob. Your surgery is the hardest decision I've ever had to make. Please forgive me for amputating your hand."

"You are forgiven." Three words. Three powerful words that imparted freedom from guilt and bitterness. Jacob was free.

## CHAPTER 30
## The Protector

A man with shoulder length unkempt hair, dirt encrusted clothes, a Colt pistol strapped to his hip, and a jagged scar that ran from the corner of his eye to his chin entered Mayor Montgomery's office and faced Peter. "I have found Johann Müller and his family. I have come to claim my reward."

Peter's bland scowl altered into a menacing sneer. "Where are they?"

"A little town called Prairie Hills in Oklahoma Territory. They own a dairy farm there." He pulled a folded paper from his vest pocket and plunked it on the desk between them. "A copy of the deed."

Peter unfolded and perused the document. "How did you find them?"

"Some contacts that owe me favors, a few well-placed bribes, and blackmailing the land office clerk."

"Very resourceful of you."

"I'll take my money. Now." The mercenary growled.

"Of course, you will." Peter pulled a wad of cash from his

vest pocket and counted out three hundred dollars into the man's filthy palm.

"Pleasure doing business with you."

"Likewise." The informant exited, temporally easing the tension in the room, and Peter called, "Simmons!" The rotund balding man appeared. "Arrange my travel to Prairie Hills, Oklahoma."

"Right away, sir." The sniveling man backed away and hastened to do Peter's bidding.

Peter turned toward his father. "Finally. Heidi will be mine."

---

Sunday morning dawned crisp and sunny. The chores were finished, and Jacob had donned his Sunday clothes, only needing help with his neck tie, and Josiah was already thinking up possible solutions for that. A little more than a week had passed since his conversation with Heidi. Jacob's inward turmoil was an active battle field, and his spirit longed to hear pastor preach truth from God's Word to his heart.

Jacob rode Shadow, adding another item to his grateful list. When he entered the church, he smiled and nodded at Heidi sitting a few rows up from the back. Then he continued up the aisle and scooted into the pew next to Josiah.

Pastor Kendrick's text was from 2 Kings chapter 5, the story of Naaman the leper. "Naaman was a commanding officer for the king of Syria. He was a man of valor, victorious in battle. The king of Syria respected him, and the king of Israel feared him."

"Because of his wealth and stature, Naaman sought every healing means available to cure his leprosy. But God was more concerned with his pride than his disease. When all other avenues failed, God used a servant girl to suggest that he visit Elisha, the prophet of the God of Israel."

"God then used a diplomatic letter from the king of Syria to the king of Israel to get Naaman to Elisha's house. Naaman expected honor and immediate healing. In lieu of meeting the officer personally, Elisha sent a lowly messenger to tell him to wash in the filthy Jordan River seven times."

"Naaman was angry because his pride had been dented. Part of his healing would be his heart, and that part couldn't be healed until he was humble. His servants who loved him convinced him to do as Elisha had bidden. When he humbled himself and obeyed, he was healed, both from his leprosy and from his sin."

"Notice that when he returned to Elisha with gifts, he professed that 'I know there is no God in all the earth but in Israel; so accept now a present from your servant.' He not only proclaimed God to be the one and only true God, but also declared himself to be His servant."

"Naaman's physical disease was fatal from a medical standpoint, but his pride was fatal from a spiritual standpoint. While both required healing, his pride had been what separated him from God and His perfect purpose for his life."

"Is your pride separating you from God's purpose for your life? If so, repent, ask for forgiveness, and humble yourself before the God you serve. He desires to use you; He desires to fill your life with joy and peace, even in the midst of tragedy."

The sermon was still drawing to a close, but Jacob could not wait. He bowed his head and entreated the God of Heaven. He now saw his anger for what it was: fear and pride. "Dear Father, my heart is open to You. Forgive my pride. I am nothing without You, but with You, I am strong and victorious. Help me to trust You more. Guide me, for my desire is to fulfill Your purpose in my life. I don't know why Your plan included me losing my hand, but I pray You will help me to accept it and grow closer to You because of it. Make me a man You will be proud of. In My Savior's Name, Amen."

The millstone that had been dragging Jacob's spirit deep underwater toward anger and bitterness broke away, and he floated to the surface and gulped the fresh air of forgiveness. Tim's recent exhortation replayed in his mind: "You are loved. You are whole. You have been and will continue to be used by God as His beloved son for His purpose."

By the time Jacob opened his eyes, most of the congregation had meandered from the building, likely heading for home and Sunday dinner. He sniffed and wiped his sleeve under his nose while he blinked away the sheen of moisture that had gathered on his eyes. His gaze lifted from his boots and ran right into his favorite pair of blue eyes.

Heidi's smile seeped through every pore of his being and ratcheted his heart rate as if he were a school boy facing his first crush. But this was no crush. Jacob's heart brimmed with love for this woman.

"Hi." Jacob's raspy tone revealed the proof of his spiritual battle, and his genuine smile announced his victory.

"Hi, back." Heidi lifted the carved box Jacob had given her for her birthday and offered it to him. When his brow furrowed, she explained with a hint of levity, "I thought you might like to borrow this. Within it lies verses on parchment. Most of them were penned by the man I most admire, but I have added a few of my own as well."

Her levity dissipated into ardency. "These verses have been such an encouragement to me these last several months, and I desire to share that same encouragement with you." She donned a matronly expression. "Take care of my box. I expect it to be returned in pristine condition."

The edges of Jacob's mouth turned upward, and the teasing twinkle in his eyes mirrored hers. "Yes, ma'am." When he received the box, his expression sobered. "Pastor's sermon this morning was meant for me. My heart, like Naaman's, was angry because it was full of pride and hurt and fear. I have confessed my sin of pride and found forgiveness."

"And now your heart feels lighter, doesn't it?"

"Yes, it does." Jacob inhaled a deep cleansing breath. "Heidi, may I be your suitor again?"

"Yes, Jacob. In my heart, you never stopped being my suitor."

Ingrid Müller approached them. "Did you ask him?"

Heidi's eyes widened. "Oh, I forgot! Seth Carter and his family have invited our family for Sunday dinner, and he extended the invitation to you, if you'd like to join us."

"Only if you'll let me walk over with you." Jacob winked and received a shy nod in return. "Great, I'll catch Emma to let her know I'll be dining elsewhere this afternoon."

Emma had already left, but Jacob sent the message with Josiah before he stowed the engraved box in his saddlebag and fell in step with Heidi for the walk through town. Her family followed about thirty paces behind them to offer chaperoning and privacy.

---

Peter Montgomery climbed from the morning stage with a demeanor even more sour than usual. The vibrations of the long train rides, the swaying and rutted jolts of the stage, and the thick coat of dust left him in a decidedly foul mood. He muttered under his breath. "Prairie Hills. Finally. Who would ever choose to live in this primitive part of the country."

He donned his mask of amiability and procured an early lunch at the café. Wishing for something stronger to drink for the task ahead, he made due with his cup of black coffee. This town was so uncivilized. No wonder that German giant thought he could hide here and never be found.

A sudden influx of traffic on the street beyond his window caught his eye, and he heard the waitress comment to another customer, "Church just let out."

Perfect. Peter threw back the rest of the coffee in one gulp, left enough cash tucked underneath his plate to cover the cost of his meal, and ambled to the boardwalk to watch the passers-by.

Peter spotted his prey and strode from the opposite boardwalk to meet her. He stopped abruptly a few paces in front of Heidi, effectively blocking her path. His voice was menacing and his face contorted with disdain. "I told you I would find you."

Heidi did not need to say a single word for Jacob to know who this fiend was. The terror was written all over her face. Jacob instinctively began to reach out and pull her behind him, but he caught himself before he touched her and instead commanded. "Heidi, move behind me." When she froze, he positioned himself between Heidi and Peter, blocking her from her attacker's view.

Behind them, Johann paled and moved to surge forward but found himself inhibited by his wife's determined tug on his arm. "Let Jacob handle this, Johann. You'll be here if he needs reinforcements. Frederick, run for the sheriff." Johann opened his mouth and closed it as he battled with indecision. "Jacob will protect Heidi. He's stronger than you think."

Still on the street near the boardwalk, Peter growled, "Move out of my way. She belongs to me."

The fire of righteous anger lit Jacob's veins. "She will never belong to you."

The arrogant Montgomery sneer distorted Peter's face, and he spoke with condescension. "So you think she belongs to you?"

"Heidi will belong to whomever she chooses."

"She doesn't have the power to choose." He spat into the dirt. "Women are weak."

"Not Heidi," Jacob contended. "She is strong, courageous, fearless. She is creative, loyal, and determined."

"Ha! If she is so strong, why is she cowering behind you?"

"She is not cowering. She is trusting me to protect her. Strength is knowing whom to trust. She trusts God, and God has placed me right here in this moment to face you."

Peter took another half step forward. "I love her. She is mine."

"You have no idea what love is. Love protects. Love cherishes. Love is kind and unselfish."

Peter's gaze traveled to Jacob's empty cuff, and he scoffed. "You're a cripple! You think you can protect her with one hand?"

Jacob gritted his teeth in determination. "One hand is all it will take to defeat you."

"You think you're a tough guy, huh?" Peter scoffed.

"Fierce enough to fight for the one I love. I will protect her."

"You have no idea who you're dealing with."

"Try me."

The anger in Peter's eyes flamed just before his right hand flew toward Jacob's jaw. In one smooth combination move, Jacob's left arm blocked the punch, and his right fist met Peter's nose, crunching the bone and spewing blood. With one punch, Peter was on the ground clutching his nose. He drew his pistol, cocked it, and aimed it at Jacob's chest, "I will kill you and her father, and she will be mine!"

Jacob swung his leg in a kicking block that moved Peter's gun hand up and away. When the gun retorted, the bullet fired into the sky away from any onlookers.

Sheriff Will Stewart took that moment to grab Peter's arm

and hoist him to his feet. "You are under arrest for attempted murder, two counts of assault and battery, disorderly conduct, disturbing the peace, and threatening our town's citizens. You're going away for a very long time. That is, if the judge doesn't order you to hang." With that, Will hauled Peter toward the jail.

Jacob turned, his anger dissipated, and concern in his eyes. "Heidi, are you all right?"

Without warning, Heidi flung her arms around his torso. "You. I choose you."

Jacob lifted his arms as if in surrender and met the eyes of her papa who smiled and nodded his wordless permission. Jacob lowered his arms and rested them on Heidi's back in a protective embrace. When she didn't let go, he rested his head against her hair and breathed in her floral scent. She belonged here. In his arms. Forever. With his mouth an inch from her ear, he whispered, "I love you, Heidi."

Heidi's breath tickled his neck. "I love you, Jacob."

Her parents were still on the boardwalk looking on. Ingrid nudged Johann with her shoulder. "Do you have any doubts now?"

"Not one."

"Then give him your blessing already. Your daughter has chosen well."

"He hasn't asked me yet."

Ingrid moved her mischief-filled eyes from her husband to the embracing couple and back. "Oh, he will. Maybe this evening, or after lunch."

Jacob could feel Heidi's heartbeat against his chest. The thundering rhythm had slowed from a gallop to a brisk walking gait. Still she clung to him. Heidi was the one. The desire to make her his wife nearly overwhelmed him.

He whispered again, "If your father gives his blessing, may I ask you to marry me?"

The soft puff of air from her laugh wafted the bow of his necktie. "Are you asking if you can ask, or are you asking?"

"Both."

Heidi gradually released her hold on him. Jacob made deliberate eye contact with Mr. Müller. He lifted his right hand and wiggled his ring finger, only slightly perturbed that he couldn't hold up the correct hand for the question. He mouthed, "Blessing to marry?"

Johann nodded, and his wife nudged him in the ribs, grinning in victory. "Or now."

When Jacob and Heidi separated, Jacob trailed his hand down Heidi's left arm to her hand. Wrapping his fingers around it, he knelt before her. "Heidi, you are my one and my only. You are the one I have been waiting my entire life for. You are my angel, and I love you with everything I am. I will love you forever. Will you become my wife?"

Happy tears spilled onto Heidi's cheeks. "Yes! Oh, yes!"

Jacob was overcome with the desire to kiss her, but he wouldn't kiss her lips, not before the wedding. "May I kiss your hand?" At her nod of approval, his lips brushed the soft skin on the back of her hand. The touch was brief and gentle. She had chosen him, and he had chosen her, and all was right with the world.

## CHAPTER 31
## *Traditions*

Heidi had chosen a Christmas wedding. Jacob was delighted that he didn't have to wait until spring to make her his bride. When he examined their house's progress, however, he realized there was still a lot of framing and finishing work to get done. Every task he'd accomplished had taken longer than he expected with one arm, but he was determined that excellence was a higher priority than speed.

At least they had four outer walls and a roof, but other than the load-bearing timbers, the interior was bare. He so wanted the house to be complete before they moved in as husband and wife! Autumn was swiftly flowing into winter, and he was running out of time.

The jangle of a harness drew his attention to the front of the house, and he slipped his hammer into his belt and stepped down from the doorway to the ground, the leap a reminder of the porch and steps that were yet to be built.

Johann set his wagon brake, and the entire family disembarked. Jacob was happy to see them, of course, but he hadn't been expecting them. "To what do I owe the pleasure of this visit?"

Johann reached into the wagon bed and removed a large tool box. "We're here to help you, son." Within the next half hour, Jacob's family, the Carters, the Kendricks, as well as all of the men present at the Langes' farm on the day of Jacob's accident piled out of their wagons with tool belts and boxes.

Overcome by their generosity in giving of their time and labor, Jacob was reminded of the verse from the story of the record-breaking rebuilding of the wall of Jerusalem in Nehemiah 4:6, "So we built the wall . . . for the people had a mind to work."

And work they did. James the delegator did what he did best, and he soon had everyone organized and productive. Frederick and Thad were there, too, and Jacob didn't think he'd ever seen more willing errand boys.

By nightfall, the interior walls were framed and covered with wood planking, the bricks for the fireplace and part of the chimney had been laid, the front door was hung, and the floor of the porch and steps had been built. All of the interior structural elements of the house were done. Jacob mentally assessed what still needed to be done: porch posts and railings, chimney, interior doors, moldings and baseboards, kitchen cupboards, the cookstove, and furniture.

The only other outstanding item was his surprise for Heidi —a hand water pump in the kitchen. He'd read about the modern convenience and decided to include it in their home. If it worked as well as advertised, he guessed he'd be installing them in homes all over the ranch in the new year.

Jacob shook hands with every man who had come and thanked them profusely. Tom Wilson, the eldest of the group, took a gander at the sky and bellowed in his deep gruff voice, "If the red sky is right in its prediction of good weather tomorrow, we'll all be back to help you finish up, Jacob. You have been a blessing to all of us at one time or another, and we'd like to return the favor."

Jacob didn't trust his voice to speak, but he indicated his gratitude with a nod and a wave of farewell.

By the end of the following day, their home was finished. The men had even driven their wagons to Josiah's workshop, loaded up all of the furniture he had built for them, and delivered every piece to its proper place.

After the ladies had meticulously cleaned the interior, Heidi opened the chest her papa had hefted inside and began hanging curtains, laying colorful rugs, and making the bed with a hand-pieced wedding ring quilt. After all of the proper goodbyes had been said, Frederick plopped down on the sofa as the reluctant chaperone while Jacob and Heidi talked and dreamed and studied the walls for the placement of her paintings.

"If we framed some of your sketches, we could hang several together like a collection."

"Sketches!" Heidi exclaimed. "Thank you for reminding me." Completely missing Jacob's puzzled expression, she scurried over to her art bag and withdrew her sketchbook. Scooting Frederick over, she sat in the center of the sofa and gestured for Jacob to sit beside her.

"Something you said the other day—I don't remember your words exactly—but something to the effect that you wished you had a way to remember what your arm looked like before your accident. Anyway, I realized then that I'd never shown you my entire sketchbook." Jacob's brows were scrunched in concentration trying to find the main thoroughfare in her off-road conversational wandering.

In answer to his nonverbal question, Heidi uncovered the first sketch she had drawn of him—the close-up of his left side while he was milking. The focal point of the sketch, where the shaft of light from the barn window had shone on him, was his left hand. Jacob was struck speechless. He gently pulled the sketch toward him and studied the hand he had lost. Every detail was perfect—the raised veins on the back of his hand, the dirt under his short fingernails, even the small scar on the side of his thumb.

"Thank you, Heidi. You had no idea God would use your gift to be a blessing to me today, but He did. This sketch is a reminder that God used a severed hand to amputate the pride from my heart. He has taught me that a one-handed man can still be whole if he is fulfilling God's purpose for his life."

"Isn't that true for all of us, though?" Heidi softly added. "We may not all be missing an appendage, but we all have weaknesses that make us feel less than whole. What an encouraging thought that God still uses imperfect people to accomplish His perfect plan!"

"God turns our broken pieces into a masterpiece for His glory."

---

The late November day held a distinct chill with low, gray clouds and a blustery wind. Jacob's visit with Heidi at the Müllers' moved from the front porch to the warmth of the family room. "To honor my German heritage, there are some traditions I'd like to include in our wedding if you're amenable."

"Our wedding should be the ceremony of *your* dreams. As long as I still get you at the end, my dream will come true." Heidi's blush tipped his lips in a smile. "So what are these German wedding customs?"

"For one, Papa will leave a penny in my left shoe to symbolize the hope of a prosperous marriage. After the ceremony, my shoe will be auctioned off, and the guests will add coins to the shoe. You must supply the winning bid to win me and return my shoe."

"German brides usually wear black dresses, but since I prefer blue, my dress is a royal blue satin. Do you mind me not wearing white?"

"Not at all. When you wear blue, the hue of the fabric enhances the color of your eyes. Is there anything else you want to include?"

"Just one. After the ceremony, the ladies present hold the edges of a long lace veil while the bride and groom waltz beneath it." She paused before she bashfully asked, "Would you dance with me?"

His smile slipped, and her gaze followed his to the arms in his lap, his right hand wrapped around the end of his left forearm. "May I think about it and let you know?"

"Of course."

Hoping to soothe the awkward moment between Heidi and Jacob, Ingrid interjected, "What? You don't want to have a Polterabend or have the best man abduct the bride?"

"No, absolutely not!" Heidi chuckled.

Jacob's brows lifted in surprise. "What is a Polterabend?"

"It's a custom from medieval times. The wedding guests shatter ceramic plates and bowls to scare the evil spirits away from the ceremony. It's just a waste of good china."

"The abduction of the bride happens after the ceremony. The groom has to find where the best man has hidden her and pay him a ransom. I'd rather stay with you."

Heidi had his rapt attention, and his eyes softened to communicate that he'd rather have her with him, too. This wedding couldn't come soon enough.

Johann entered the house and shucked his winter coat. "Jacob! Just who I'm looking for. I need to leave town on business for a few days. Would you be willing to help Frederick with the milking until I return?"

"Sure, I'd be happy to help." Johann nodded and plodded

into the kitchen. Jacob whispered to his fiancée, "What was that about?"

Her expression was as confused as his own. "I have no idea."

Johann Müller left Prairie Hills for four days. No one seemed to know where went or why, but he returned and resumed his routine as if he'd never left. Something about the way his eyes twinkled when he thanked Jacob for covering for him made him wonder what that trip had been about.

---

Concern creased Luke's eyes when his gaze followed Julie while she waddled around the kitchen, her shoulders tilted backward to compensate for her extended belly. "The coffee pot is full, and the stew is warming for lunch. Ingrid is providing lunch for us, so don't wait for me." Julie ambled to the coatrack and began donning her winter outerwear.

Luke met her there and laid his hands on the upper sleeves of her coat. "It's only two weeks before Christmas, and our baby could come anytime. Are you sure this outing is a good idea?"

"Luke, I'll be fine. I've had no contractions yet, and the last-minute wedding details still need to be planned. Besides, with winter here and a newborn coming soon, I may not be able to visit with my friends again for a while. Emily will be be driving me in the buggy, so I don't even need to ride Cinnamon."

"You were planning to ride Cinnamon?" His words were laced with alarm.

"No, but don't you feel better that I'm not?" Julie playfully swatted him with the end of her scarf. "Stop worrying. I will be fine. Truly." She tapped his chest with her finger. "And if the baby comes, I'll know where to find you."

Luke tried to keep a serious face, but her teasing always disarmed him, and this day was no exception. The edge of his mouth twitched until it gave way to a lopsided smile. "All right. Have fun, and stay warm." He leaned in and kissed her. Then he splayed his hand and rested it on her belly. "Stay safe, little one."

"I'll only be gone a few hours. I'll be home before dinnertime. You won't even miss me."

"I already miss you."

Julie smiled and rolled her eyes at him. "You're crazy."

"Crazy about you."

"Emily's pulling up. Gotta go." Luke grabbed his coat and followed her out to help her up. After he bundled her lap in a fur blanket, he stepped up on the rail for one more quick kiss.

Emily snapped the reins and set the buggy in motion. "What was that all about?"

"Luke is overprotective the last month. He did the same thing when I was expecting Matthew." Julie shifted to face Emily. "Did you know he was with Emma and me when I miscarried Buck's first baby?"

"No, I didn't know that."

"Seeing me so hurt traumatized Luke, I think. Doc thought I might never conceive again. That's why Luke hovers like a mama hen. He loves me."

Soon they arrived at the Müllers and were ushered into the warmth while Johann cared for the horses. Heidi was including them as Jacob's family in planning her wedding day. Her desire to add a few German wedding traditions would make their ceremony beautifully unique.

Heidi was running through her list. "And after the ceremony, the bride and groom waltz together." The list continued, but Julie's thoughts stopped on the waltz.

With finger sandwiches and tiny German pastries on her delicate china plate, Julie found Heidi alone on the sofa with her notebook in hand and sat next to her as gracefully as her condition would allow. "Heidi," she asked quietly, "have you discussed the waltz with Jacob?"

Heidi's pencil halted mid-letter, and she turned her full attention to Julie. "I have mentioned it. He's supposed to let me know."

Julie opened her mouth to comment, but winced instead. "Oooh!"

Heidi's eyes widened. "Julie! What is it?"

"Um. My water broke. Emily, I'm going to need a ride home." Julie seemed to be the only calm one in the room. The other ladies started fluttering around her. Ingrid called for her husband to bring the buggy around. Emily wiped up the puddle. Emma collected the winter clothing and bundled Julie as if she were a toddler. Heidi wrapped a few extra sandwiches for Luke's dinner. "Ladies, I'm fine." The instant she was settled on the buggy seat, another contraction circled her belly and squeezed. "All right, Emily, smooth and steady."

"How can you be so calm?"

"Would you rather I panic?"

"No."

"Okay, then. Just get me home."

Luke met the buggy and swept Julie into his arms while Emily opened the front door for them. Aunt Emily scooped up Matthew and dressed him warmly. As soon as Emma arrived to help Luke, Emily drove Matthew the short distance to their house and sent James for Doc. "Luke will want to be husband more than doctor right now."

Just before midnight, Julie and Luke welcomed Rebekah Noelle Hamilton into their family. She resembled her daddy with her wisps of blond hair and blue eyes, but Julie didn't mind a bit. Their baby girl lived up to the meaning of her name: "captivating beauty with joy."

When Jacob visited Heidi to share the happy news of his niece's safe arrival, Heidi was overjoyed. "Rebekah Noelle. What a beautiful name!"

"Mama and baby are both healthy, and Luke couldn't grin any bigger if he tried."

"How does Matthew feel about having a little sister?"

"He adores her."

Ingrid's voice carried to them. "Jacob, you'll stay for dinner, I hope."

"Yes, ma'am, I'd be happy to."

After the meal was finished, Heidi's papa leaned back in his chair. "Jacob, we have a family tradition we would like to continue with you and Heidi." At Jacob's nod, he continued. "On the evening before your wedding, our family would like to meet the two of you in your new home and have a prayer of dedication for your house and your marriage."

Jacob smiled at Heidi, lifting the edges of his mouth enough to uncover his dimples. "That sounds like a lovely tradition."

---

The final week of Jacob's bachelorhood crawled by, and Heidi had been so busy with last-minute preparations he had barely seen her. He spent his extra time with his family. Even Tim had surprised him by arriving on the stage for his wedding. Tim had been in secret communication with Pastor Kendrick and offered to officiate the wedding ceremony. Jacob was elated, and Heidi wholeheartedly agreed. Josiah had been chosen as his best man, but Jacob had inwardly wanted Tim standing with him, too. Now he had them both.

At night, while lying in bed, he contemplated Heidi's request to dance with him. His left hand was missing. If he couldn't hold her hand, how could he dance? There must be a way. He still hadn't had a chance to discuss his concerns with his soon-to-be bride.

## CHAPTER 32
## *The Waltz*

On the eve of their wedding, Jacob met the Müller family in the house that would become his and Heidi's home on the morrow. They gathered in a circle, and Johann prayed, "Our Father, You have brought these two young people together, and tomorrow they will become one. Please bless their new family. Remind them to trust each other, but trust You above all, in the good times and the hard ones. Help them to grow closer together as they grow spiritually closer to You."

"Give Jacob wisdom as he leads their family. Bless Jacob and Heidi with children who will love You as they do." Jacob peeked at Heidi and found her looking at him. He raised an eyebrow, winked, and she blushed.

Oblivious to the interaction, Johann continued, "We dedicate this house to you. May you take these walls of wood and stone and use them to be a blessing, not only to Jacob and Heidi and the generations to come, but to others You bring into their lives who need hospitality and love and compassion. May Your love abound here. In Jesus' Name, Amen."

"Before we say goodnight, I would like to present you both

with a gift to make your new home complete." He retreated to the spare bedroom and returned with a wrapped flat parcel that he handed to Jacob. "This is to remind you of the strong bond of family. Even when they are not with you, they still shape who you will become with their enduring love."

The gift was too large for Jacob to unwrap while standing, so he sat on the sofa, Heidi beside him, and untied the twine holding the paper in place. Supporting the weight of the gift with his left arm, he used his right hand to pull away the paper.

Jacob's hand flew to his mouth. Heidi leaned in and beheld what Jacob had seen—a artistically detailed painting, specifically a portrait of a family. A husband and wife sat on a porch swing watching their two dark-haired boys, about eight or nine, playing catch while a furry little dog romped between them.

*Why had Jacob reacted so strongly?* Heidi wondered. When she studied the painting further, she found her answer. The husband looked exactly like Jacob if he were to grow facial hair. His brown eyes gleamed with the same intensity she saw in Jacob's, and his arm was lovingly and protectively holding his wife close to his side. The woman in the portrait radiated joy and love as she watched her boys play. Heidi's eyes searched the corner, and her suspicions were confirmed. The artist was Miriam Collins. Jacob was holding his family's portrait.

Jacob looked up to meet the eyes of Heidi's father. "How did you find this?"

"Months of letters and telegrams. Most of your mother's paintings are part of a frontier collection in a gallery in Kansas City, but I found this one held by a private collector. Once he heard your story, he was willing to sell it to me, wanting to get this portrait into the hands of its rightful owner."

"Your business trip." Jacob made the connection. Johann nodded. "This is second only to Heidi herself as the best wedding gift ever." His eyes misted, "I didn't think I'd ever see my parents again or own any of Mom's paintings. You have given me back something I thought I had lost forever. Thank you."

Johann pulled a nail and hammer from his large pocket. "Now you must decide where to hang it."

Jacob and Heidi debated for a moment before they chose the wall in the dining area where Jacob's parents could watch them, and maybe someday their grandchildren, grow in the love they had fostered in Jacob. The portrait was hung, and the house felt like home.

---

When Jacob entered the bunkhouse later that evening, Tim and Josiah were in the middle of a game of checkers. Tim was staying in the bunkhouse, too, since he had traveled alone to be there for his brother's big day. For a few days, life had felt like old times. Jacob hadn't realized just how much he needed Josiah and Tim and their camaraderie as he anticipated the transition to life as a husband.

Jacob's enthusiasm was evident by his grin and the near bounce to his step. "Remember whose turn it is and put your boots on. There's something I need to show you at my house."

"What is it?" Josiah's brows crinkled in curiosity.

"Our wedding gift from the Müllers."

Tim stuffed his feet into his boots. "Okay, but what is it?"

"You'll have to come with me to find out." Jacob lit a second lantern and walked with a quick stride toward his new home, his brothers in step behind him.

Several minutes later, the trio climbed the front steps and entered Jacob and Heidi's house. The groom-to-be rounded the dining table and held his lantern aloft. Josiah and Tim stepped up to examine the painting.

Tim noticed the resemblance of the man on the canvas to Jacob, though the woman didn't look much like Heidi.

Assuming Heidi had painted it, he blurted, "Heidi wants you to grow facial hair and have two boys?"

Josiah just stood there and absorbed the image. He reached up as if to touch the man and woman, though his fingers stopped before they made contact with the canvas. His voice held a wistful tone. "I used to beg you to play catch with me, and Mom and Dad would sit and watch us while Ruff would try to steal our ball and run off with it if one of us missed the catch. I'd almost forgotten what they looked like—well, Mom." Josiah glanced at his brother. "You look just like Dad."

Tim's face was scrunched in confusion. He rested his hands on his hips and tried to process Josiah's comments. "So, the bearded man is your dad?"

Jacob nodded and pointed to the boys in the scene. "This is me, and this is Josiah. Our mom painted this portrait of our family. It used to hang in our living room growing up. I'd thought we'd never see one of her paintings again, but Mr. Müller searched and found this one. Apparently, most of her others are in a museum gallery."

"Mom's paintings are in a gallery?"

"Yep. In Kansas City. One day, we'll have to travel there together and see them."

---

The wedding day had arrived. Josiah had been up early and had the pot of coffee ready for Jacob. Tim sat across from Jacob and sipped his own cup of coffee. "Marriage is all about unconditional love. Chuck your pride out the window and choose what is best for Heidi. She'll be doing the same for you, so you won't be neglected, I promise. Serving each other and putting each other first is what strengthens a marriage, for that is how God Himself designed marriage to work. Love Heidi when she's sweet; love her when she's not; love her when she cries for no reason because she's nine months pregnant; love her when she's grumpy because she hasn't had a full night's sleep in months."

Laughter filled the space between them. "Okay, I get the message."

"Protect her, cherish her—"

"And love her unconditionally." Jacob finished.

"Exactly." Tim gestured with his coffee cup and raised it to his lips, satisfied that Jacob was armed with the wisdom he had gleaned during his first year of marriage.

---

A light snow was wafting outside as Jacob stood at the front of the church with Josiah to his left and Tim standing center-stage behind him. Angels in paintings wore white garments; his Christmas angel was wearing blue. Heidi glided down the aisle toward him on her father's arm, and her eyes melded with his. The awe and love he felt for her expanded his entire chest.

Just as an artist could envision a painting when it was still a blank canvas, Heidi saw him not for what he was, but for what he could be. She infused him with hope and courage. His desire to protect her and cherish her for a lifetime was a natural result.

When Mr. Müller gave Jacob Heidi's hand, Jacob lifted it in his right hand, laid it gently on his left forearm, and covered it with his hand. Pastor Timothy O'Brien presided over the ceremony, and their vows were witnessed by God and those gathered with them.

At Tim's pronouncement of "You may kiss your bride," Jacob tugged Heidi close with his left arm, glided his fingers to the nape of her neck, and touched his lips to hers gently, sweetly. The frisson of desire surged all the way to his heart.

When he pulled away, Jacob leaned near her ear, the puffs of his breath whispering against her hair, "I love you, Heidi."

"And I love you, Jacob." Her blue eyes shone, confirming that she meant every word.

"May I be the first to introduce Mr. and Mrs. Jacob Collins," Tim resounded.

When Jacob offered his arm, Heidi slipped her fingers around his bicep, and they shared another smile. The buggy for the ride to Tom Wilson's barn was waiting for them at the foot of the church steps. The venue of the annual church social had been offered for their reception to keep everyone sheltered from the winter elements.

On the drive over, Jacob's smile faded slightly. "Heidi, I would love to waltz with you, but I'm not sure how. I want to hold your hand in mine, but whenever I switch hand positions, my feet get tangled up." Heidi looked unflustered. So beautiful. So confident. He loved that about her.

"Does the end of your left arm hurt?"

Surprised by the change in topic, he replied honestly, "Not usually, but sometimes I can feel the pain in my hand. I know that sounds daft."

"Not at all. It's phantom pain—nerves sending messages to your brain from your hand that is no longer there," Heidi stated matter-of-factly.

Jacob lifted an eyebrow. "How do you know about that?"

"Luke lent me a book."

One side of Jacob's mouth lifted in a smile, "Of course, Luke lent you a book."

"If I wouldn't hurt you if I touched your arm, our problem is solved. We can dance normally, and your feet will know what to do."

"My arm really doesn't bother you, does it?"

She looked down at the empty cuff at the end of his left

sleeve and shook her head slowly. "No, your missing hand is a constant reminder of your selfless courage."

His heart swelled. Truly he was the luckiest man alive to have this woman's affection.

When the guests had all gathered, the ladies present held the edges of a German lace veil aloft in the center of the room. Jacob held out his right hand. When she placed her hand in his, he led her to the space underneath the veil's canopy.

Heidi whispered to Jacob, "This is my first dance."

"Mine, too."

"You've never danced before?"

"Family members don't count. I've been saving my first waltz for *you*."

Jacob faced Heidi and slowly lifted his left arm. Heidi carefully placed her palm against the inside of his forearm and gently wrapped her fingers around the end. Her hand was soft, and her touch was featherlight. Jacob closed his eyes, captivated by the feel of her skin against his. "Is this all right?" Heidi asked shyly.

Jacob's dimples smiled at her when he reopened his eyes. "Perfect. I can almost feel your hand in mine." Jacob and Heidi danced effortlessly in three-quarter time. For all the times Jacob had felt lonely in this very barn, he was now sharing his first waltz with his wife.

---

When the reception concluded, Tim pulled the buggy up to the front door and disembarked as Jacob and Heidi exited the barn. He engulfed Jacob in a hug. "Congratulations, Jacob. I'm proud of you. Keep that knot tied tight."

"I will."

Tim turned to Heidi and gave her a one-armed hug. "Welcome to the family."

"Thank you."

Extending his closed hand toward Heidi, Tim lowered his voice and uncoiled his fingers away from his palm to reveal two small pieces of cotton batting. "I would be remiss and quite uncaring if I did not offer you this comfort." Heidi's brow crinkled in question. Tim's eyes twinkled in amusement. "They're for your ears. Jacob snores." His straight face burgeoned into a grin just before Jacob shoved him.

After a shared laugh, Tim bowed and gestured toward the buggy. "And now I will be the silent chauffeur for the remainder of your journey."

Though Jacob knew Tim's silence for a half hour would border on the impossible, he offered Heidi his hand to assist her climb into the back seat, rounded the buggy to the other side, and scooted close to his bride. He intertwined his fingers with hers just before the buggy lurched into motion.

So the impossible wasn't quite so impossible, for Tim did not break his vow of silence. Jacob and Heidi kept their conversation to the wedding and their guests, cognizant that while Tim's mouth was closed, his ears were still in good working order.

When they approached their new home, Jacob leaned in close to Heidi's ear and whispered, "Wait for me." Then his lips brushed her ear before he disembarked. Jacob had always envied the way his married brothers would encircle the waists of their wives and lift them from any wheeled conveyance, but his missing hand would not dissuade him from an alternate version of this expression of care and closeness.

Thankful for the lower height of the buggy, Jacob approached Heidi and slid his left forearm beneath the voluminous folds of fabric under her knees and wrapped his right hand behind her back and secured her waist. With ease, he lifted her off the seat and against his chest. Heidi's arm instinctively circled his neck, and her touch broadened Jacob's smile.

"There is one more wedding tradition that cannot be overlooked."

"Oh?" A smile tugged at the corners of Heidi's mouth.

"My bride must be carried over the threshold." Jacob ascended the porch steps and bent his knees slightly to align his hand with the door latch. He swept through the doorway and heard a baritone chuckle and a snap of the reins just before Jacob lifted his boot heel to shut the door behind them.

Once away from all prying eyes, Jacob kissed his wife and set her feet softly on the floor with a wink. "Welcome home, Mrs. Collins." After hanging up their coats, Jacob turned to Heidi, who slipped her arms around him. Her gaze was full of warmth and love. Jacob reached for a wayward blond curl, mesmerized by the silky feel of it between his thumb and forefinger. "I was right, you know."

"Right about what, exactly?" Heidi's lifted brow and teasing smirk could not hide her smile.

"What I said to you the morning after we met. You *are* my angel. God brought you here to me all the way from Germany and Pennsylvania. And I'm thankful." His voice softened to a whisper. "So very thankful." Jacob's thumb caressed Heidi's cheek before his fingers slipped toward the nape of her neck. Moving his gaze from her eyes to her smile, Jacob lowered his head until his lips met hers.

Heidi had definitely been worth waiting for. Her enduring faith in God had overcome her fear and bolstered Jacob's own trust in Him. Jacob had found the one his soul loved, and he knew their marriage was God's design. God had redeemed the imperfect canvas of their lives and painted a masterpiece.

# Acknowledgments

Putting this long-awaited sequel into print is a milestone I could not have achieved alone. Those who helped make this book possible deserve my highest gratitude.

First, I would like to thank the wonderful man who encouraged me to pursue publication of these stories in the first place. My husband Bob has been my faithful supporter in this endeavor. His teasing persistence that my story needs a jousting scene keeps me laughing, but his serious comments have greatly shaped this story.

My friend and sister-in-law, Cindy Bower, has been my primary advisor throughout this process and I highly value her insightful feedback and honest comments on each revision. Most authors can only dream of an editor who so fully understands their purpose, but Cindy shares my passion for developing a story with a faith-filled message designed to touch the heart. Thank you for being on this writing journey with me.

Holly Talley performed the monumental task of the final edit. Her years of experience teaching composition enabled her to polish my manuscript into what it is now.

The lovely young lady on the front cover is Savannah Talley, the daughter of my editor. Savannah, like Heidi, is a talented artist in varied types of media, but the detail in her pencil drawings in particular is exquisite. She was gracious in allowing me to pepper her with questions about her craft, her subjects, her tools, and her technique. Her vivid imagination allowed her to see the sketched scenes with Jacob and describe what detail she would emphasize and how she would compose each sketch. She is currently studying commercial art at a Christian college, and I am eager to see how God will use her amazing talent.

The admonition to focus on becoming the man or woman God wants you to be while waiting for a spouse was based on a popular sermon by Pastor Jim Schettler titled, "Seven Steps to Perfect Dating." He was my youth pastor, then my church's senior pastor (the Campus Church at Pensacola Christian College). Through the years, I heard this particular sermon several times, but the catchy points contain timeless truths. This one is "Don't look for the right one. Be the right one, and you'll find the right one." In other words, if your heart's desire is to grow in your relationship with God, He will make sure you find the one He has chosen for you. By the way, my wonderful husband Bob was worth waiting for, and Pastor Schettler is the one who performed our wedding ceremony.

Finally, I would like to acknowledge my readers. Without your unfailing encouragement, *Heidi's Faith* may have never been written. Fear can manifest itself in many ways, but God's perfect love casts out fear. Trust Him for your eternity. Trust Him for your todays and tomorrows. He is faithful. Always.

# About the Author

An Amazon best-selling author, a four-time novelist with five-star review status on Goodreads and Amazon, and a former freelance writer for *Abekamazing Homeschool Magazine*, Jill's writing engages the heart of her readers and leaves them empowered to fulfill God's plan for their lives. Jill's novels seamlessly weave a page-turning story with the truth of God's unconditional love.

Jill and her husband recently celebrated their twenty-seventh anniversary. After working as an RN in cardiac critical care for thirteen years, Jill received a much prayed-for promotion to full-time Mom. Both of their boys joined their family through the gift of adoption.

Because their oldest son is a Leukemia survivor, and the youngest is a Type-1 diabetic, Jill's nursing skills are still used on a daily basis. Jill is also a homeschool mom, loving her opportunity to teach and to cherish the one-on-one time with her high school boys.

When she can find some free time, she enjoys playing her flute, piano, and cello. She and her family love their church in Florida and serve in the music and children's ministries there.

Jill has had a secret wish for many years to write a story that would inspire readers by reminding them of a God who loves them unconditionally and longs to have a personal relationship with them. Publishing her first book was a dream come true. In the fall of 2024, Jill will publish her fourth novel in the Rugged Cross Ranch series.

Follow Jill on Social Media:
  Facebook ~ Jill Dewhurst, Author
  Instagram ~ jilldewhurst.author
  Author Pages on Amazon, Goodreads, BookBub
  Author's Website ~ www.jilldewhurst.com

  facebook.com/DewhurstPublishing
  instagram.com/jilldewhurst.author

*Also by Jill Dewhurst*

**Rugged Cross Ranch series**

Julie's Joy

Emily's Hope

Laura's Redemption

Heidi's Faith

# Rugged Cross Ranch

**Julie's Joy**

Finding Joy . . .

Julie Peterson had been born into a family of faith and privilege, but when her dad decides to move his family West to homestead near his sister's ranch in northeastern Oklahoma, disaster strikes, leaving Julie a nine-year-old orphan. Rescued and cared for my a migrating Indian village until her uncle found her years later, Julie has learned to find joy even when life turns out differently than she hoped. Meet her now as a young woman, returning home to the Rugged Cross Ranch. Though she has faced many hardships in her young life, Julie spreads joy to all around her. When the biggest tragedy of all strikes, will her joy be extinguished forever?

Buck Matthews, the second oldest brother on the ranch, has given up his dreams of a family, knowing no woman would accept his heritage. When Julie arrives on the ranch, their friendship reveals they have a great deal in common. Would Julie be willing to accept his love?

Follow God's sovereign hand through this story of faith, family, and redeeming love. Be inspired to trust the One who loves us all unconditionally.

## Emily's Hope

Finding Hope . . .

Emily Kendrick, the pastor's oldest daughter, has willingly put her dreams on hold for her family. She had assumed the responsibility for managing the household and teaching her siblings when her mom died. Now she is ready for the next chapter of her life to begin. When God asks her to wait even longer, will she place her hope in God and trust His timing for her life?

James McAllister is the oldest of the brothers on the ranch. Though he enjoys his position as foreman, the title he truly desires is husband. He has patiently courted Emily for several years, understanding how much her family needed her. When the time finally comes for him to ask Pastor Kendrick for her hand, James does not get the answer he expects. Will he be willing to wait for Pastor's and ultimately God's blessing?

Follow God's perfect plan through this pioneer story of hope, trust, and family.

**Laura's Redemption**

Finding Redemption . . .

Laura Kendrick stubbornly refuses to follow her expected path as a pastor's daughter. Her unwavering desire for adventure causes her to reject the idea of marriage and motherhood. When her life is threatened, will the sacrifice of her rescuer be enough to convince her heart to accept his unconditional love before her final opportunity is gone?

Tim O'Brien is the third oldest brother on the Rugged Cross Ranch. Content with his life as a cowboy and wrangler, will he be willing to give up the life he knows and the woman he loves to follow what God has asked of him?

Follow God's plan of redemption woven through their story and be inspired to give your heart to the God who loves you.

Made in the USA
Columbia, SC
06 January 2025

49013045R00200